D1596892

Blue Horizons

**Center Point
Large Print**

**This Large Print Book carries the
Seal of Approval of N.A.V.H.**

ॐ श्री गणेशाय नमः

Blue Horizons

Faith Baldwin

Center Point Publishing
Thorndike, Maine

This Center Point Large Print edition
is published in the year 2000 by arrangement with
Harold Ober Associates.

Copyright © 1942 and © 1970
by Faith Baldwin Cuthrell.

All rights reserved.

The text of this Large Print edition is unabridged.
In other aspects, this book may vary from the original
edition. Printed in Thailand. Set in 16-point Plantin type
by Bill Coskrey.

ISBN 1-58547-033-3

Library of Congress Cataloging-in-Publication Data

Baldwin, Faith, 1893-
    Blue Horizons / Faith Baldwin.
        p. cm.
    ISBN 1-58547-033-3 (lib. bdg. : alk. paper)
    1. Large type books. I. Title.

PS3505.U97 B58 2000
813'.52--dc21

                                        00-027738

WITH LOVE AND ADMIRATION
FOR MY FRIEND
KATHARINE COLLINS PANCOAST
AND IN LOVING MEMORY OF
THOMAS J. PANCOAST,
THIS LITTLE BOOK
WHICH I WISH WERE
WORTHY OF THEM.

Chapter 1

The countess was shooting craps.

She sat cross-legged upon the patio tiles, near the swimming pool. Her almost adequate bathing suit was a short serial—in two bright parts. Dividing them, her midriff was brown as bacon, thin as an excuse. Her small, equally brown face was surmounted by an expensive confusion of hair which looked like a gray chrysanthemum in a strong wind. Diamond bracelets clanked one upon the other upon each tiny wrist, and in one ear she wore a hoop of rubies . . . the exact color of the enamel on her fingernails, her toenails, and her big mobile mouth.

Her difficult name was Frieda de Szombathely. Those who had known her for a long time called her Fritzi. More recent acquaintances were likely to call her Zombie, for short. She had been born, however, twenty-six miles out of St. Louis, sixty-seven years ago.

She had never been a pretty woman, but now nearing seventy she was possessed of a distinguished ugliness, in miniature, her high cheeks, her narrow green eyes, her heavy dark brows and strong inquisitive nose, more arresting than in her youth.

The countess made her point, and laughed. Her opponents were two men, one old, one young, one rich, one poor, one fat, one thin. Warming the dice between dry, hard palms, she reflected that whereas she had once preferred her men rich and old, she now wished that she could afford them poor and young. She rolled the dice, and smiled at Lanny Martin, approving the brevity of his trunks, the width of his shoulders, the depth of his chest and the insolence of his eyes.

"Darling—" she hadn't the remotest idea of his name—"darling, you owe me forty-two dollars!"

The older man spoke. His name was Howard Toller, he had a noble stomach, a hairline that had retreated with his discretion, an excellent sun tan, and a denture which was perfection.

"He won't pay you, Fritzi," he warned her gently.

Lanny yawned. He said amiably, "Perhaps she'd take it out in trade?"

They were alone, these three, on the synthetic banks of the bright blue pool. The patio stretched high, wide, and handsome to all points of the compass. Coconut palms leaned to the wind, great pottery jars held exotic bloom, umbrellas blossomed in bright profusion, and the sapphire sky was an arched and distant roof. Behind the crapshooters lay the white stone pile of the house and before them shaven lawns ran to a half-moon of beach and the aquamarine sea. Far out, on the indigo edge of the Gulf Stream, the fishing fleet rocked in the swells. Gulls screamed by the bathing pier, and quarreled on the beach, and a sleepy pelican bobbed placidly past, dreaming of fish.

The countess snapped her predatory fingers.

"Little Joe," she coaxed, "come on, Little Joe."

Little Joe obliged, and Lanny sighed.

"What a woman," he murmured admiringly.

8

The golden sun shone down, nearing mid-heaven. There must be, mused the countess, any god's number of people in that enormous house but she had not met them. She and Howard Toller had arrived late on the previous evening, by car, from Palm Beach. The countess had been tired, melancholy from a forced parting from her personal maid, and suffering from a stupendous hangover. She had therefore demanded a snort of Scotch and a good bed. These had been tendered her by an impersonal and competent maid and she had slept like the dead until two hours ago. Waking, she had listened to a mockingbird singing somewhere close at hand. She had little fondness for nature. The sun was too bright, the bird too insistent. She rang a bell vigorously and the meager breakfast to which she was resigned had appeared in due course. After which she had selected the passion flower and bamboo bathing suit and sallied out to look for trouble.

The dice were still hers. She rolled them expertly and regarded resultant Big Joe. "Come seven," implored Lanny devoutly but Big Joe came rolling in.

"I'm bored," said the countess. "I need a drink." She lay flat on the tiles, face upward and closed her eyes against brilliance. "Our hostess—I suppose we have one? . . . I wouldn't know—is she lunching with us?"

"Bobbie?" asked Lanny. "Oh, she'll be home presently . . . she's been in Boca Raton for a couple of days—"

"These Americans!" remarked the countess with

9

disapproval, and Howard Toller chuckled. He had been in love with Fritzi thirty-odd years ago. He still liked her. It amused him to witness how conveniently she had forgotten the facts of her life and her birth after meeting Breda de Szombathely in Budapest. It amused him even more to contemplate the unseemly haste with which she had recalled her nativity when such a recollection became urgent.

"Remember St. Louis?" he asked gently.

"Is that her background?" inquired Lanny, enraptured. "I thought she was born in a glass case in a museum."

The countess reached out and struck his hand sharply with her bony little fingers. She said, "Bobbie . . . ridiculous name. Sounds like a chorus girl, circa nineteen-ten."

"Philo Vance," remarked Lanny. "Do you read cards or just look into crystals?"

Howard Toller fished a pack of cigarettes from a pocket in his bathing trunks. He lit one, and inserted it between the countess's spectacular lips. He asked, "Have you forgotten already? . . . Roberta Wilson Scott Martin Rivers. *And* my cousin."

"My stepmother," added Lanny, "for the record."

"How clannish," said the countess peevishly. "Where's my drink . . . or has the staff walked out?"

Lanny rose. "I'll track one to its chilly lair," he promised pleasantly, "and don't forget you owe me my revenge, countess."

He sauntered off in the direction of the house and the countess sat up, her thin knees hugged to

10

her flat chest. "Nice boy," she said cordially, "who in hell is he?"

"Lanny Martin," said Howard Toller, "and he must be about thirty-six. He's very charming, utterly no good. Bobbie adores him."

"But where, exactly, does he come in?"

"My dear Fritzi, I told you all about this ménage when I proposed bringing you here."

"I didn't listen. I didn't care. I would have gone anywhere, with everything found. You know that. Have you forgotten that I lost my last shirt at Bradley's? Or that Priscilla Wright took Marie in exchange for my contract debt? Poor old Marie—she's been with me for a thousand years. But I can't afford her now and she's very practical."

"You still have your diamonds," he reminded her, "and a smattering of rubies, emeralds, and such."

"All that will stand between me and relief for the next twenty-five years," she said sharply; "you can't count the Paris house, or the Brittany place, or the Cannes villa . . . or even the moldy mausoleum which was in Breda's family since the flood—"

"I grieve for you," said Toller.

"You wouldn't care about marrying me?" she suggested. "After all, you've been a widower for six years, you could do with a devoted wife."

Her eyes were greener than ever, they glittered with malice—and some anxiety. But Howard Toller looked profoundly shocked.

"Good God, no!" he said.

"Thanks. Well, I tried," she said amiably. "Go on,

11

tell me about Bobbie—and Lanny."

He explained patiently. "Bobbie's my cousin. Her first marriage was for love. She had defied a stolid, settled, well-to-do family by going on the stage—if you can call it that—but a struggling young lawyer snatched her out of the front row a few months subsequent to the event and married her. The result of that union was one son, Jonathan Scott. When Jon was about seven his father died, and shortly thereafter Bobbie's father, my uncle, having invested in little gadgets which became necessary to the automotive industry, made more money than even she could spend. So she remarried, at thirty-two, for amusement, one Lansing Martin, who brought to the marriage unfailing good humor, a zany sort of charm, and a son by a previous marriage who must have been about seventeen at the time. That's Lanny, who now owes you upward of fifty bucks. The marriage lasted seven years. When Bobbie divorced Martin she insisted upon keeping Lanny. Martin didn't care. You're likely to meet him, by the way, if you stay here long enough. Bobbie's sorry for him now that she's no longer married to him. Besides, he entertains her. He's always a little plastered, eternally broke, and invariably amiable. Bobbie gives Lanny an allowance. He's supposed to be writing a book or something. He has been known to work at short intervals . . . he gets on beautifully with Bobbie, and Jon tolerates him . . ."

"Jon? Oh, her own son. Where is he?" asked the

countess.

"He's an architect," said Toller, "and a good one. He's in New York—here comes your drink."

A muscular manservant, with the air of a conscientious nursemaid in the park was trundling a bar wagon toward them. When he reached them the countess placed her order and a moment later taking the proffered glass in her hand she weighed it carefully, together with her thoughts.

"Any more husbands?" she inquired.

"Rivers. Bobbie married him when she was forty-five. He was fifteen years her junior, a friend of Lanny's. She's rented this place in Miami Beach in order to avail herself of the existent Florida divorce laws."

"Complicated," commented the countess, absorbing her drink, "and rather disgusting."

She had been married to her Breda when she was twenty—and grand climax to the grand tour of Europe. She had remained married to him until his death, a decade previously. Marriage had not interfered with her whimseys nor with his. Neither had ever reproached the other. They had been mutually affectionate, courteous, and understanding for nearly forty years.

She set the glass down beside her and turned her head a little. Her eyes widened. "Who on earth is that?" she demanded.

The woman approaching them was small and plump. She wore superbly tailored raw silk slacks, her bare feet were thrust in hand-sewn platform shoes, her shirt was bright silk, and a close, matching turban concealed her hair. She was smoking, and she waved the long holder at them, cordially.

"Merely your hostess," said Toller, lumbering to his feet.

The countess stayed where she was . . . if she ever had any manners she had exchanged them for manner. She watched with detached interest the cousinly embrace, and smiled briefly at Mrs. Rivers.

Toller performed the introductions. Bobbie Rivers said distractedly, "Give me a chair. I'm ten pounds too heavy to commit yoga . . . or is it yogi? How are you, Howard? Have you seen Susan? Where on earth is Lanny? I am perfectly distracted." She looked, as Howard pulled a long chair forward and she sank into it, completely serene. A small, round, pink and white face and round turquoise eyes. She pulled off the turban. Her hair was short, curly and an unconvincing red-gold, verging on pink. But it became her.

"I'm so glad you could come," she told the countess vaguely. "I hope you'll stay a long time. You too, Howard. Is there any Vichy on that wagon . . . I'd like a glass. Where's everybody?"

Toller gave her the Vichy. He said calmly that he hadn't seen Susan and that Lanny had left the patio a moment ago.

Bobbie counted on her fingers. She said, "Alison Palmer was here when I left . . . No, I think she's gone, she said something about having to go to Delray. But Dick Farmer is staying on. My doctor," she explained to the countess. "Perfectly wonderful about glands. And I expected Elsie down—yesterday, I think. Or perhaps tomorrow. Or is it next week?"

"Jonathan's girl," asked Toller, "the glamour kid?"

"So suitable," said Bobbie, "but they can't make up their minds. . . . Yes, it's next week." She looked baffled. "I'm all mixed up," she admitted superfluously. "It's Evelyn's fault. Most ungrateful."

The countess fixed her with a bright green eye. She remarked, "This is wonderful. Who is Evelyn?"

"My secretary," said Bobbie, "haven't you met her? Oh, I forgot, I fired her in Boca Raton and you just came—when *did* you come?" she asked Toller.

"Last night," said Toller, "Fritzi and I—"

"Fritzi? May I call you that, baroness?"

"Don't demote me," said the countess, "it's all I have left."

"Princess . . ."

Toller chuckled. He said, "Countess. The name's de Szombathely, in case you've forgotten."

"I have," said Bobbie, horrified, "instantly. Fritzi, if you don't mind."

"I don't," said the countess. She was entertained, she was pleased. She liked her hostess. She was slightly on the wacky side but Fritzi liked her. No mean judge of human nature—barring her own, far too human—Fritzi discerned generosity, kindness, and a childlike appeal in the round blue eyes.

"Good," said Bobbie. "Well, have fun. There are the cars," she said. "We might go to the Brook Club tonight and of course there are always the boxes at

Hialeah . . . I mean, anything you want to do—I simply must find Lanny and Susan."

She was gone, as suddenly as she had come.

"Is she always like that?" demanded Fritzi. "You'd better give me another drink."

Toller obeyed. "Always," he said, "only a little more so."

"Who is Susan?"

"Bobbie's sister. Somewhat older, entirely sane. Shrewd, practical, and a very nice person," said Toller, "but she won't approve of you."

"Does that matter?"

"Not very much. Susan runs the house, manages the always altering staff . . . any house, of course . . . the one in New York, the one in Aiken. She's lived with Bobbie ever since Scott's death. She never married, not even me."

"Have you asked her?"

"Years ago. When we were all youngsters."

"Why wouldn't she marry you?"

"First cousins. She said it was biologically unsound."

"What isn't? And who," demanded Fritzi, "is this? Prettiest girl I ever saw."

Mr. Toller, sprawling in the lounge chair vacated by his hostess, looked once, twice, and rose, with haste. He said, "I don't know. I hope she's a house guest. I'd like to frame her—"

"I can well imagine."

"Picture frame," he said severely, "and hang her on the library wall."

16

"Library?"

She was neither very tall nor very short, the girl coming toward them across the patio. She wore a blue linen skirt and jacket and a white blouse. She carried a blue linen hat and her honey-gold hair was bright in the sunlight. She walked beautifully, her figure was flawless. Flawless, too, her skin and coloring, and astonishing the fact that her eyes, now that she was close to them and they could remark them, were a dark and unusual brown.

She smiled impersonally.

"I was told," she said pleasantly, "that I'd find Mrs. Rivers here."

"She went toward the house a moment ago," said Howard Toller. "If I can assist you—"

"Thank you," said the girl, "but I can find my way."

"Wait a minute," said Mr. Toller. "I'm sure I know you . . . I mean, I'm certain I've seen you. The Stork?" he asked hopefully. "Twenty-One . . . the St. Regis?"

"I'm afraid not," said the blond girl pleasantly. "I live here, you see. All the time. In Miami Beach. I'm from the real estate office."

She smiled again and departed, in the direction of the house.

Toller sat down.

"A good try," said Fritzi. "Have you forgotten you're a year older than I?"

"I did," he said, "for a minute. I wish you wouldn't remind me. I could eat that girl, with cream."

"Wolf her down," suggested the countess.

"I might," he said happily, "buy a place here. Any place. If I did I'd need a real estate agent, wouldn't I?"

"You need," said Fritzi kindly, "a keeper and a guard. What about going to the races? You could do with a bit of distraction. Yesterday at Bradley's someone gave me a good horse in the fourth—"

Chapter 2

Josephine Bruce walked through the patio and up the step to the dining terrace, partially roofed, the tall pillars heavy with bougainvilleae. She was smiling a little, remembering the eager, fat man and the thin ugly woman. Then her smile faded. She thought, I shouldn't come here, ever—

Curious how much it still hurt, despite the changes, despite the resignation, despite everything.

She hesitated on the terrace and a man rose from one of the big chairs and tossed aside his newspaper. He wore a striped bathrobe over bathing trunks and greeted her with every evidence of pleasure.

"Miss Bruce," he said, "how wonderful."

"Mr. Martin." Josephine smiled at him. "I was looking for Mrs. Rivers. Her secretary called the office from Boca Raton and said she wanted to see me today . . . around lunchtime."

"She's just home," said Lanny, walking beside her. "I haven't seen her yet. We'll send someone to find her. Let's go into the house."

The French doors of the great living room

opened on the dining terrace. Flowers filled it, sun-light, air, salt from the sea, fragrant with roses.

"Sit down," said Lanny. He went to pull a bell cord and speak to the maid who answered. "Miss Bruce," he said, "to see Mrs. Rivers."

Josephine said, standing by the windows and looking across terrace and patio to the sea, "I'm afraid I made an informal entrance, I took a short cut. But the one servant I encountered thought Mrs. Rivers was on the patio."

Lanny said, offering her a cigarette, "Look here, I forgot. I'm not speaking to you."

"No, thanks. Why?"

"I'm still sore. You wouldn't go to the Brook with me."

She said, "I explained why, Mr. Martin."

"I ignore your explanation. I thought that real estate agents did everything to please a client."

She said, smiling, "I'm hardly a real estate agent, although I work in a real estate office, and some-times show properties. It happened that I knew more about this one than anyone else . . . and Mrs. Rivers is our client, strictly speaking."

"That's the trouble," he said, laughing at her. "You always speak strictly."

She shook her head, still smiling. She disapproved of Mr. Martin. She knew a good deal about him . . . his life was the sort of book you find lying around open on the best tables—but she liked him, rather. He was entertaining . . . if you knew how to keep him in his place. She thought she knew. She was twenty-two and she had been working since she was eighteen.

"If you'll come upstairs, Miss Bruce?" suggested the parlor maid, reappearing.

"Wait a minute—"

"Sorry," said Josephine, and went from the room into the square hall and up the curving stairway to the cluttered, sunny boudoir which Mrs. Rivers called her office.

Bobbie was sitting at a desk. It was piled with papers. It had a look of chaos. So had she. She had run her fingers through her hair until it stood out wildly around her face. She said, as Josephine came in, "I'm so glad to see you. Do sit down."

Josephine sat down on a couch piled with books, unopened mail, phonograph records, and pillows. She asked quietly, "Is anything wrong, Mrs. Rivers?

"Everything. That wretch, Evelyn . . ."

"Miss Gainford?"

"Yes, my secretary, you met her. Well, she's gone, cleared out, bag and baggage. Baggage," added Bobbie, "is rather good, I think."

"She left you?"

"I fired her," said Bobbie, "at Boca. We went up there for a few days. My aunt's there . . . she's ninety-nine or something. Anyway, Evelyn was too impossible. She's dreadfully spoiled. That comes of hiring your friends' children . . . she's the daughter of a woman I've known years—not that I ever liked her much. They lost everything in the crash and Evelyn took a secretarial course or something. Well, that's neither here nor there. She came back here yesterday, packed and left. I gave her two months' salary . . . I'm sorry for them," said Bobbie vaguely, "but—"

Josephine said firmly, "What did you want to see me about, Mrs. Rivers?"

"See you?" Bobbie focused her eyes on the girl's lovely face. "Oh, that. Something about mice. . . . Or was it bed linen? I don't know. Susan can tell you . . . I'm distracted, I—"

She leaned forward and her face changed. She asked, "You type, don't you, and write a good hand? I like my personal letters written in long hand."

"Yes," said Josephine, startled, "but—"

"It would be wonderful," cried Bobbie, "will you do it? I mean you'd save my life, you're the very person."

"The very person for what?"

"To take Evelyn's place," said Bobbie impatiently. "Why didn't I think of that before? You live here— or don't you?"

"Yes," said Josephine, "I live here."

Bobbie rose, came over to the couch, pushed more things aside and sat down.

"You know everyone and everything. You would be such an enormous help. Susan looks after the household end. All you'd have to do would be to keep the guests straight—who is leaving, who is coming—and plan for them . . . trips, amusements, you know what I mean. Write my letters, arrange things. What do they pay you at the office?"

Josephine told her, and Bobbie shook her head, horrified.

21

"But that's ridiculous. I'll give you what I gave Evelyn—and of course, you'd have your suite here and—"

Josephine said quietly: "It's a great deal more than I'm getting, as you know. But it would be temporary . . . and I am not at all sure that the office would take me back, Mrs. Rivers. I have to think of that. I have my mother to consider, and she isn't well . . . also, I couldn't leave her."

"You wouldn't be leaving her," said Bobbie, "you could see her every day, if you like, you would have time off. There would be weekends now and then. Surely there is someone who would look after her if you had to be away."

Josephine said hesitantly, "I think that could be arranged but—"

Bobbie said, "Then it's settled. And it isn't temporary, not at all. I decided last night to buy some land and build a house. I don't want this one," she said, "it's too big, it isn't at all the sort of house I'd buy. Not that I don't like it," she added quickly, fearing to hurt the girl's feelings, after all little Miss Bruce had found the house for her, "but it just isn't my type. I have been thinking—about taxes and all that . . . I'd like a house here. And I'd need someone to supervise," she went on. "I wouldn't be here all the time, and while it was being built. . . . Of course my son would build it."

Josephine felt dizzy. She said, "Then it would hardly need my supervision."

Son? But Lanny Martin was Mrs. Rivers's stepson.

22

She couldn't imagine him building anything but a doghouse, and that metaphorically speaking.

"He's an architect," said Bobbie, "Jonathan, I mean. He'd draw the plans and all that. But his work is in New York." She took the girl's slender hand in hers and held it. "I'm at my wits' end," she said, smiling, "you've no idea what a favor—"

Josephine said, after a moment, "It's very tempting. Of course, I'd have to talk to my mother."

"Run home," said Bobbie suddenly, "and ask her. I'll ask Susan to have Evelyn's room ready for you, meantime."

"Hadn't I better find out what it was you wanted originally?"

"Susan will know." Bobbie rose and opened the door to the hall. She called, "Susan, Susan, are you there?"

Susan Wilton came unhurriedly down the hall. She was a tall spare woman with pretty gray hair and direct blue eyes. She smiled at Josephine, whom she had met during the house-hunting period, and asked quietly, "What is it, Roberta?"

"Didn't we want to ask Miss Bruce something?" inquired Bobbie. "You told me about it—before I went to Boca. Evelyn remembered and phoned from there."

"I could have telephoned, it would have been simpler. It was about the linen inventory. I checked the real estate office's inventory against the one I made," said Susan, "and there is a discrepancy . . . not very much: half a dozen pillow slips for the main house, and a like number of sheets and some things in the servants' quarters—mattress pads, mostly. I'll get you the list."

Bobbie said, impatiently, "Oh, let it go. Susan, I've asked Miss Bruce to take Evelyn's place . . . I'm certain that she'll be marvelous."

Josephine said hastily, "I've explained to Mrs. Rivers that I will have to talk things over with my mother. It's a very kind and flattering offer but—"

Someone knocked. A voice murmured that Miss Thelma Oberlin and Count Fyodor de Todleben had just arrived by car.

"Susan, you go—No, I will. Thelma's so sensitive," said Bobbie, "and this new Russian acquisition—"

"Baltic Russian," said Susan, "of, I imagine, German extraction. You'd better go, Bobbie."

Bobbie departed, the door slammed, and Susan smiled at Josephine Bruce.

"Well," she said, "do you feel competent to take us on?"

"It's more money," said Josephine soberly, "than I'd earn in years in the office. But . . . no, I don't feel competent, really," she answered honestly, "and—"

"It isn't hard really. Just a ringmaster's job," said Susan. "You crack the whip, and see that the customers are entertained. Half the time my sister doesn't know whom she's asked here or why. You straighten that out, look after the social mail and the bills—all but the house bills. They're in my province. I think you might find it fun, once you were used to

24

it, and I imagine," she said, with her wide pleasant smile, "that you could do with a bit of fun."

Josephine sighed. She said, "I—I don't know, Miss Wilton."

"You're afraid my sister will change her mind? She won't. After you grow to know her you will realize that underneath all the—the clutter of the exterior there are some very tidy rooms. She knows what she wants. But there's one thing she won't want."

"And that is?"

Susan walked over to a window and stood looking out at the water. She asked, over her shoulder: "You've met Lanny Martin, haven't you?"

"Yes, of course."

"I had forgotten," said Susan, "he met you first . . . His stepmother sent him down ahead to prowl around real estate offices . . . and then sent *me* to view the results. Well, you are a great addition to any real estate office, my dear," she added. "And I now recall a telephone conversation I overheard the other day—"

Josephine said, somewhat defensively: "Mr. Martin called me at the office and asked me to go to the Brook with him last night. I refused."

"If you come here," said Susan thoughtfully, "you needn't refuse. My sister won't mind. She will, in fact, be delighted. She likes you. Frankly she has been trying to settle Lanny with some nice, sensible girl for years."

Josephine made a face. Her astonishing dark eyes were very bright. She said, "I don't know that I like the description . . . and besides on the mere evi-

25

dence of an invitation to the Brook Club, are you assuming—?"

"I never assume. I was warning. As long as it is Lanny it's all right. But if it should happen to be Jon—"

"Jon?"

"Jonathan Scott, my sister's son by her first marriage. She has," said Susan thoughtfully, "rather more in common with her stepson. But she is inordinately proud of Jon. She has even selected his wife for him. Normally Jon wouldn't be here during the season, or at the most he would fly down for only a few days. But Roberta's taken it into her head to buy some land and build and of course Jon will get the job. Knowing Jon as I do I dare say he would far rather not—but his firm will have something to say about that. And that is where Evelyn came in—and went out."

"Evelyn," asked Josephine, rather dazed, "you mean Miss Gainford?"

"Exactly. The quondam secretary. She has known Jon for years, of course. During the six months she was with my sister, she saw very little of him. This wasn't exactly to her liking and it appears that she has been writing him . . . keeping him informed on this situation and that and suggesting that he take a holiday and keep an eye on things. My sister, when she learned this, was considerably annoyed and jumped to the conclusion—it wasn't much of a leap—that Evelyn had motives of her own. You follow me, I think?"

"Quite," said Josephine. She was pink, under the cream-gold of her skin. "Mr. Martin is open season. Mr. Scott—I believe you said—is closed."

"Not just the way I would put it," said Susan, "but I think you understand."

"What," demanded Josephine, "makes you think that I would even harbor the remotest interest in either Mr. Martin or Mr. Scott?"

"Lanny," said Susan reflectively, "is attractive enough, I suppose. Jon's a darling. Maybe I'm prejudiced. I wouldn't know. The point isn't so much that they, singly or together, might attract you but that you would attract them. Or don't you look into a mirror?"

"I've looked in it for twenty years."

"I like you," Susan told her, "and have since we met in the office. That is why I'm warning you. I perceived that you had a quantity of that misnamed commodity common sense under your very lovely hair. If you hadn't I couldn't talk to you like this. So don't be angry. Think it over. I believe you would find the position both profitable and amusing. And as permanent as you'd care to make it, provided you fitted in and were competent—which I believe—and provided you listen to this Cassandralike warning and are not too annoyed to ignore it."

"Thanks," said Josephine. "I'm sorry I lost my temper, a little. If you'll give me your inventory and your notes I'll take them to the office. And I'll talk to my mother tonight."

"Have you had lunch?"

"No, but that doesn't—"

"Suppose you come down with me and we'll have ours on the terrace. I don't know about the others. Trays by the pool, or in bedrooms, or off to lunch on the terrace at Hialeah. I never know, which is one reason why my job just isn't as easy as it sounds."

Josephine shook her head, smiling. "I think," she said, "I'll go back to the office. I can get a coke and a sandwich on my way. Just now I've a good deal to think over."

"All right," said Susan and walked with her down the hall, "but remember, if you do come, you have an ally."

Chapter 3

Josephine walked down the curving stairway, stopping for a moment to look down into the big square hall, filled, like the rest of the house, with sunlight and flowers. An elderly butler, paunched and gray, uniformed and pompous, paused to approve her leisurely descent. He was over sixty, he suffered from neuritis and a hair-trigger temper, he had served Mrs. Rivers under the wise direction of Susan Wilton for upward of ten years, reasonably content with his lot . . . quantities of tea, a nip of the best brandy when off duty, ample tips—if somewhat smaller of late, and good living quarters. But his mind was troubled by the tenor of the times, his heart torn by the agony of the country he had left forty years ago and of which he was still a citizen,

28

and his dignity disturbed by the lack of reverence accorded his station by his fellow, if inferior, servants whose gypsylike propensities he greatly deplored. Mrs. Rivers's house—any house occupied by her—was more or less a lunatic asylum but he accepted that as part of the phenomenon known as American life. A bachelor, by choice, he still had a keen eye for a pretty ankle and hence when Josephine arrived at the last stair he smiled at her in a zippered sort of way, greeting her with the staid deference shown to a lady. He had an unerring capacity for recognizing the gentry.

"Good morning, Miss Bruce," he said and moved pontifically toward the door. "A very lovely day," he added, as though he had created it.

"It's beautiful, Wycherly," she agreed, smiling, and went out the great door cool and trim in her linen suit, small, poised and efficient.

Wycherly looked after her with increased appreciation. When, before Mrs. Rivers's arrival, he and Miss Wilton had reached Miami Beach with the staff to set the house in order Miss Bruce had been of the greatest possible assistance.

He watched her walking down the wide palm-bordered drive and turned and went his way. He did not see her pass through the open gates and pause at the stone posts, he did not see her put up one small hand to touch the carved lettering which read "Blue Horizons."

Josephine walked down Collins Avenue until she picked up a jitney going her way. She got in and sat beside a man with a toothache, a woman with a baby, and a little girl with a cold. She got out on Lincoln Road and walked a block or two to the real estate office. Lincoln road was crowded. Traffic was a sluggishly moving stream and pedestrians an equally slow surge.

Josephine watched the people, strolling under awnings and archways . . . window shopping, window wishing. Women in printed silks, in linens, women in tailored suits, hatless women, women wearing straw hats, flower hats, toques and turbans. A girl in gray flannel slacks, high-heeled, toeless shoes on her stockingless feet, and a silver fox coat to her hips. A girl in what looked like a modified sarong. A fat woman in a pink cotton dress, dragging a screaming small boy in a sailor suit by one grubby hand. A woman getting out of a Rolls-Royce in front of one of the shops, beautifully dressed and talking voluble French to her bored, anemic male escort. Another Rolls-Royce with the G.B. license on it.

Josephine never tired of Lincoln Road. She had grown up with it. It was the crazy, star-spangled dream of men who were both visionaries and doers come true. Sometimes it had the quality of a dream still. All the lavish display of luxuries, jewels and frocks, hats and cosmetics, toys and flowers—the shining windows, the fanciful architecture . . . restaurants and motion picture theaters, banks and business offices . . . pastel colors under a peerless sky, cream and rose and pale yellow, turquoise and sepia . . . and the living green of palms.

For three months of the year Lincoln Road blossomed like a flower of stone and steel and then slept in the sun until the next big, short season woke it to teeming life again.

Josephine went into the real estate office. It looked like the entrance to a small private house, chaste and white, with a small, unobtrusive legend on the windows. In the window was a colorful dioramic presentation of Miami Beach from enlarged photographs, with the addition of miniature palms. No more, no black slates advertising bargains, no photographed houses, no price marks.

She went through to the room she shared with several others and found it deserted. A clacking typewriter announced that Edna, Mr. Seymour's secretary, was back from lunch in the Seymour office. Josephine opened the door and went in and Edna pushed the red riotous hair from her tanned forehead and said, "Hello, stranger."

"Hi," said Josephine, "where's everyone?"

"Feed bag. Bill was in and out a moment ago. He thinks he has the Durkin sale clinched. He was looking for you. Said he'd be back."

"Here he comes," said Josephine, and disappeared to powder her classic nose. The sound of a hurricane, the tempestuous heralding of a whirlwind, accompanied by sound effects, that was Bill Gamble, the youngest partner of Seymour and Company . . . Bill, who when a forceful and new salesman had had his cards printed "Gamble with Gamble."

She emerged a little later to find Bill sitting on

Edna's desk swinging his long legs. He was a stocky, personable young man with sun-bleached hair and crooked eyebrows over very blue eyes. He had a battered hat on the back of his head and was graphically describing his previous difficulties with old Mr. Durkin. "First he says he'll sell, then he comes down and says he won't. So I informed the prospect, bet's off. Then he staggers down here and says, 'Well, for forty thousand, provided it's all cash.' Who in hell, I figure, ever heard of that much cash? I had lunch the other day with Richards . . . Dun and Bradstreet lists him at about seven millions. But who paid the check? I did. Richards had left his wallet on the piano or in the swimming pool or on the bridge of the *Elmira*. . . . Hi, Jo, light of my life. Hast et?"

"No, I forgot—I've been at Blue Horizons with Mrs. Rivers and—"

"Why don't you make Nat or someone take over?" Bill inquired, getting off the desk. "Why should you run your legs off for her?"

"I don't mind. Want to feed me? I've something I want to ask you."

"The answer is yes," said Bill rapidly, "but this is so sudden. May I have six bridesmaids . . . and a flower girl? Edna here will do, she'd look lovely in flowers."

"Scram," ordered Edna, "I've work to do, if you haven't. Mr. Seymour's coming back from his fishing trip. Mr. Corley is getting over his grippe and things will start humming."

Bill tucked Josephine's hand under his arm. He

said, "Well, the Durkin deal is in the bag. We can afford lunch; let's go."

They walked out into the hot sunlight, down Lincoln Road and across to a small, tucked-away restaurant reached through a patio. There were tables on the outdoor terrace and palms and the sound of water falling into a basin from the height of a tall fountain.

"The sky," said Bill, "is the limit." He scanned the menu. "How about a drink?" he asked hopefully.

"You know I—"

"Sure. But someday you'll break down. I'll have a Manhattan . . . better make it two," he told the waiter.

"Bill—at midday!"

"Well, today's special. Besides, you were going to ask me to marry you. Don't go away, Bert," he told the waiter kindly, "you know Miss Bruce always proposes in public. She'll have jellied soup, stone crab salad and iced tea. I don't approve, you understand, but that's what she always orders. Bring me the blue plate and a mess of greens to keep up my vitamin content. Now, scat."

He leaned back and grinned. He said, after a moment, "You're looking stirred. What's up?"

She had known him for a dozen years, ever since his parents had moved to the Beach from Tampa. They had gone to school together, to the coeducational academy where small girls of ten could look at big seventeen-year-old boys with admiration and hero worship. Then Bill had gone on to the university and when she was fourteen Josephine had gone

33

north. But when after college he returned to get a real estate office job and she had come back to join the League and do all the things her friends did, as a matter of course, Bill had been right on her doorstep. She was eighteen then and she had had a marvelous time until she was eighteen and a half.

Bill had got her the job, her first, the one she now held.

"How's your mother, Jo?"

"About the same."

"I'll drop in to see her, one of these days," he promised, and drank the two Manhattans, one at a time.

"I wish you would. Bill, I'm serious, I want your advice."

"Don't marry him," he said instantly, "even if he does make twelve thousand a year. He doesn't love you. Not as I love you, Toots. Look, ever since Uncle Al left me the wherewithal to buy into the outfit, I've had big plans . . . and there's no reason why we shouldn't get married now. I have the interest in the business, sure, it isn't much but it's something—we can't know from year to year how it will cut up but its bound to show us a profit, as long as the firm stays in the black. Then there's my drawing account and commissions. The Durkin deal will net me a new jalopy. And enough over for a honeymoon. What about Cat Cay? You'd like that, wouldn't you? Or Pete would let us have his boat and we could go down off Bimini fishing. Don't speak. Don't say a word. I know all the answers. We'd take an apartment and your mother will be comfortable with us.—How about it?"

She said, smiling and unastonished, for she had been hearing all this for a number of years, and recently, every time Bill closed a deal, "You're sweet, but the answer's the same. No."

"Same reason?"

" 'Fraid so, Bill."

"You're fond of me, you don't love me. Oh, hell," he said, discouraged and eying the blue plate with detached horror. "Now, why did I order this?" he inquired. "I don't know why I waste my time with you, Jo. I suppose there are prettier gals—not that I've ever seen one. I know there are more reasonable—" He broke off. He asked anxiously, gravely, "You're not trying to tell me you've fallen in love with someone else? Thurman, for instance?"

"So that instigated the crack about twelve thousand a year?"

"Yes . . . why not? Oh, he's all right, coming young lawyer and all that and his practice will go up in leaps and bounds. Leaps from matrimony into divorce, bounds because his clients have been out of bounds. But you *can't* like that stiff."

"My good Bill," she said with spirit, "I hardly know him. I never laid eyes on the man before and until he came in to rent the bungalow for a client that day last autumn. . . ."

"Well, if it isn't Thurman or some glamour boy you've run into, what is it?"

"Mrs. Rivers has offered me a job."

"What kind of job?" asked Bill, pushing back his plate. The sunlight filtered through the palm fronds and made a checkered pattern on his tow head and brown face.

"Secretary. You know. Do her letters, keep her check book, arrange her parties. There's more money in it than I've ever dreamed—and she said it might not be temporary. If I fitted in, maybe I'd go north with her. . . ."

He said, "I don't like it at all. She's liable to hire you for a couple of weeks and then kick you out. You know the time we had until she saw Blue Horizons . . . she didn't want anything her sister and that heel of a stepson had picked out. That reminds me, I remember what's-his-name giving you the eye."

"Lanny Martin?" asked Josephine, smiling. "He gives everyone the eye. I wouldn't worry if I were you."

Bill said, scowling, "If you resign your job with us and anything goes haywire with this other proposition—"

"There are other jobs," she said defensively. "I'm a good secretary and typist and I *can* show houses. I like 'em. I know about them."

"Sure, none better. But the setup? There's such a crazy crowd going and coming at the Riverses," he said, "and—"

She said, "No crazier than anywhere else, and besides, how do you know?"

"I read the papers and draw my own conclusions."

Josephine was silent. She said, after a moment,

"Every year I think I can't get enough stone crabs. Let's go to Joe's some night and eat until we blow up!"

"Okay by me, baby. But, look, you aren't serious about this job proposition, are you?"

"Never more so."

"What about your mother?"

She said, "I'll have to talk to her, of course. But can't you see, Bill, with this extra money and my living—I'd live at Blue Horizons you see—we can afford to have Cousin Agnes. She and Mother get on marvelously, Agnes adores her. I've racked my brain for ages, wondering how it could be managed. Agnes hasn't anything . . . she lives with that dreadful sister-in-law and absolutely slaves."

He said shrewdly, "She'd go on slaving if she came to live with your mother. Sorry, don't mean to hurt your feelings."

"That's all right. I know Mother's demanding. But it's different, Angie wouldn't mind—for Mother. She loves her, and she hates that old harridan in Fort Lauderdale. It would be a perfect arrangement. I could afford to run the apartment for the two of them and pay Agnes a little . . . I mean spending money, enough to make her feel a little self-respecting and independent. I feel so responsible for her, Bill. Mother doesn't, but I do. After all, if Father hadn't persuaded her to invest—She did have a little income, you know, and she handed over her entire principal."

The brown eyes were troubled and the sweetly formed mouth shook.

37

"Skip it," said Bill hastily. "Your father believed the bubble wouldn't burst. Everyone did, I expect. And he lost everything and a little bit more too, so—"

"I know. Well, that's the way it is. Then if I did go north with Mrs. Rivers, I'd know Mother was taken care of and happy. Or if I didn't go, I'd be here on a salary."

"That sounds screwy. Salary from whom and for what?"

"From Mrs. Rivers. She's going to build, she said something about wanting someone here to supervise. For a while anyway."

"Build! Baby, why didn't you say so? Where . . . bay front, ocean front, island? For Pete's sake, why keep it from me! When do I see her?"

"She likes the office, the business will come to us, don't worry. But her son's going to be the architect, so he'll have something to say about it."

Bill said raptly, "Now you're getting to important matters."

"Not to me, that is, not as much. Bill, what do you think about my taking the job? It's a risk, I know, but—"

He said, "It's up to you. Personally I don't like the idea of your being thrown with a bunch of mugs—"

"How do you know they're mugs?"

"If the stepson—what's his name?—Martin is any example."

"Oh," she said, annoyed, "he's all right. You saw him only a couple of times, back in late December . . . you hadn't a chance to know what he's like."

38

"I'm a great judge of human nature," he said. "Look, about this building deal—"

Josephine sighed and drank her tea. She shouldn't have mentioned that. Not now, not if she really wanted advice. Bill was a bird dog for business. That was what made him a good salesman, what had induced Seymour and Corley to accept the small legacy and admit him to the firm.

He was talking and she paid no attention. About the Richards holdings on the bay front, about the Herbert tract on the ocean front, about the new developments on several of the islands in which his firm had an interest. He broke off suddenly.

"You're not listening."

"No."

"But—" he looked at her, his eyes wide—"did you say you'd live at Blue Horizons?" he asked.

"Yes. Didn't you get the point? That's why I thought of Cousin Agnes."

"It didn't percolate. Holy cat! But when am I to see you?"

"I don't imagine Wycherly will throw you out if you happened to be walking along Collins," she said.

"Secretary permitted male followers. No bloody fear!"

She disregarded him with distaste. "And where," she inquired, "did you pick that up?"

"Barkeep," he said, "very British."

"Well, I don't like it," said Josephine. "And don't be silly. There's no reason why I can't see people when I'm free. Besides, I'll have time off, I'll be at the apartment. . . ."

"And I can take you to a movie," he prophesied, "and maybe run to one drink at the Beachcomber, if my takings have been good, and then get you back in time to put your employer to bed."

"I'm not to be her personal maid."

"You may find out differently," he suggested; "you'd be surprised what secretaries are expected to do. It's a good thing Lanny Martin didn't decide he needed one. Blonde with brown eyes . . . and other specifications."

"Bill!"

"Oh, I'm sorry," he said. He looked at his watch. "I've got to see a dog about a man," he explained. "Suppose I drop in tonight and we'll hash this over."

He paid the check, asked the waiter about his wife's arthritis, and they went from the patio into the blaze of light on Lincoln Road. Walking back to the office, he asked, presently, "Telling the boss when he gets back?"

"Not until I talk to Mother."

"That means, you'll talk her into it." He added gloomily, "I suppose it is a break. But I'm not sure that it isn't the wrong kind. You'd better marry me, Jo. It would be better than having Corley bark at you—he does, I've heard him."

She said, "He's never forgiven my father. They had a terrific row years ago. But he's been very fair to me. He didn't say no when you asked him to give me a job."

"Oh, fair enough, the old so-and-so. Better," he

40

went on, "than walking Mrs. Rivers's sheep dogs in the cool of the evening."

"She hasn't any sheepdogs. She hasn't any dogs at all. She's allergic or something," said Jo, smiling against her will. "And if she had half a dozen of 'em, there's plenty of room on the grounds. . . ."

Her voice trailed off. He said, "Poor kid," gently, took her hand and squeezed it. "But there's one thing . . . Blue Horizons. You're going to hate being there. Plenty."

I won't," she said valiantly. "Why should I? It's nothing to me—now."

"Okay," he said again, "it's up to you."

Chapter 4

Night came softly to Miami, a brief nostalgic dusk, a deepening into starry darkness. Lights bloomed along Lincoln Road and in the palm gardens of the hotels. Lights shone on swimming pools and were brighter than day in the restaurants and cafés and clubs. A cool wind talked in its sleep among the palms and life stirred along the highways and boulevards.

The apartment in which Josephine and her mother lived was tall, white, modern. Their rooms were few, their conveniences many. In the good-sized bedroom, which they shared, Venetian blinds shut out glare and midday sun. The living room, which served also as a dining room, was large and furnished with the good pieces they had been able to save from the wreck. Josephine wished sometimes that they had saved none at all, but had been able to buy new, little by little. The rather massive furniture looked wholly out of place in the apartment. It was not—what was the word?—functional.

Besides, every day her mother remembered something . . . she remembered just when Joseph bought that, and where; how much he paid for it and why . . . what occasion it commemorated, whether a spending spree or an anniversary, or just a day on which he had expressed a wish for an eighteenth-century powder table.

When Josephine came in her mother was sitting on the Empire love seat near the living-room windows, in the dark. She often sat in the dark, to Josephine's acute distress. It was a mute reminder that she, Josephine, was late. It was a mute reminder that nowadays Mrs. Bruce had no soft-footed servants to tiptoe in and turn on the lights for her. Not for four years . . . when the last had left her . . . the last, sole survivor of many.

Josephine automatically put her finger on a switch and as the light glowed, her mother spoke.

"Oh, it's you, dear," she said, with her unfailing sweetness tempered by underlying martyrdom, "I didn't hear you come in. You're late, aren't you?"

"Not very. Are you hungry?"

"No," said her mother, "I wish I had more appetite . . . but I haven't."

"If you would only take your tonic regularly."

"I try," said Mrs. Bruce plaintively, "but it chokes

me. And what is the use? Sitting here, day in and day out, as I do."

She did not. She had numerous friends, and they had not forgotten her. They came to take her driving, to take her to the Beach or Surf Club for luncheon, or to their own houses. But she would not always respond. There were many days when she "preferred" to be alone. She did not wish to be a burden. She did not wish people to feel that they must consider her, especially as she could not return their hospitality. Josephine had heard this over and over again for years. She sometimes wondered how her mother's friends—who heard it also—could endure it. Most of them did. The real friends, the loyal ones. Besides, when she was in the mood no one could be more amusing and charming than Alva Bruce.

Josephine took off her things, washed, combed her hair, and went into the tiny kitchen. Her mother rose, sighing, and Josephine ran out. "I'll move the table," she said. "Here. You can set it."

She did the ordering before she went to work and saw that there were cold things, and soup ready to be heated, for her mother's lunch. Dinner must be hot and substantial, otherwise Alva would not have one good meal a day. Alva's breakfast was a mere matter of fruit juice and black coffee, even in the old days of trays and personal maids.

"Women alone," the doctor had said, "get into bad eating habits. Especially your mother's type. You'll have to look out for that as best you can, Jo, my dear."

Josephine fixed a vegetable salad, broiled chops, creamed last night's baked potatoes, whipped cream for the gelatine dessert and made iced coffee. When finally, they were at the table, "What have you been doing today?" she asked. "Did Fanny come?"

"Yes. We went for a short drive and stopped for tea. She has a new car," said Alva, "and the most enormous diamond bracelet I have ever seen. At least four inches wide . . . execrable taste."

Alva's diamond bracelets and all the things Joseph had showered upon her had gone the way of everything else in their personal crash. Poor, misguided Joseph, she thought, always missing him yet unable to think of him without that spark of anger and resentment, sinking more and more money into crazy developments, sure that boom days would never be over. Losing so much at the time of the hurricane, pulling out again, losing more during the debacle of '29 but then managing to be on top once more. She'd never dreamed that there would be a time when he wouldn't pull out. They'd always had their ups and downs, and they'd always lived as if it were always up. The banks had retained their faith in Joseph . . . until just before the end.

She still had her pearls. She put her hand to them now. They were creamy and glowing against her fine fair skin. She was as blond as Josephine but her eyes were a cool, dark gray. She was a thin small woman with a good, if meager figure. Her hands showed her age. She was fifty-eight. Two sons had been born prior to Josephine. One had died at birth and one

44

when he was three months old. Alva was fond of saying, "If my sons had lived." If her sons had lived they would have been financial geniuses like their father but with less recklessness, less faith in a personal future.

"Darling, do eat your nice chop."

Alva ate with every appearance of reluctance masking a perfectly normal hunger. And presently, having cleared away, brought her mother cigarettes, and lighted her own, Josephine said, "Look, I have something to tell you. I saw Mrs. Rivers today and . . ."

"Mrs. Rivers?"

"You remember. At Blue Horizons."

"I had forgotten her name. Well?"

Josephine told her, briefly. The salary, the duties, the arrangements which might be made.

"Perhaps it is a risk. But I have a good record at the office and if anything happens I'm sure I could get another job. You know how I've managed to fill in, when work was slack . . . typing for Miss Harboard and the others . . . there's always something. And I ran into Mr. Hubbard the other day—"

Hubbard was a banker. He had been a close friend of Joseph Bruce. Hubbard's bank, Mrs. Bruce considered, had ruined the Bruces. She said hotly, "How you could even *speak*—"

"Mother, please! Let's not go into that again. He was very nice. He asked about you, said he wished you would see him and Mrs. Hubbard."

"I wouldn't," Alva said dramatically, "if they were

45

the last two people in the world."

Josephine sighed. She went on after a moment, "Well, anyway, he suggested that if I grew tired of the office there might be a place for me at the bank. You know he offered . . . before . . . he was the first—"

"As if I would permit you!" said her mother.

"That's neither here nor there," said Josephine. "The point is, there will be something I can do if this other proposition folds up. Of course I'll hate being away from you. But you and Agnes will have such a good time . . . and I wouldn't worry about you. I'd run in often, evenings, as often as I could . . . and there would be weekends. I could sleep on the couch. And I thought that maybe if things turned out as well as I hope, if I could save something, I'd buy a little car—Agnes drives—and then this summer you'd be a lot more independent."

Her mother said slowly: "I don't suppose you can afford to refuse." She looked tragically at her daughter. "But—could you *bear* to live at Blue Horizons?" she asked. "I don't see how you could, not for all the money—" Her voice trailed off. She added, "I shut my eyes whenever I have to pass it . . . but you young people are so callous, so hard."

Josephine flushed, her heart was tight with sorrow and anger. She said, after a moment: "I don't like it, I won't like it, and I'll never get used to it. But that's a crazy attitude, and I'm perfectly aware of it. It's so changed—the Bowens altered it in many respects. I've told you that. And besides, as you say, I can't afford to be—sentimental. I spoke to Bill about the

46

arrangement."

"What did he say?"

"Well, he didn't like the idea." Josephine relaxed a little, the tension at the back of her head lessened, and she laughed. "He thought I'd better marry him instead."

I'm being clever, she thought, disliking herself, to get my own way, I hate it but there it is. She's always been afraid I'd marry Bill. . . .

"And throw yourself away," asked her mother energetically, "with your background . . . and the opportunities. . . ."

"What opportunities?" Josephine asked incautiously and immediately regretted it, for her mother said mournfully: "Those you should have had. Of course," she added, "if you are with Mrs. Rivers you will meet people—"

"People?" repeated Josephine. "You mean with money?"

Her mother said unhappily, "You do me a great injustice . . . if you are suggesting that I would want you to marry for money."

You did, thought Josephine, or rather you married the man who, you thought, would make money . . . he did, too . . . you were right.

Aloud she said, "Sorry, I didn't mean to be cross. Yes, I'll meet people. I've already met a few. But the eligible men, dear, the ones with the bank accounts are old or married or both."

"Didn't you say Mrs. Rivers has a son?" asked Alva with an attempt at complete carelessness.

Josephine burst out laughing. Really, she thought, she's priceless, poor darling. She said, "I told you she had a stepson. I don't imagine he has anything more than she gives him. He doesn't work, he seems to subsist on air or something. As a matter of fact, she has a son of her own. I didn't know that until today. He's an architect and will be coming down to talk over building plans."

"Building plans . . . has she bought Blue Horizons?"

"No, she's buying some land and building. No one could add to Blue Horizons, not after the Bowens. But don't be hopeful about Mrs. Rivers's son, darling, it won't wash."

"Why?" asked her mother openly. "Is he married too?"

"I believe not. But he's spoken for," said Josephine. "At least his mother speaks for him. She doesn't want him entangled with secretaries. That is a tip, straight from the stables. Besides," she added, "he's probably very dull and very unattractive, and even if he weren't, it wouldn't matter."

Her mother asked slowly: "Josephine, you're not really in love with Bill."

"No, darling; not really. Not at all."

"If only," her mother mourned, "you could have a season north. There was a time when I might have asked Ellen Johnson to take you. She was a bridesmaid at my wedding and your father and I went north for hers; I was matron of honor. She was married, that summer, in the church at Bar Harbor."

Josephine had heard all about Ellen Johnson. Moreover, she had met her. She thought that a charity season with her mother's capitalistic old playmate would be perhaps the most fearful punishment any spirited girl in her right mind could imagine or endure. She said briskly: "Well, I can't go north, except in a secretarial capacity, angel, so—"

Her mother said, after a moment, "I can't say that I like the idea, but if you're so set on making this change naturally I have nothing to say. You are, after all, the breadwinner in the family," she added with her most courageous and wistful smile.

Josephine, who loved her but who knew her, flesh and bone, mind and spirit, could have shaken her.

"All right," she said, "I'll telephone. Now. And then call Agnes."

Chapter 5

For the next few days Josephine was busier than a bookie on Widener Cup Day. She notified the office of her intention to leave and Mrs. Rivers of her intention to arrive. She superintended the moving in of Cousin Agnes—plus two canaries, a trunk, the family photograph album, much knitting, and innumerable small bags—and officiated at her own moving out. She endured, during this time, the quiet tears of her mother and the calamitous prophecies of young Mr. Gamble, who haunted her doorstep at every opportunity, but who, eventually, drove her and her modest luggage to Blue Horizons.

49

Her entrance was not, she felt, auspicious. In the first place, the day dawned accompanied by the sort of weather which Floridians deeply resent and never mention . . . cold, chill, with an off-sea wind, and whitecaps scudding over gray water. Wycherly met her, looking as pleased as was compatible with the dour arrangement of his features together with a badly swollen cheek, the result of a recalcitrant tooth, lending him a ribald, lopsided look and moving Bill Gamble to barely concealed merriment. Bowing from his increasing waist, Wycherly reported that Mrs. Rivers would see Miss Bruce later in the day as Mrs. Rivers and some of her house guests were at the Bath Club for luncheon and bridge. Miss Wilton, however, was at home.

A younger manservant appeared and took up the burden of the bags, and a small, trim maid, wreathed in professional smiles but with a wary eye, arrived to show Josephine to her quarters. Thus surrounded by an audience Josephine could do no more than shake Bill Gamble's hand firmly and bid him good-bye.

"Thanks for bringing me," she said.

" 'S all right," he assured her, if with the utmost reluctance. "Y'understand I don't approve?"

Wycherly's eyebrows elevated and the little maid exchanged a knowing look with the houseman, who was, temporarily, her big moment.

"Thanks again," said Josephine hastily, "and I'll be seeing you."

"When, exactly?" inquired Bill.

"I'll let you know."

She wished he'd go, for heaven's sake!

He said, looking around, "It still looks familiar."

Josephine signaled the maid. Wycherly had said, solemnly, "And this is Rhoda," so Josephine said, beckoning, "All right, Rhoda," and prepared to ascend the stairs.

Bill grunted and presently went out through the door Wycherly held open, in readiness.

A little later Josephine took stock of her rooms. They were very pleasant, the bedroom, not large but extremely cheerful, an adequate bath, and a little living room. The master and guest rooms of Blue Horizons were all arranged en suite and this was one of the smallest. But she liked it, and the wide windows overlooking the patio and pool and the ocean.

Rhoda lingered. Should she unpack? But Josephine thanked her, smiling. She would see to that herself, she said, and Rhoda after a moment of disappointment rallied and departed. Luncheon would be at one-thirty, she suggested.

She wanted to talk, thought Josephine, and get her bearings. She doesn't know quite how to place me. I'm Staff. But not Servants' Hall. It was easy with Evelyn Gainford, her status, as friend of the family, was definite. Me, I'm not pigeonholed.

She unlocked her bags and proceeded to put into the good-sized closet and bureau space her various possessions: sport clothes, linen frocks, an afternoon dress, simple dinner dresses . . . hats, shoes, lingerie,

51

toilet articles, photographs, the double one of her mother and father, a small framed snapshot of Bill.

Her personal, treasured portable typewriter stood severely upon the delicate piece of furniture which was presumably a desk in the living room.

Someone knocked and Susan Wilton came in.

"Are you comfortable?" she asked, smiling. "I hope so." She looked around the room, frowning. She had ordered flowers, but they were not in evidence. She went on, "My sister will be home later in the afternoon. Meantime, I suggest that you orientate yourself." She stopped. "I forgot," she added, "you already know your way around. Do you like the rooms?"

"Very much."

Anything, Josephine thought, would have been better than the big corner suite, the one she remembered best. But that was now Mrs. Rivers's, and she would have to enter it sooner or later. Stupid to be so unwilling, to feel resentment and horror, such tearing agony at the thought of walking across a threshold.

Susan Wilton said, with utmost gentleness, "You were very brave to come here, my dear."

Josephine looked up quickly and Susan said: "You see, I didn't know the whole story until a day or so ago when I stopped in your office—you weren't there, of course—on a minor matter and happened to meet Mr. Gamble. We discussed the change you were making."

Josephine said wearily: "Bill shouldn't . . . I mean,

52

oh, I know the Bowens changed things considerably, apparently they didn't mind—" she broke off, this was very difficult for her—"but I didn't think when Mrs. Rivers rented the house from them that anyone would feel it necessary to give her chapter and verse. I thought perhaps I wouldn't be brought into it at all."

"You haven't been," said Susan. "My sister doesn't know—and I didn't, as I said, until just the other day. I realized that you were familiar with Blue Horizons, but I thought it was because of your activities in the real estate office. We don't know any local people, we don't even know our landlord . . . you may remember all the negotiations were conducted by your office."

She went to the door and turned to smile at the girl who seemed suddenly forlorn, desolate even, standing by the windows looking young and alone.

"I hope you'll be happy here," she said; "there may be some confusion and difficulty at first. People—come and go. They are not always the people I'd like to see come," she added carefully, "but this is a careless and gregarious household, as you will learn. And you can always come to me if you are troubled in any way. I hope you won't be, but if you are, you'll remember that I'm here."

"You're very kind," Josephine told her sincerely.

The door closed and Josephine sat down in a deep chair bright with glazed chintz, yellow background, turquoise birds, near the windows. She remembered this room, of course . . . it had pleasant associations

53

for her. Yet her eyes filled with silly tears and her throat felt dry and tight.

Idiot, she told herself.

After all, she had asked to show Blue Horizons at the time the Bowens decided to rent it and go to South America. She thought it would be good for her. Face things, and you're the stronger for it. She remembered the first time she had taken a prospective client through. It was like walking on swords . . . what was the story of the girl who walked on swords, The Little Mermaid? But she had braced herself and the second time it had not hurt so much.

Well, it wouldn't hurt now. Why should it? You had to think of a house as a shell . . . she hunted for the right phrase in her mind . . . only atmosphere mattered, the people who made that atmosphere. Not the house itself.

You had a jewel case, it contained the things you most loved . . . when they were gone, the case didn't matter. It was empty, it served no purpose.

She was very angry to find that she was crying.

She went into the bathroom and washed her face and eyes in cold water. She powdered, was lavish with lipstick, and returned to arrange her typewriter, and put out notebooks and sharpened pencils.

Rhoda knocked and entered, bearing two vases of flowers, a fat round one, a tall thin one. Miss Wilton had sent them in, she said, and put one on the dresser and one on the desk. She lingered, again ready to talk, half friendly and familiar, half on guard. But Josephine, thanking her, dismissed her

54

without words. Hers would be, she foresaw, a difficult position.

Rhoda, departing with no word to carry belowstairs, left the door open and the countess looked in. She cried, at the doorway: "Hello. I know you, don't I?"

Her flat green eyes were curious but her wide red mouth smiled.

"We met," Josephine said, "quite informally, on the patio, one day. I'm Josephine Bruce, from the real estate office," she added, feeling rather strange, a sort of Lawks-a-mercy-can-this-be-I sensation. "But Mrs. Rivers has engaged me as her secretary."

The countess came in and shut the door. "So that's it." She spoke her own name carelessly. "Not that you'll remember," she added. She sat down and offered Josephine a platinum cigarette case with a little crown of rubies and diamonds ornamenting the shining surface. She wore white flannel slacks, a bright red shirt, and a navy coat.

She said, "A pretty girl like you should be doing something else—or someone. Do tell me about this household."

"I'm afraid I can't," Josephine said, smiling, "as I arrived only half an hour ago."

The countess looked grieved.

"But I thought you were an old friend," she began.

"You've confused me with my predecessor," Josephine told her. "No, indeed. I'm a local product."

"Local?"

"Like oranges in Indian River. I was born in Miami Beach," she said, "and Mrs. Rivers plucked me out of my job to take over the secretarial duties."

"How too disappointing," said the countess. "I thought you would be able to—how do you say it?—dish the dirt."

Josephine laughed. "I don't say it, just that way," she countered gently, "and even if I were in a position to—dish it, I—"

"Wouldn't?" asked the countess and exhaled a lungful of smoke.

"That's right," Josephine admitted.

She felt slightly jittery. Perhaps you didn't go about your new duties in this way. If she antagonized one of Mrs. Rivers's guests, she might be fired before night.

The countess chuckled. "I like you. I wish I could afford you." She looked at her watch, which was mostly diamonds and rubies but still managed to tell a little time. "Good God!" she exclaimed in horror. "I'm due at Hialeah. But Howard went off somewhere this morning. Have you ten dollars?"

Josephine blinked.

"I think so," she began uncertainly. . . .

The countess fished in a flat red handbag and produced six dollars and forty cents. "With any luck," she said, "I'll pay you back tonight. Howard won't lend me any more. He's as tight as my mother's corset." She elaborated on what else Howard was until Josephine's small flat ears burned.

A girl wandered past the door, stopped and came in. She was pretty in a sulky way, slightly unwashed, her long fair hair disheveled. She wore green pajamas, and said negligently, "Hello, you two." She regarded Josephine beneath heavy lids. "Competition," she said sadly. "Where's everyone?"

"Bath Club or races," the countess told her.

"Pop?"

"He said something about Palm Beach when I encountered him this morning."

"Oops," said the girl, and departed as suddenly as she had arrived. The countess grinned at Josephine.

"House guest," she explained kindly, "daughter of one Dr. Richard Farmer. She flew in yesterday from Nassau. Flying somewhere else today. This place is a tourists' camp. She and Lanny Martin were out all night doing the town. Her name's Jean. From the way she looks this morning," she added reflectively, "Jeanie with the dark-brown taste."

She rose. "What about the ten?" she reminded Josephine.

Josephine fetched her purse. She had twenty-two dollars. She gave a new ten dollar bill to the countess, with misgivings. And the countess laughed.

"If I win," she said, "I'll split with you. If I lose, well, you may get it back provided Howard's amenable. I think he will be, when he learns to whom I owe it. You remember Howard, don't you? Elderly satyr, leering over his stomach? He's one of my dearest friends," she added, "damn him," and vanished brightly into the corridor.

Josephine's mind staggered. She felt as if she had been hit on the head. But hard.

The rest of the day was comparatively normal. She lunched with Miss Wilton in the breakfast room . . . "dining room's too big, patio's too cold, terrace too windy," explained Susan, and afterward sat in Susan's living room with her and talked of a number of trivial things. At about four-thirty Bobbie Rivers returned from the Bath Club together with two elderly female house guests, a Mrs. Carter and a Miss Terry. She took Josephine to the alleged "Office" and handed her a stack of mail. "I've made notes," said Bobbie proudly. "Would you like to work in here?"

Josephine looked around. The clutter dismayed her. She said, "I think perhaps it could be managed in my own rooms."

"Good," said Bobbie vaguely. "I can't find anything anyway. Suppose you come in every morning while I'm having my breakfast tray and we'll talk things over. Now tonight"—she closed her eyes in an effort to remember—"Dick Farmer, his daughter, my stepson, the countess, Howard, and I are going to the Brook. The rest will dine at home. At eight. You might arrange bridge after, if they seem inclined. Otherwise you may have some suggestion."

So the pattern of her days was set. Fill in, arrange contract or other amusement, and answer letters. Bobbie's notations were clear. "Refuse," she had scrawled across three invitations. "Say I'd

58

love to have her come for the first week in March. . . . Tell him I won't pay the bill, the lamp shades are not satisfactory. . . . Tell this organization I sent a check last month."

Josephine did not see Lanny Martin until after breakfast on the day following her arrival. No one breakfasted downstairs, trays were customary. She had asked Rhoda to bring hers at eight, to Rhoda's horror, as few trays found their way upstairs before ten. And after breakfast and her bath she dressed and went downstairs. The sun shone again, and it would be some time before she could appear in Bobbie's room with her notebook.

The day was gold and blue. Josephine walked across the patio across the lawn to the strip of beach and sat down with her back against the retaining wall and looked out to the Gulf Stream, dark and lovely, a strip of crumpled indigo ribbon. Some of the fishing boats were already there. She had brought toast from her tray for the gulls and they screamed about her, lovely in the air, awkward on the ground, their cold, inhuman eyes regarding her with icy greed.

An hour passed, Josephine dreamed—and re-membered.

"Hi," said Lanny, and came to sit beside her and fill his pipe.

"Hello."

"I haven't laid eyes on you," he said reproachfully, "of course I knew you were here. Bobbie told me. What a break . . . for me, I mean. How about a spot of night life tonight?"

Josephine shook her bead. "It isn't one of my duties, I'm afraid. Besides, Mrs. Rivers has said that I may go home for the evening."

"I'll drive you there, and wait," he told her eagerly. "Don't be like that."

"Like what?"

"Efficient and brush-offing," he explained. "Bobbie will love to know I'm in good company. She said so, last night. She said, 'Lanny, for heaven's sake why don't you amuse my little Josephine?'"

Josephine laughed.

"I doubt it."

"Frankly," he said, "she's disturbed over Jean. Have you seen Jean by any chance? Her father's the best gland man in the East but he should have gone to work on hers ten years ago. Bobbie doesn't like Jean."

"And Jean likes you?"

"She's crazy about me," said Lanny pleasantly, "but then she's crazy about any man." He grinned shamelessly at Josephine. "Look," he said, "if Bobbie sends you a signed memo to the effect that you can go out with me tonight after you've been home—?"

"All right," said Josephine.

"Then relax and look as if you had something to look forward to—other than a shot of cold poison," he suggested. "Good heavens, what is the good Fritzi doing up at this hour?"

The countess, in startling pajamas, was strolling

across the lawn toward them. Her hands were full of money.

She said, "Hello, Lanny, you're looking very pretty this morning." She said, "My dear, I hit the daily double, right on its two noses. Here's your ten and your winning."

Josephine took the ten and waved aside the fifty-six remaining dollars.

"But I promised," said the countess firmly. "And if I hadn't won you might have whistled for the original stake."

Josephine shook her shining head. Fritzi groaned.

"Stubborn woman. Lanny, you won't get to first base with her . . . or aren't you trying? Josephine—you don't mind, do you—look, here's a thought. Take it, put it away and when I come borrowing again, you can lend it back to me, a little at a time."

"Better take it," advised Lanny, "she has bulldog blood."

Josephine took the money, and put it in the pocket of her jacket. Fritzi sighed with relief. "Now," she said happily. "I always know where to go . . . when Howard's stuffy. Which is almost all of the time. Here he comes—leer and all."

"Why," Mr. Toller greeted them, "if it isn't the dream girl in the patio."

Josephine reflected how odd it was to live in the same house with people and never see them. She smiled at the fat man, and Lanny warned soberly: "Lay off her . . . money won't buy her and you're not beautiful enough to arouse her aesthetic sense."

61

"But who *is* she?" asked Howard, intently.

Lanny explained, and Howard said sadly, "Why is it that all *my* secretaries look as if they had been weaned on cold tea with a pinch of alum?"

Josephine looked at her watch and rose. She said, smiling, "I'm sorry but Mrs. Rivers is expecting me by now, I think."

They watched her walk up the lawn. Lanny sighed, "There goes something."

"You can't afford her," said Fritzi briskly.

"And you can't afford me," Lanny told her calmly.

"*I* can afford her," said Howard, with gloom, "but she wouldn't consider it. Lanny, I'll take you on at tennis."

"Okay," said Lanny, coming to his feet, "but don't hold me responsible for your stroke—including one of apoplexy!"

Josephine went up to the big corner bedroom where Bobbie Rivers, her breakfast tray on her knees, was conferring with Susan Wilton. Bobbie wore a blue bedjacket over her nightgown, her pink hair in a blue snood. The bed was strewn with letters, wires, a couple of newspapers, and six photographic proofs. She pointed to them dramatically.

"Send them back," she told Josephine, "they give me the horrors. I look fifty years old."

"You are," said her sister, "and a bit."

"I know it, Susan, but must I look it in my pictures?" She added, "The letters can wait. Nothing important. That wire's from Jon, he says hold everything, he's trying to get away—" She turned to Josephine. "My son," she explained. "I talked to him the other night, and told him the plans I had made. He doesn't agree. I thought that you, Susan and I would go out this morning and look at some of the sites which have been suggested. Eleven I told the real estate office. That nice Gamble boy is going along. If I find the right one Jon can't object."

"He can," said Susan, "but his firm will object to his objection."

"Be ready," Bobbie told Josephine, "at ten of eleven, will you? Better bring a notebook. I can't remember places. And take the letters with you, they can be attended to later. There's nothing there I have to tell you about."

At a little after eleven Susan, Bobbie, and Josephine drove up to the real estate office in the big, chauffeured car. Susan had flatly refused to go with Bobbie in the little car. "Not the way you drive," she had told her sister. "I'd like to live a little longer although I'm sure I don't know why."

Bill Gamble was waiting for them. He greeted Bobbie and Susan with charming deference and Josephine with decorum. He said, "Just on time. I've a list here of several sites which I am sure will interest you."

The Sunset Islands, Star Island, Indian Creek Drive, bay front, ocean front . . .

Toward one o'clock Bobbie discovered her site, with considerable frontage on North Bay Road and on the bay itself. She said plaintively, "My feet hurt.

63

And I like this. Who owns it?"

Bill, holding his breath, told her.

"Could I have an option on it," asked Bobbie, "or something—until my son gets here, that is? I'd have to have his advice."

"How much are they asking for it?" asked Susan with regrettable practicality, before Bill could answer.

He told them that too.

"Ridiculous. He'll have to come down," Susan said.

"We'll do our best," Bill pledged, "but of course this is a pretty choice situation . . . and as Mrs. Rivers is certain she'd prefer bay front—"

"I don't want to be on the ocean, always," said Bobbie, "too noisy. Too many waves, all that sort of thing. It's all right for the season. And I don't like islands. No. This is just what I want. Ever since we went to Gertrude Watkins," she told Susan, "I've been determined to build my house on the bay."

Susan said, "Well, you can't make up your mind in ten minutes, Roberta. Suppose we go back and talk it over. Jon may have other ideas."

"It's my house," said Bobbie crossly, "even if Jon builds it. And he'll build it my way too." She turned to Bill. "See about an option, will you?" she said. "And have all the figures ready for Mr. Scott when he arrives. And now," she said, "I'm dead . . . let's go."

Bill signaled Josephine with his eyebrows. Will she or won't she? he inquired. Josephine shrugged hers, in effect. I haven't the least idea, was what they conveyed. Susan, catching the little byplay, smiled. Nice

64

youngsters, she thought. I hope the girl isn't silly enough to fall for Lanny. She was fond of Lanny but she didn't like him. She liked Josephine.

Bobbie sent Susan and Josephine down to lunch with those of her guests who were not at the races or the Surf Club . . . four, to be exact. A married couple who had arrived late the night before, en route to South America, and the two elderly women whom Josephine could not tell apart. After luncheon she and Susan were summoned to the office where Bobbie sat, a luncheon tray beside her, and pored over the sketches she had been making and now displayed.

"White stone," she said, "and you enter directly on the patio . . . dining terrace on the right and on the left a sort of outdoor living room. Pillars. Then the drawing room, library, and indoor dining room, and a terrace on the bayside. Oh, damn," she said, "where's the swimming pool?"

"Wait till Jon comes," said her sister soothingly.

"I sent him a wire," said Bobbie absently, "I said, 'come at once have bought land.' That will bring him. Look, Susan, about the bedrooms . . . yours, mine, Lanny's, Jon's—and a couple of guest rooms . . . never more than two," she said finally. "All these people are driving me crazy!"

"Why do you ask them?" inquired her sister.

"I don't know. They ask themselves. Do you think Howard and Fritzi are staying indefinitely? Of course I asked them to but I didn't expect they would. And I haven't laid eyes on Thelma and her

Baltic problem for days."

"They left yesterday," said Susan, "having had a wonderful time."

"I wish they'd all go," said Bobbie. "I think I'll do my own bedroom in mauve and blue and yellow . . ."

Toward two o'clock the following morning, Lanny Martin and Josephine returned to Blue Horizons. After Josephine had seen her mother they had gone out to Marden's Riviera, and had returned to drop in at several of Lanny's favorite informal haunts. Coming in, quietly, they were not speaking. Josephine's face was bright, and her eyes black with anger. She carried a little wrap over her arm, and walked ahead of Lanny, a slender figure in a black-and-white print dinner dress.

"Wait, don't go upstairs mad," he said, laughing, very sure of himself.

"I'm not angry," she told him; "merely disgusted."

"You can't blame a guy for trying, and you're so darned pretty—"

The hall was dimly lighted. Neither saw the tall man stroll out from the library and stand there, in the archway.

"Look," said Lanny, caught her hand and swung her close to him. "I'm crazy about you . . . I'm not eligible. You know that, you're a practical girl. But we could have a lot of fun together. Like this—"

He drew her close, and kissed her, very expertly.

Josephine freed herself and slapped him, hard.

"That won't do," said Lanny softly, "for I could

66

cost you your job. Or don't you like your job?"

"What is her job?" inquired Jonathan Scott, and moved forward into the light.

"Jon, for Pete's sake!" exclaimed Lanny, and held out both hands to his stepbrother, astonished and unabashed. "Where'd you drop from?"

"New York, by plane, a little while ago. No one was up or about when I came in, except a houseman who took me to my rooms. He told me you were out so I came down to wait, over a highball. I wanted to talk to you. It appears, however, that I interrupted—"

"My brother, Jonathan Scott, Miss Bruce," said Lanny, grinning. "Miss Bruce is Bobbie's newest and most decorative secretary. And she is delighted, I'm sure, at your sudden appearance. Or weren't you watching?"

"I was watching," said Jonathan, acknowledging the introduction. His eyes were ice blue and unsmiling. He was the best-looking man Josephine had ever seen. "Perhaps," he added, "Miss Bruce would like to go upstairs . . . as it's fairly late."

"I would like it very much," said Josephine, with cold fury, "thank you, Mr. Scott. And good night."

He had looked at her as if she . . . as if she and Lanny . . . She hated him. She thought, And he dismissed me as if I were a—

If he stays here, she thought, I won't. Job or no job. She went up, carrying herself tall and straight, her head very high. Lanny, looking after her until she disappeared, whistled.

"Sorry," he said, "you had to witness my shame. I

67

must be slipping."

"I'm not interested," said Jonathan, "in your affairs. But you might have had the decency to exclude Mother's employees."

Josephine heard that, at the top of the stairs. Don't mind me, she thought, I just work here. She could manage Lanny Martin. And manage him she would, perhaps in a way she hadn't intended, if only to show Jonathan Scott that she was unmoved by his interference or disapproval.

Chapter 6

When on the following morning Rhoda knocked, Josephine opened her eyes with the distinct sensation that she had never closed them. She called, "Come in," drowsily, and managed to drag herself out of bed and into the bathroom while Rhoda set the tray on the bedside table. When she emerged again Rhoda was still there. She said, as Josephine crossed the room, "There's a note, Miss Bruce."

A note, and a cluster of gardenias, waxen pale, dewy. They had been put on the tray and their scent was apparent and poignant. The envelope lay beside them and Rhoda's eyes were bright with curiosity. They were pretty eyes, dark and quick, but this morning the lids were swollen and very pink.

Josephine clambered back into bed and looked, startled, at the other girl. "What's the matter, Rhoda," she asked, "is anything wrong?"

She did not especially like her; nor for that matter,

except for Wycherly, any of the Rivers staff. She suspected them, despite Susan's watchfulness, of gossip, cheating, and the sly backstairs habits of the parasite type of servant, greatly on the increase during the last decade. But her heart, which was easily moved by unhappiness, spoke for her.

"It's nothing," said Rhoda, sniffing.

Josephine repressed an impulse to ask the girl if she was not happy in her situation. That was Susan's province and not hers. Instead, she said kindly: "But you've been crying."

"It's Holmes," admitted Rhoda, in a burst of confidence.

Holmes was the houseman, general factotum, and errand boy, who operated under Wycherly's direction.

"Is he ill, has he left?" asked Josephine.

"No," said Rhoda, "he hasn't, Miss Bruce. Not that he isn't worked to death in this house." She paused but Josephine, pouring black coffee, made no comment. "It's the horses."

"Horses?"

Rhoda looked irritated. Miss Bruce, her attitude said clearly, must know what horses are. Great, shining creatures with four legs and—sometimes—a disposition and desire to run faster than other horses. The story came out by fits and starts. Holmes had been playing the horses. Not that everyone didn't. Holmes had lost not only his shirt but his pants. Which was all the more distressing as he and Rhoda were planning to be married in the summer and maybe buy a chicken farm on Long Island after they had worked for a while as a couple.

Josephine said, "I'm sorry. But you know, of course, that he shouldn't, that he can't afford it?"

"Them that can," said Rhoda, "always wins, or it seems as if they do. But the ones that could use a bit extra, they lose. Holmes has been lucky up to now, Miss Bruce. He had almost two hundred put away since the start of the season. He knows a couple of the grooms at Hialeah. But someone he met on his last night off gave him a tip and he went overboard, with everything he had, on a long shot. If he'd won we'd be sitting pretty—but he lost."

There was little Josephine could say beyond the usual commiseration. She thought, That's the other side of racing, the side that hasn't anything to do with glamour and pretty women and lunching on the terrace, sunlight, flamingos and flowers and the sleek swift creatures lined up at the starting post. This was the side too well known by the little people, those who rarely, if ever, saw a track, who did not walk up to a Mutuel window to put their two dollars on the uncertain nose of a starter, but who, instead, placed their little bets with the ubiquitous and illegal bookie.

"It's not fair," said Rhoda hotly, "the way we have to slave and scrimp—and other people have it easy. Holmes plays the dogs too, but he's broken about even on them this season. We all do," she added, "Mr. Wycherly too, and Cook and the others . . . everyone does."

"I don't," said Josephine, "and you shouldn't."

"That's easy to say, miss," said Rhoda defiantly, "but everyone likes a bit of excitement and some money that isn't come by as hard." She sniffed again and lingered. "Did you forget your note?" she asked.

"No," said Josephine, and laughed outright. "Run along," she said, "and I'm sorry about Holmes."

"It's from Mr. Martin," Rhoda said gently and closed the door behind her, disappointed but at least able to bear a bit of news kitchenward. "And he came to the pantry at a quarter to eight, in his swimming trunks and said, 'Put these on Miss Bruce's tray, will you, Rhoda, there's a good girl.'" Wycherly wouldn't approve but she wouldn't tell him, the old dodo. Nor would she tell anyone that Mr. Martin had given her a dollar. Mr. Martin was so good-looking. Not, of course, as good-looking as Mr. Scott whom, as she was new here, she had seen for the first time this morning, going out through the patio to join Mr. Martin. But Hilda said—Hilda was Mrs. Rivers's maid—that Mr. Scott was stand-offish. Mr. Martin wasn't, not by a jugfull, thought Rhoda, speeding downstairs, her heart a little lighter. There was always another race.

Josephine opened the note. It said simply, "Forgive me, won't you? One too many Scotches and, besides, you're very tempting, you know. I promise I won't offend you again. What about an early swim?"

She lay back against her pillows and thought, You're darned tootin' you won't!

She had gone to bed believing that she could not

71

stay in this house a minute more than she could help, that she never wanted to lay eyes on Lanny Martin again, much less Jonathan Scott. She had thought, I can resign when I see Mrs. Rivers . . . before she gets a chance to fire me, before Scott tells her that he saw me in the hall with Lanny early this morning, and what he saw . . . I could talk till doomsday and not be believed. Mrs. Rivers thinks Lanny's pure gold. If I told her what he said to me coming back in the car, and afterward, she wouldn't believe me. Or if she did she might think he had every right to say anything he wanted to me . . . or any other girl. Jonathan Scott wouldn't tell her that I smacked Lanny down, literally. Girls don't do that any more. It sounds fishy. Perhaps he didn't see that part anyway. I don't know. I don't care. I'll take the job at the bank.

But there was Cousin Agnes, happily settled in the little flat—Josephine couldn't bear to send her packing back to Fort Lauderdale, to her sister-in-law's unpleasantly triumphant "I told you so!"

They were contented together, companionable, Agnes and Mrs. Bruce. Agnes would listen patiently hour by hour while Alva complained, remembered, dwelt on past glories and present obscurity. Agnes would feed her the clue lines, "Do you remember when we all went off to Cuba on an hour's notice?" or, "Do you remember the summer we spent in Europe and what Joseph said to the Lord Mayor of London?"

That sort of thing.

It was admittedly unhealthy to encourage Alva Bruce to live in the past, yet it was better, Josephine thought drearily, than leaving her alone, most of the day, miserably rebellious in the present.

She rose, went to the windows and looked down at the patio. Lanny was in the pool and someone was coming up the beach from the ocean. Jonathan Scott. She had not realized how tall he was, taller than Lanny, heavier. His dark-red hair was copper in the sunlight and he carried himself with a sort of unconscious arrogance. Her mind stiffened with resentment against him. Why did he have to come, she thought, and spoil everything?

But just what had he spoiled, what had he said? Nothing, but the repetition of her name and the suggestion that she run along to bed and leave him with his half brother. No, not what he had said, but the way he had looked—as if she were too trivial to consider . . . as if she could be brushed away like an insect, she thought furiously.

She'd show him. Where's your fighting spirit, my girl, she asked herself, and your pioneer ancestors? I won't be done out of a good job, she told herself, firmly. I won't. Not just because a man looks at me with—with indifference and annoyance. I'll make myself so indispensable to Mrs. Rivers that even her precious son can't dislodge me. I'll handle Lanny Martin with kid gloves. He'll be sorry he ever saw me, much less suggested—

She took the gardenias and laid them on the dressing table, watching herself in the mirror, her familiar reflection, the creamy skin, which never tanned but warmed to a pale peach-gold, the brown eyes, dark with anger, the honey-golden hair . . . You're not so bad at that, she told herself, quite without vanity. And put one of the gardenias over her ear.

She put on a bathing suit, the new one, demure, full skirted, golden yellow printed with little brown palm trees, took her cap from the dresser drawer and a pair of dark glasses. She put on the gay bathing shoes and a toweling robe and went, swiftly, quietly, down the back stairs, the bathers' stairs, and out by the small door to the patio.

Jonathan Scott was sitting on the edge of the pool talking to Lanny. He said, "You're up bright and early considering your large evening."

"I thought we'd discussed all that. I explained, didn't I?"

"No necessity to. Pretty girl comes to work for Mother, so you make a pass at her as a matter of course. Next time it will be one of the maids. I wouldn't be at all surprised it if had been," said Jonathan. "I remember last season in Bermuda when I flew over for a couple of days and the local girl left suddenly . . . Susan went around like a black cloud for days but she's very loyal. She never said a word—to me, that is. I hope she said plenty to you. After all, you're not a kid."

"You are," said Lanny carelessly, "compared with me, so where do you get off anyway, lecturing?"

"Nowhere. I'm just warning you."

"About what? You don't want to get the girl fired,

do you? Not that Bobbie would. She doesn't care what *I* do. It's what you do. If you were in my shoes—or had been last night, and tales were carried, poor little Jo would be sent packing. But I don't count. I'm the prize clown around here, court jester," said Lanny, with considerable bitterness, "I sing for my supper. When I sing off key, which I do occasionally, it only amuses Bobbie."

He wondered if this would be the right time for a touch, and decided against it. Old Jon was hardly in the mood. But he had plenty of what it takes. His grandfather had left him a very good income, with considerable principal in trust. The firm, of course, didn't pay him any upper-bracket salary. Bobbie had wanted to buy Jon into the firm or buy him one of his own but Jon wasn't having any of that. He got his job on his own merits and held it the same way.

Someday Jon would be very rich, thought Lanny gloomily. Bobbie would leave him her money—minus various legacies and enormous taxes . . . and if she doesn't leave me something, said Lanny to himself, I might as well jump in the pool and hold my nose till I drown, right now. But Bobbie was good for another thirty years, he reflected. Susan, originally inheriting as much as Bobbie, probably had more now. She didn't spend it. And so it would all go to Jon and his heirs.

Speaking of possible heirs—

"Seen Elsie lately?" he asked carelessly. "I thought she was coming down."

"This week or next," said Jon absently. "Who's

that?"

Lanny sat up.

"That's Jo," he said, with delight, "and pretty cute. Or don't you think so?"

He rose hastily, and went to meet her. He said, when he had reached her, "You're looking very festive. Gardenias become you." He lowered his voice, smiling. "Does it mean I'm forgiven?"

Josephine looked at him with apparent frankness.

"Of course," she said. "I—it was pretty silly of me. Very cinema. But I was angry. I still am."

"I'm a fool," he said with contrition. But his eyes laughed.

"You are," she agreed serenely. "But now that you've found it out perhaps we can be better friends . . . on that basis?"

Jonathan Scott had risen to his full height. He must be over six-three, she thought, but he's so beautifully proportioned you aren't conscious of it at first.

"Good morning, Miss Bruce," he said.

"Good morning." She smiled at him briefly and sat down on the edge of the pool. "It looks cold," she commented.

"Not as cold as the ocean. Why you two spend your time in pools," said Jonathan, "I wouldn't know."

"Don't like waves," said Lanny, "too much trouble."

"And you, Miss Bruce?"

Ice blue, his eyes. She remembered them vividly.

She said, "I like a good fight, occasionally," rose, and looked at him, smiling.

He walked beside her down to the beach, across the strip of golden sand to the curling foam at the water's edge. The storm had blown over but the breakers were still high, rolling in, green at the undercurve, white at the crest.

Josephine waded in, took a breaker easily, and swam out with long even strokes. Jonathan followed her but Lanny sat down on the beach and watched them, his arms around his knees. The pool was more to his taste. Placid and unresisting.

Out beyond the breakers Josephine floated, her arms behind her head. It wasn't cold now, it was warm, just the right temperature, and the cradling swells rocked her gently.

Jonathan spoke, close beside her.

"Aren't you rather far out?" he asked.

"I don't think so; I've swum ever since I was a child. And it doesn't alarm me to be over my head," she said.

He retorted instantly, "That's a species of double talk. You were referring to last night, I think."

Her heart quickened, this was a challenge, in the open.

She said slowly: "I was hardly—over my head, in any sense of the word. I am afraid you misunderstood. Lanny"—she stressed the personal name and he noted it—"had been drinking a little too much. So he made a mistake. A natural one, perhaps, as most girls in my position are considered fair game.

No closed season. I did my best to correct his error and I think he understands; there's no need to make an issue of it."

He said shrewdly, "You are speaking of my mother?"

"Exactly," said Josephine. "However, if you feel that she should hear of the incident, I'd rather tell her myself." She added, with open scorn, "But I think Lanny can take care of himself."

Jonathan Scott flushed. "I am sure of it. I wasn't thinking of Lanny."

"Thanks," said Josephine. She turned over and started swimming for shore. She said, over her shoulder, "I appreciate your interest in the welfare of the helpless working girl, Mr. Scott, but I can take care of myself too."

He did not follow her in and she emerged from the water, dripping and exhilarated. She took off her cap and waved it at Lanny.

"It's grand," she said, "you ought to come in."

"I've a bad heart."

"Nonsense. I've seen you play tennis."

"It's very fast," he said, "when you're around."

"It's too early in the morning for that sort of thing." She sat down beside him, fished in her robe for a cigarette. She said, looking out over the water: "Mr. Scott swims very well."

"He does everything well. He's a good guy," said Lanny, "even if we don't always see eye to eye on everything. He's too damned serious. Reaction, I suppose, from Bobbie and her crazy entourage. Besides, he's eaten up with ambition. He doesn't want people to think that the Wilton money has anything to do with his eventual success. And it won't, either. The kid's smart. But he thinks he's handicapped. I could do with a handicap like his, and have a lot of fun spending it."

She said idly, "He's very attractive."

"Is that so?" Lanny retorted. "I might have known . . ."

"But not my type."

"What is your type?"

"I wouldn't know," she answered, sifting sand through her fingers, "I haven't met him yet."

"That's your error," said Lanny; "we're not exactly strangers. Well, poor old Jon. He's engaged, you know."

"I didn't," said Josephine.

"It hasn't been announced. I don't know why. But it's settled, all right. Same girl, all along. Dancing school, country club, proms, that sort of thing. She'll be here presently. Personally I shudder for him."

"Why?"

"Oh, I can see it all," said Lanny. "Ceremony at St. Thomas's. Whopping big reception. Detectives and wedding presents. Honeymoon in Hawaii. Apartment on Park or Fifth and a little place in Connecticut. A couple of saddle horses and four children. Braces on their teeth. Best schools. You know. The prospect gives me the horrors. When, if ever, I have the d.t.'s it won't be snakes that I'll dread, it will be a vision of the correct life for the conventional, well-heeled gentleman and his equally correct wife."

Josephine laughed. "You make it sound very dull. What's she like?"

"Who? Elsie? Trust a woman to ask. You'll find out. She's amiable, dynamic, and dark. Mind of her own. Iron hand, velvet glove, all that sort of thing. I can't stand her myself," he said.

"I don't believe it," said Josephine. "I think perhaps you once liked her very much but she wouldn't look at you."

His jaw dropped.

"Do you read tea leaves too?" he inquired.

"No, but there was something in your voice—"

"I'll have to learn the sign language. Oh, well, years ago—when she came out. She's twenty-four now—she was eighteen then—but it was just a flutter. An error of judgment on her part; mine too. Hi, Jon, are you ever coming in?" he shouted. "I'm starved!"

Josephine cached her cigarette in the sand, flung her robe over her shoulders and rose. She said, "I have to be going, your mother will want me soon." She smiled at him, walked back to the pool and dove in once to wash off the sand, rose, and went across the patio to the little door and the back stairs. The gardenia had disappeared, she had pulled it off with her cap. It had, however, served its purpose. All in all, she thought, going back to her room, a profitable morning.

Chapter 7

Josephine had been with Mrs. Rivers for some time when Jonathan knocked and came in. His mother's face was illuminated when she saw him. She asked, "Why haven't you been in sooner?"

"I was. With your tray."

"But you didn't stay. Oh, I'm sorry . . . this is my son, Jonathan Scott." She patted Josephine's hand. "This is Josephine Bruce," she explained. "I wrote you about her. She's saved my life."

"Then I am very grateful to her," said Jonathan. "Miss Bruce and I have met before," he added, "last night, for a moment, and again this morning."

"That's nice," said his mother. "Now, Jon, about that bay-front site."

He asked, "Is your heart really set on this, mother?"

"Of course."

"But why? Originally you decided to come here—on personal matters," he said, "just for the season. You haven't been here long enough to know what you want or if you want it . . . Personally I'm opposed to the idea. Haven't you enough houses?"

"Not nearly. I did consider Palm Beach. But there's something about this place. I went to Delray recently and Boca Raton . . . the Lindsays tried to sell me the one and the Eberlings the other. But my mind's made up. Wait until you see the site, Jon," she said coaxingly, "you'll fall in love with it just as I did."

"I doubt it," he said. "It isn't that I don't like the Beach . . . but somehow—"

She said, "You don't want to build a house for me, Jon!"

He said, smiling, "But I do. I've already built one, haven't I? The Adirondack lodge, which you rarely inhabit."

"But this is different . . . and I promise you a free hand, Jon. You can't refuse."

"Scarcely," he admitted good-naturedly; "I'd lose my job if I did. The firm's not getting too many such orders nowadays. All right, I'll look at the site today, then we'll talk it over. If you decide to go through with it, I'll engage a local associate firm, as is common practice since we're not licensed in this state. They'll do the actual letting of contracts, I'll draw the plans and act as your go-between. If I know you, there'll be plenty of go—"

"I can't be with you this morning," said Bobbie distractedly. "I've the hairdresser coming and the Carters are leaving for Palm Beach. That leaves just Howard and Fritzi, everyone else has gone. Lanny's planned lunch at Hialeah before the races. Josephine, telephone Mr. Gamble, will you, dear, and arrange to go out to the site with Jon this morning? There's my party at the Surf Club tonight, for Fritzi, to meet people here . . . it's one way of canceling a lot of obligations. Tomorrow we'll talk plans, Jon, and you can see Mr. Rennard—he's the lawyer," she explained, "you know. Frank got him for me, very nice person . . . sympathetic."

Josephine rose. "I'll phone now," she suggested. "When do you wish to go, Mr. Scott?"

"Eleven?" he asked. "I've a call or two to make— I'll take your car," he told his mother, "if there's anything left of it."

When Josephine had gone, Bobbie, lying back on her pillows, in the wild disorder of a bed strewn with papers and sketches, letters and magazines, said happily: "It's so comforting to have you here. And Josephine's such a help, very different from Evelyn. I got her out of the real estate office, or did I tell you? She has an invalid mother or something . . . and a young man. You'll see him this morning. Not that she's confided in me. Not the type. But I saw him looking at her the other day. Do you like her, Jon?"

"I've hardly met her," he said, smiling. "But were you quite wise, I wonder, engaging someone of whom you know so little? There must have been dozens of girls . . . or I could have found someone for you."

"Oh, nonsense," said his mother, "we know all about her—I simply couldn't stand Evelyn Gainford a moment longer, she was terribly officious. She—"

"Yes, I know," he said, and smiled. "You caught her writing to me, so you thought she had dark designs. And you didn't like it. Therefore you fired her. She came back to New York in a parlous state. I took her to lunch—"

"Jon, you didn't!" wailed Bobbie.

"I did. I got her another job. So forget it."

"You know," his mother said, "Evelyn and Elsie hate each other. They came out the same year and then of course when the Gainfords cracked up—she'd do anything to cut Elsie's throat, if she could,"

"Don't worry about Elsie."

"Have you seen her?"

"Of course. She's very busy with war relief work, and most efficient. Red Cross, thrift shops, all that sort of thing. But she said if she didn't get down this week, she'd be here next."

"And you'll stay?"

"Darling," he said mildly, "I'll have to stay if there's a job in prospect. The firm isn't turning down jobs."

"Then it all works out," said his mother placidly. "Hadn't you better run along?"

He rose and then stood looking down at her. She was completely gullible, addlepated, and emotional. He felt more like an older brother than her son. He loved her very much. She went through life like a dragonfly, bright and aimless, skimming surfaces. Well, let her stay that way. In depths, she would drown.

He asked, "Lanny given you any trouble?"

"Of course not," she said briskly, "you're so hard on him sometimes, one would think you years older. He amuses me, and I'm fond of him. Naturally there's always some woman—I was worried last summer. You remember Harriet Simpson, a pretty widow—with a dreadful reputation? But nothing came of it. Then just a few days ago that dreadful little Jean Farmer joined her father here and practically threw herself at Lanny's head—"

"Why was that so terrible?" asked Jonathan, smiling, "She's over twenty-one, isn't she, and there's plenty of money, on her mother's side."

"But she's a wretched child," said Bobbie, "and she'd ruin him. I'd far rather see him married to someone without a cent."

"Mrs. Simpson was, as I recall it, in just that situation."

"But she wasn't *nice*," said Bobbie firmly. "A nice girl, I mean, someone steady. He has talent, he really has. If he married the right girl something might come of it. A play or a book," she added vaguely, "or even a movie. Those people make pots of money. Now, a girl like Josephine Bruce, perhaps. And he's quite interested in her, you know."

"I didn't. Is he?"

"I've eyes in my head."

"Pretty eyes."

She smiled at him. "But I suspect Josephine has too much sense."

"The kind spelled the other way? Perhaps she thinks he has money," he suggested, "in which case—"

"Oh, no, she doesn't," said Bobbie, "I won't have anyone marrying Lanny for the money he hasn't. What with taxes and all I can't leave him very much, it wouldn't be fair to you."

"Please," he said, "let's not talk about—"

She said energetically, "A little income perhaps. And if there were a nice practical girl—oh, do run along, darling, I simply must get myself up."

Jonathan, under Josephine's direction, drove the small car to the office where they picked up Bill Gamble and proceeded to the bay-front site. Walking around, his hands in his pockets, Jonathan listened patiently to Bill's sales talk.

"I have the figures here," said Bill, producing them.

"Pretty high," Jonathan commented. "Asking price, cash down, taxes at present . . . it all mounts up."

"No encumbrances," Bill reminded him, "a wonderful buy. Property is still going up. You couldn't find a better site, not if you searched with a fine-toothed comb. What about it, Jo?"

She was looking out over the dancing sapphire waters of the bay. The city of Miami rose opposite, tall towers, a lovely broken sky line, dreaming into the blue.

"It's lovely," she said, "a perfect place for the right house."

Jonathan nodded, put the papers in his pocket. "My mother has an option, you tell me?"

"That's right."

Jonathan grinned. "She forgot to mention it," he murmured. "Well, I'll talk to her. If she can't be dissuaded—"

Bill looked at him with acute dislike.

"You'd like to dissuade her?" he inquired.

Jonathan said nothing for a moment; then he spoke. "As I was saying, if she is determined, then of course we'll get busy. I'll talk to Mr. Rennard, and to Mr. Thayer."

"Rennard. Oh, the lawyer. Thayer's the architect, isn't he?"

"Yes," said Jonathan briefly and led the way back to the car.

On the way from the office Josephine was silent. And Jonathan spoke, making conversation as they drove.

"There is great natural beauty here, the waterways . . . all this immensity of water, ocean and bay, Indian Creek, the canal, the lakes . . . water and sky and trees are an unbeatable combination. But there's an artificial quality, a suggestion of world's fair, of impermanence, overbuilding, a feeling that the bubble may burst . . . and in certain quarters a touch of Coney Island."

She asked evenly, "How much do you know about the Beach?"

"Very little. Only what one reads and hears. I've been here, of course, several times, but never to stay long. Why?"

She said, "It was a dream, you see. In nineteen-five it was a strip of beach and a dense mangrove swamp. If you knew it and had seen it grow you would feel differently. Those of us who have find much to deplore, but this we must accept, with the coming true of the dream. Because we love it, and believe in it."

He asked, interested, "You were born here?"

"My father," she said, "came here as a young man, in the wake of Collins and Fisher and those who made growth possible. He saw their vision and believed in it." She forgot to whom she spoke, and smiled, remembering. "My mother used to say that my father hardly knew I was about to make my appearance because during the months before I was born his chief interest was the building of the causeway—begun in nineteen-seventeen, finished in nineteen-twenty."

They had turned in at Blue Horizons and Jonathan stopped the car and sat silent looking at the house. He said regarding the great façade, softened by flowering vines: "Still, why my mother selected this—it's incredible."

"You don't like it?" Josephine asked, with silky courtesy.

He replied absently, not noting her tone: "No. It's half Florida, half Hollywood, wholly opulent. The setting is lovely, I grant you, and the landscaping very good. The house, in its way, has charm. But it's an incredible barn of a place. I have been wondering ever since last night who on earth built it . . . it has that new-rich exhibitionist look which gets under my skin."

Josephine was scarlet. She said rapidly: "My father built it in nineteen-fifteen. It was one of the first great show places. He planned it, lived in it, loved it. I was born," she said, "in the room you now occupy . . . and my father—" her voice broke—"my father died there, in Blue Horizons. He had lost it, and he couldn't endure that. So he stood by the windows of the room which is now your mother's, and looked out over the ground he loved, and to the ocean beyond . . . and died."

"Died," repeated Jonathan, bewildered and shocked.

"He shot himself," said Josephine. "You were mistaken about Blue Horizons . . . it has known everything that any house could know . . . love and hope and birth, disaster," she said, "and death."

Before he could speak, before he could move, she had opened the door, left the car, and was running the short distance to the house.

Chapter 8

The big hall was deserted. Josephine racing upstairs caught a glimpse of Holmes on the patio, saw Rhoda's skirts whisking by. She reached her door, went in and threw herself on the bed. She was, she told herself, too angry for tears, a complete fool. Why had she permitted Jonathan Scott's criticism of Blue Horizons to upset her?

After the first shock, the incredible horror of her father's suicide, she had spoken of it to no one . . . not even to Bill, nor to her closest friends. Alva Bruce, after an illness following the tragedy, had not mentioned the manner of her husband's passing and it was tacitly understood between her and Josephine that Joseph Bruce had died a natural death.

The insurance company had paid the claim. There was no suicide clause in the policy. The sum involved was not so large as you would expect a man of Bruce's financial standing to carry. But he lived always on a shoestring, as far as ready cash was concerned. His money was put to work for him . . . and, when his last failure came and there was no more money, nothing except his wife's jewelry, Blue Horizons already mortgaged heavily, and the police, he had killed himself.

Not cowardice, the eighteen-year-old Josephine had assured herself, over and over in the dark hours following, never cowardice. But courage . . .

He had been an extraordinarily vital man, with a touch of genius and so much persuasive charm that even his business enemies loved him. He was big, virile, and informed with such tremendous enthusiasm for every new project that he carried others with him. He believed. You had to believe, perforce.

No, not cowardice. If he died, there would be something for Alva and Josephine, an anchor to windward. And there had been. Enough in cash to pay the necessary expenses and insure the rent of the little apartment; enough in trust to provide Alva with a small income.

Her jewels had brought more, but not much. A forced sale at that time could not return the owner more than a fraction of the sums paid for workmanship, and for the prestige of the shops where the jewels had been purchased.

Josephine thought, He'll think I was bidding for sympathy.

She remembered the shocked look in Jonathan's eyes as she had spoken, too disturbed for caution, shattering the precedent of reticence.

Someone knocked at the living-room door. "Who is it?" she called, not caring. Rhoda perhaps, or a message from Mrs. Rivers or Susan.

"Jonathan Scott," he said. "May I see you for a moment?"

Josephine closed her lips on the instant negative. Sooner or later she would have to face him. She rose and went into the adjoining room, her hands on her tumbled hair.

When she opened the door, he stood there looking at her, embarrassed and contrite . . . "If I could come in, a moment?"

She stood aside, and he entered, to stand in front of the windows, the sunlight bright on his red hair.

"I'm very sorry," he said, "you must know that. I had no idea."

She was embarrassed for him. He means, she thought, to be kind.

"It was my fault," she said. "I don't know why I broke out like that—I don't, as a rule."

He said, again, "I'm sorrier than I can say. If I had known . . ."

"Mrs. Rivers doesn't," she said swiftly; "I'd rather she didn't. Miss Wilton knows . . . she heard it from outside recently. I don't believe Mrs. Rivers even dreams that I once lived here. You see, afterward, the Bowens bought the house and made extensive changes. The swimming pool was one. We—got along with the Atlantic Ocean."

He said gravely, "I hurt you, I expect, very much."

"I was foolish to permit it," she said. "You must for-

91

give me . . . and now, please, shall we forget about it?"

"If you say so." He waited, wondering if she would care to talk to him about the tragedy. He thought, She looks so young, and vulnerable. To move about the house in which you were born, an employee of the people who had rented it, to walk in and out of rooms which had seen your childhood and your growing up and your unhappiness. He thought, She has spirit and courage. But she shouldn't tie herself up in knots, perhaps if she talked about it—?

He waited but she said nothing. The subject was closed, as far as she was concerned, he decided, with a wholly illogical sense of irritation.

He said, formally, "Wycherly had several messages for us. It appears that Aunt Susan has gone to an art exhibition at the library and to luncheon and will be out until late afternoon. And we are to join my mother at Hialeah."

She asked, startled, "I?"

"You were specially mentioned," he said.

Josephine glanced at her watch.

"It's later than I thought," she began hesitantly.

"I've asked Wycherly to give us lunch on the terrace. As soon as you are ready. Then we'll drive out. We'll make the first race."

She joined him outdoors a little later. She had changed to her blue linen suit, and carried a light coat over her arm. She was hatless, her dark glasses were in her purse.

Wycherly had laid the table for two, to the left of the pool. Palms whispered, and the waves spoke softly to the sand and the fishing fleet patrolled the Gulf Stream. The sun was brilliant on the blue water of the pool, and the air smelled of salt and flowers.

A Scotch-and-soda for Jonathan, iced tea for Josephine, redolent of fresh mint, hot chicken broth, cold roast beef and horseradish, a salad of vegetables and avocado, and for dessert fresh strawberries and cream.

Yet she might have been eating the sugar sand of Florida. Every mouthful choked her. She was twenty-two years old, she was sitting under a cloudless sky, palm trees shaded her, the broad blue waters danced for her entertainment, and somewhere a bird was singing. A grave and handsome young man made necessary small talk. Yet she was utterly unhappy.

First, she thought, he finds me struggling with Lanny Martin, like Rhoda on her night out—only she wouldn't struggle. And then I go to pieces and tell him the story of my life . . . make, in other words, a bid for his sympathy. Well, I don't want his sympathy or any part of him.

"You're sunburned," she said with an effort. After all, there was no sense sitting there like a gargoyle, wolfing lunch, mute and hostile.

"I can't," he said, "achieve a good tan. Like Lanny, who always looks like something done in bronze." Was she mistaken or unduly sensitive, did the corners of his mouth twitch a little, as he spoke of Lanny, did his absurdly blue eyes regard her speculatively? He went on smoothly, "I always stop short of blistering, thank heaven. Luckier than most red-heads. You don't tan either," he added politely.

Silly conversation. What do you use against the ultraviolet rays? Oil? Tannic acid? How interesting.

She suppressed a desire to giggle hysterically.

"No; it's odd, too, as I'm out in the sun most of the time," she said.

He looked at her impersonally.

"You look," he said calmly, "rather like a peach. That even, rosy-gold."

Josephine felt the betraying color rise and could have slapped him. She asked coolly. "You flew in, didn't you, the other night?" And wished instantly that the strawberries had choked her.

"Midnight. That is, we were due at midnight but we were held up, and an hour late." He looked around but Wycherly had vanished. He added, "I've been meaning to speak to you about the other night."

She said hastily, "Hadn't we better go soon, your mother will be wondering . . . ?"

"There's time. Look, I—"

"We've already discussed it," she said, setting her firm little jaw.

"Not quite enough. If Lanny's been annoying you . . ."

"I explained," she said, "and he's apologized." She lifted her eyes and looked at him squarely and he was startled, not for the first time, by the contrast of their dark velvet brown and dark brows with her skin, and the pale gold of her heavy hair. "It was natural that you would misunderstand."

"I didn't."

"Didn't what?"

"Misunderstand. You see, I know Lanny. He's very susceptible."

Anger flared within her again. Her father used to say, "Jo, you've inherited my temper. But I licked mine years ago. Try harnessing yours early. Spirit's one thing, and bad temper's another."

She asked stonily, "Is that in the nature of a warning?"

"Perhaps," he said. "I don't want to see you— hurt."

"That's very kind," she began, with deceptive sweetness and Jonathan, looking at her, laughed suddenly. His lean face broke into lines of pure merriment and his eyes were warm and amused. He seemed much younger, shaken from his natural gravity.

"Now you're mad again!" he said.

Wycherly came up before she could answer. He reported, slightly reproving, "Mr. Martin just telephoned from the clubhouse, Mr. Scott."

"Did you tell him we were on our way?"

"I indicated as much," said Wycherly gravely. He was fond of Jonathan Scott. He asked, as Josephine rose, "I wonder if you would do me a great favor, sir."

A moment later Jonathan joined Josephine in the hall. He said, "I have Wycherly's six bucks in my pocket. And the name of the nag he's playing across the board. I wish I could reform him . . . but it seems to be in his blood. Shall we go?"

Traffic was heavy on the way to Hialeah. They passed stands bright with flowers and golden with oranges. They moved in a stream of big cars, little cars, jalopies. And in due time drove down the palm-bordered avenue and a parking space and walked to the clubhouse, Jonathan fishing in his pockets for the passes with which Wycherly had entrusted him.

They found their party upstairs in the upper boxes, Bobbie and Fritzi, Howard Toller and Lanny Martin, who greeted Josephine as if he hadn't seen her in a week.

"Sit down. I've a horse for you in the third. Can't fail."

"I don't bet," she said absently, looking out over the track. It was fast, the sky was flawless, the sun shone, and a little breeze ruffled her hair. She felt, as always, the thrill of excitement, the tightening of her nerves, the catch in her throat. Out on the little green island, the rosy flamingos strutted, were reflected in the clear water. Flowers bloomed, people went past on their way to the betting windows. The grandstand, the boxes were crowded. And now the horses were going to the post.

"You missed a good lunch," said Bobbie, smiling at her son. "I was afraid you wouldn't come out. But I couldn't wait to hear what you thought . . . of the site, I mean. It's perfect, isn't it? The more I think about it—"

He said, "It's all right. We'll talk about it later, in detail." His eyes were thoughtful, centered not on

96

the track, or the people or the horses, but on Lanny and Josephine, Lanny's dark head close to the girl's, his eyes alive with mischief, and his own special brand of caressing insolence.

Fritzi sighed. She asked, "How much money have you?" and turned her flat green gaze on Jonathan. She thought, He's rather devastating . . . but it would be like a steeplechase. Too many obstacles, you're beaten before you begin.

Laughing, Jonathan displayed his wallet. "About a hundred dollars," he answered.

"Howard," she said gloomily, "has tied the purse strings into so many knots it would take a Houdini to get a nickel out of him. I'm broke. You wouldn't care to split a bet with me on the next, would you?"

"I'd be delighted," said Jonathan gallantly, mentally kissing all or any part of his money good-bye.

"She's a dreadful gambler," said his mother, "but maybe you'll win. I want you to place fifty for me on the next . . ."

He could hear a little of Lanny's low-voiced conversation.

"I haven't seen you in years."

"You exaggerate," Josephine said mildly. "It was this morning."

"Seems years. Old Jon has no business monopolizing you. I'll report him to Washington."

She said, "I wish I were a flamingo."

"Good Lord, why?" inquired Lanny blankly. "And if you think you can put me off that way—"

"It must be wonderful," said Josephine, "to wear

97

pink all your life."

He said, "We're going to the Surf tonight . . . I want every dance."

Josephine laughed, "Aren't you mistaking me for a house guest, Mr. Martin?" she inquired.

"Lanny. Only girls who hate me call me Mr. Martin." He raised his voice. "Bobbie," he said, "Josephine's coming to the Surf tonight, isn't she?"

"Of course," said Bobbie absently, and squealed as her horse rounded the turn.

"But—" began Josephine.

Bobbie tore her gaze from the track. She asked, "Didn't we discuss table plans? I meant to. After the races, when we get home, then. Perhaps it would be a good thing if you went out early and—Come on," she shrieked suddenly and rose to her feet, "come on, Boston Man!"

"All your dances," said Lanny in Josephine's ear.

Chapter 9

Josephine arranged the place cards at the Surf Club early. It was a big party, and later there was dancing in, tonight, a Hawaiian setting, palms, hula girls and the soft, memorable wailing of guitars. Bobbie's guests included hordes of people from Miami Beach, some of whom Josephine knew very well, and two carloads had motored down from Palm Beach. Josephine, dancing with Lanny, catching a glimpse of the studied nudity of Fritzi, all her bones exposed, felt as if her own simple frock were a Mother Hubbard. But Lanny, holding her close, thought otherwise.

"You're beautiful," he said, "you should always wear yellow . . . or blue, or pink, or black. Anything. Or," he added calmly, "nothing. Hold on, that was an inevitable wisecrack. Look at Fritzi, shaking a mean calf. Not half bad for an old girl; she must be a thousand years. She's looking at Jon as if she could devour him. How do you like old Jon, by the way?"

"Very much."

"In a tone that says not at all? Don't mind me, I'm not sensitive. Besides, we're friends, not relatives. But he's a swell guy really. How about another night out, just you and I?"

"Better not," said Josephine.

"You haven't forgotten?" he asked sadly.

"What was there to forget?" she inquired.

Later Jonathan asked her to dance. He danced, she learned, quite as well as Lanny, better perhaps, not so intimately. You didn't have to be on your guard with him. They spoke little, negotiating the big crowded floor. Once he said: "I like this place."

"It's lovely," she said, "the bright tiles and the arches and the sense of space and dignity . . . I haven't been here in years."

She stopped. There I go again, she told herself angrily. Joseph Bruce had been a member of the Surf Club, of the Bath Club, of Indian Creek Golf Club. She remembered Alva crying tragically, "You mean we have to give up our memberships? But we'll never see *anyone!*"

Jonathan asked presently, "Shall we go look at the pool? I remember it as especially attractive."

They stood, a moment later, on the edge of the pool and looked down in its lighted, translucent depths. And he said quietly, "This was just an excuse. You don't look like a cactus, Josephine."

"Cactus?" she repeated, astonished.

"Yet you are. Lovely flower, encompassing thorns. You don't trust me, do you? Is it because our first encounter was not very auspicious? That was Lanny's fault," he said, without rancor. "Do you think that we could be friends? I'd like to be, you know."

She said uncertainly, "Why—I—"

"We're going to work together. And it will be work. I know my mother. She'll lose the first fine edge of her enthusiasm after the ground is broken for the house. I don't mean that she won't want it. She will. But she will turn it over to me. That means I'll be staying on here, for two months, three . . . and then coming down at intervals. It means, too, that Mother will change her mind a dozen times a day. The house won't be at all as originally planned. You'll be in on it all. So, if we're going to be thrown together, isn't it better to be friends, or, don't you think so?"

Lanny joined them, so quietly they did not hear him until he stood beside them. He said, "You two! I'd enjoy throwing you in the pool, Jon. This is my dance, Jo, and we're all going on to the Brook presently. It's a good thing I won this afternoon, be-

100

cause I'll lose tonight. How'd you come out with Fritzi, Jon?"

"Fritzi?"

"The countess. You know. Dracula's daughter."

"She lost," said Jon, grinning.

Lanny took Josephine's hand and swung it lightly. He said meaningly, "Don't let the tropical mood and the Miami atmosphere fool you into forgetting you already have a girl, Jon. You can't have mine."

He tilted his head and looked at his stepbrother. Jonathan, half smiling, stepped back from the pool. "Come on, Jo," said Lanny, "before I succumb to my baser instincts and push him in."

She thought, going back to the dance floor, I'd forgotten about the girl. Not that it makes any difference. And he is nice really, he means to be friendly. I've been stupid, too sensitive.

Bill used to tell her that. He was always saying, "You're too sensitive, darling. Snap out of it. I know you've had a rotten time but it's silly of you to brood about it and to think that people are slighting you or are sorry for you."

Well, they did, they were.

She discovered Bill at that minute, galloping gaily past with a pretty dark girl in his arms. His eyebrows shot heavenward when he saw her and he made wild carefree gestures. Lanny looked after him in amazement.

"Isn't that . . . ? It is! Lochinvar from the real estate office. What's *he* doing here?"

She asked, "Why shouldn't he be here?"

101

"I didn't mean that," he said hastily.

"I should hope not," Josephine said severely.

"He's making for you," said Lanny, resigned, as the music stopped. "How about giving him the slip?"

Bill, arriving, overheard and favored Lanny with a grin. "No, you don't," he said; "this is where I came in."

They had met, a number of times at the office in the house-hunting era. Lanny shrugged. "Okay," he said, "but I'll be waiting. We're due at the Brook in half an hour, Jo."

"First names?" asked Bill, a moment later. "Is that part of your job?"

She said, "It's an old Rivers custom. He doesn't mean anything, he's harmless . . . who's the girl?"

"That's the Durkin child," he answered, "didn't you recognize her, all grown up and hair-do by Arden? She's a honey. Durkin's throwing the party in recognition of the sale. The place was a white elephant, he never expected to get it off his hands . . . with cash. He doesn't need the dough any more than I need sedatives. Honey, you look marvelous. And is this part of the job too?"

"Apparently."

"What about the sale?" he inquired anxiously.

"Sale? Oh, the bay-front site. I think it will go through."

"I liked Scott," he said, "sound guy, knows his business. When are we having a date?"

"I don't know," she said, "I didn't expect I'd be wanted around, evenings. I thought I'd be sent to bed

102

with a tray, you know, upper servant sort of thing."

"Steady," he warned; "I know that tone."

"I don't mean it, really. Mrs. Rivers is marvelous to me, I like her and I'm crazy about her sister. I'm going to see Mother tomorrow afternoon, if I can manage."

"Me," he said firmly, "or have you forgotten?"

"I'll phone," she promised, "but things are happening faster than I expected. It's a variegated sort of job."

Days passed. Things went on happening. Bobbie said, smiling at her, "I don't know how I managed without you." And Susan patted her shoulder approvingly. Guests came and went. The right rooms were found, the right entertainment. Bobbie, having joined the Surf Club and engaged a cabana, felt it incumbent that her guests use it, as well as the Blue Horizons' pool and the wide ocean. There were motor trips. There were night-spot sorties. And always letters to answer, invitations to accept or decline, engagement books to be kept.

Josephine saw little of Jonathan for the next week or so, and far too much of Lanny. Jonathan was busy with his associate architects, and the sale of the land was going through the usual red tape, lawyers, consultations, title searching, negotiations. But the plans were being drawn and Bobbie called Josephine into conferences too. Josephine knew all about things down here, she said, brushing aside the qualifications of the Florida architects, she knew all about climate and prevailing winds.

About ten days after the Surf Club party, Josephine, taking her early swim—she had little time for swimming during the day, came up on the beach which Lanny, as a rule, decorated, and found Jonathan waiting for her.

"Lanny couldn't make it," he said, smiling.

Josephine said nothing. Lanny had been very drunk at the Howard Toller farewell Jai-alai and Beachcomber party last night. She had avoided him as much as possible, and Jonathan had brought her home early.

"It was nice of you," she said, "to give me an excuse—"

"Never heard so much noise in my life," he said. "And Lanny's third zombie was a little too much."

Walking back to the house with her, "Mother's made some changes in the plans," he said. "I hope they'll be the last but I doubt it. Perhaps sometime today, if you have a moment . . . I have some ideas about the terrace. She wants a loggia there and a formal garden. I'd like to talk it over with you."

"That will be fun," she said sincerely, smiled at him and went upstairs.

After she had conferred with Bobbie and made plans for the day, Josephine went to her room with a sheaf of letters. She would be free to work there until lunchtime. Fritzi looked in and asked, "Anything left of the fund?" and Josephine gave her the last three dollars. Fritzi shook her gray head. "I'll have to speak severely to the horses," she murmured. "This leaves me flat. And we're going, you know, damn it, tomorrow . . . I can't change Howard's mind. It's Nassau or nothing."

Writing Bobbie's letters Josephine found herself preoccupied, remembering Jonathan, his hand on her arm, his tall copper head bent as they walked up to the house together. She pushed the typewriter aside impatiently and leaned back in her chair. Her heart raced, and she thought absurdly, What's the matter with me, am I ill?

Ever since the night at the Surf Club, standing by the pool, hearing him ask, "Do you think we could be friends?"

Yet she had disliked, she had even feared him, she had guarded herself against him. And now, just thinking about him—

It was crazy, it was beyond all sanity. You didn't fall in love like this, all at once, from one minute to the next, walking from the beach to the house. Or did you? Or had you known all along, ever since that first night, seeing the tall figure standing in the archway, hearing the quiet voice? Was that love, that instant antagonism, and anger, that sensation of struggle . . . as if you were some wild helpless thing suddenly confronted with capture?

But she couldn't, she mustn't. She was tired, after last night, she wasn't herself.

Susan came in, ready to go out. She had forgotten something, she said. Would Josephine, when she saw Wycherly, tell him that the Mathers were coming to tea, with six house guests . . . "I have to rush," said Susan, "I'm late."

"I'll find him at once," Josephine said and went out and down the stairs.

Wycherly was there, the door was wide open and a girl was standing there, her luggage around her. She was saying, "I know I'm not expected . . . I simply forgot to wire . . . do you think Mrs. Rivers will forgive me? *Jon* . . . Jon Darling!"

Josephine, on the curve of the stairs, saw Jon come out of the library, which he was using for a work-room; saw the dark girl run forward and throw her arms around his neck; heard her cry, in a soft, husky voice, "I missed you so much, I couldn't stand it. So I packed my bags and flew."

"It's Elsie," exclaimed Susan, on the stairs behind her. "She didn't let us know. Josephine . . . if you'd see—the rooms over the garden, the suite the Carters had—and tell my sister."

She passed her, and Elsie Meredith looking up, relaxed her grip on Jon and said, "Aunt Susan, how heavenly to gee you!"

Find Rhoda. Find someone. Go into the rooms over the garden, see that they are in order. Note paper. Flowers on the table. Tell Bobbie. By all means go and tell Bobbie now, this minute, that her future daughter-in-law had arrived.

Josephine's lips felt stiff. She talked to Rhoda, heard Holmes coming upstairs with the bags. She went to Bobbie's door and knocked. She thought, Well, that's over. I was in love, crazily in love for five minutes, for half an hour. But I can't be now. He belongs to someone else. I'd forgotten that. I won't, again.

Chapter 10

Josephine walked into her apartment a day or so later, toward dusk. She found her mother sitting in the big chair by the living-room window reading aloud while Cousin Agnes, with flying fingers, fabricated a large gray sock. There were pleasant odors from the little kitchen, and an atmosphere of complacency, pervading and comforting.

"Darling," explained her mother, "I'm so glad to see you but we didn't expect you." And Agnes asked, getting to her feet, "Can't you stay for supper?"

"I'd love it," Josephine said.

She took off the jacket of her print dress and sat down on the hassock at her mother's feet.

"You both look very peaceful," she said wistfully.

"We are." Her mother's hand touched her hair for a moment. "How did you manage to get away?"

"Oh, there's a big do . . . I begged off." She swallowed, hard, in determination. "Mr. Scott—that's Mrs. Rivers's son, remember?—is giving a party at Indian Creek for his fiancée . . . who arrived a couple of days ago by plane. Hers. She piloted it," Josephine explained, "she's quite a girl."

Lanny had forgotten to tell her that Elsie Meredith was a licensed pilot. He had forgotten to tell her a number of things about Elsie which, since her arrival, Josephine had been finding out.

"Fiancée?" repeated Alva. "I thought . . . that is, you didn't say—"

"It isn't official," Josephine told her. "You know, one of those since-childhood romances, which everyone takes for granted. In another stratum of society you'd say they'd been walking out, ever so long."

"I wouldn't," corrected her mother. "Tell me what you've been doing."

Josephine roused herself from the sense of apathy which had haunted her for the last two days and gave a chapter and verse report of her activities. Alva listened with genuine interest. She liked to hear about gaiety and excitement. It created an atmosphere which she understood and in which she thrived although it was no longer hers. She had a hundred questions to ask. Where did you go, then? Did you say you saw Mary Ingram? What did she wear, how does she look after her operation? Someone told me she was quite gray. I haven't seen her in years. Did you run into Dorothy Anderson at the Surf? I heard they'd resigned, but couldn't believe it. Of course he did lose heavily last year on that real estate development. . . .

Josephine answered abstractedly, and Agnes called from the kitchen. She asked, "You like the goulash hot, don't you, Jo? I mean pepper, not stove, hot."

"Hotter the better," Josephine answered. Cousin Agnes's Hungarian goulash was famous. She thought, But now Mother will tell me about it for the millionth time.

Alva said happily: "I shouldn't eat a thing. I've put on two pounds since Agnes came. But her goulash! Joseph was always crazy about it, he used to beg her

108

to make it every time she visited us. I don't suppose you'd remember the time the cook left because she wouldn't have strangers in her kitchen? Of course it was our good old Jennie who gave Agnes the recipe in the first place but she's improved on it. . . ."

"Sit still," said Agnes, coming out, "I'll set the table. Things aren't quite ready anyway. We're having early supper, we thought we'd go to the movies."

"It's Bette Davis," Alva explained. "I didn't want to miss her, but of course now that you're here, Jo—"

"You must go anyway," Josephine said, "I expect to leave early, I've some accounts to do."

Alva cried, "You don't keep accounts!"

"Not household ones . . . don't look so agitated, angel. Miss Wilton does all that. But I've been given charge of the personal checkbooks recently . . . as it seems that Mrs. Rivers forgets to fill in her stubs and hence there's always a terrible uproar at the end of the month."

The telephone rang and Josephine rose to answer it. She said, "Yes—Oh, hello—wait a moment—" and turned to explain to Alva.

"It's Bill, he called me at Blue Horizons and was told I'd gone home for the evening . . . he wants to see me, here."

"Ask him to supper, if he can come." Alva sighed. "Now I suppose you'll insist that we go to the movies after all and leave you two alone."

Josephine laughed.

"Don't be martyred," she advised, "you know

you're dying to go." She spoke into the transmitter. "How about supper? Hungarian goulash. Yes, of course. Oh, twenty minutes or so."

Agnes was setting the table. She was a big, comfortable woman who had long since given up worrying about waistline. Hers was practically nonexistent. She was almost sixty, but had the round, trusting face of a child, curiously young and innocent, under her iron-gray hair.

"Mother," Josephine began hesitantly, as Agnes vanished into the kitchen.

"Yes? Isn't it time for a news flash? Turn on the radio, dear, will you?"

Josephine said, "In a minute. Look, I've been wondering. Well, it's about the job. I don't know—perhaps it would be better if I tried to get into the bank, after all."

Alva gasped. "You mean, you don't *like* it with Mrs. Rivers?"

"Of course, very much. But it's so uncertain," Josephine answered, feeling her way. "Naturally it sounded quite perfect at first. But now I'm not so sure. When they go north—"

"But," her mother interrupted, "I thought you believed you might go with them. Has that been changed?"

"Nothing's been said."

"They're staying down late, aren't they?"

"They intend to, through April anyway, possibly May . . . now that Mrs. Rivers is building this new house."

110

"You'd be crazy to give it up," her mother said firmly. "Or is it because of something personal? They treat you well, don't they?" she asked anxiously. "If they don't, then of course you must leave at once. But you've seemed so happy. I thought you were—like one of the family."

"I wouldn't want to be," said Josephine, "and it's a little too soon for that, isn't it? Yes, I'm treated well, don't get ruffled, mother, no one is doing anything that would offend your sense of caste."

"I don't understand," began Alva; "I didn't say anything about caste. You," she informed her daughter, "are as wellborn as anyone in that household. Better, I dare say. And a few years ago—"

"But this isn't a few years ago," Josephine told her wearily, "and we aren't discussing my social position. It's just that I'm not sure . . . and so I wondered if the bank job wouldn't be safer. It isn't something I can pick up when I need to, like knitting."

"I don't understand you," her mother admitted. "When I argued against your taking this position, and spoke of the very things which now trouble you, the uncertainty of the position and of its future, you argued that you could *always* get another job, if not back in the real estate office, then in the bank."

"We seem to have changed sides," said Josephine, trying to smile; "you were against it, as you said, and I was for it. Now it's the other way round."

Her mother frowned and lowered her voice.

"Agnes can't go back to Fort Lauderdale. Not now, anyway."

Josephine's heart tightened. She asked, "Why?"

"George—that's Tom's brother," her mother explained, "has arrived . . . with his wife and children. He's lost his job. Of course Tom took him in and will keep him. There isn't room for Agnes as long as George is there. There's talk of his finding work and moving into a place of his own as soon as it's feasible. But you know how things drag out. He said, when he came, that he intended to look for work on the West Coast or near one of the new camps . . . immediately. But he hasn't lifted a finger."

Agnes's personal life was complicated. Tom Baxter was her sister-in-law's second husband. When Charity—who utterly belied her name—was married to Agnes's brother, Agnes had made her home with them. When her brother died, she had gone on living with her sister-in-law because, at about that time, her small capital had been swept away in the debacle preceding Joseph Bruce's death. Charity had made it as difficult as possible for her. Agnes had pinch hit in the housekeeping, superintended a long dynasty of indifferent maids, looked after the one spoiled child. And when, two years ago, Charity, astonishingly, had remarried, Agnes had remained. Baxter was a good-natured, kindly creature, a builder by profession, a settled bachelor. Or, so he thought until Charity decided to weave him into the pattern of her life. He was good to Agnes and stood between her and Charity's petulance and petty tyranny. But it was not to be expected that he would turn his own brother away on

112

the assumption that Agnes's decision to live with her cousin Alva might be on a temporary basis.

Alva was reminding her daughter of this. She ended, "After all, you persuaded us into this, Josephine."

"I know."

No, Agnes couldn't return and if Josephine gave up her job she couldn't live here. They couldn't afford it, there wasn't room. Her mother was saying patiently, as one explains matters to a child: "It would be completely dreadful for her. She's very happy with me, and I'm fond of her, even if she hasn't an original thought in her head. She's good. She fusses over me and I let her, because she likes it. She rubs my back at night and heats a glass of milk for me before she goes to bed. She likes to be read aloud to while she knits. And we do get out, to the movies occasionally, even for a dinner now and then, as a change. We were hoping that you'd manage the car, before summer."

"I intended to," Josephine said. Her mother was right, of course, and her volte-face could be easily explained by the fact that in this brief time she'd grown accustomed to companionship, to someone with her every day, every night, someone who would listen, agree and sympathize, and so would not easily become resigned to returning to the former arrangement, during which she was alone—except for excursions into her old world—most of the time.

Josephine thought, If only she'd stuck to her guns, scolded me for changing my mind, that Blue Horizons was the last place. . . .

She knew perfectly well that, if Bobbie Rivers kept her on through May, at any rate she would have saved enough for a car and over; enough to keep them while she looked for other work and, perhaps, with prices lower in the summer, out of season, she could manage a somewhat larger apartment, in a less expensive district so Agnes could stay on whatever happened. It was a matter of mathematics. She was getting three times as much as she had at the real estate office. The expenses of the apartment, and food for two, figured up to little less than her old salary and the rest was sheer velvet.

"Don't say anything to Agnes," she told her mother hastily; "it was just a crazy idea, perhaps."

Her mother said reprovingly, "I should say so. Unless . . ." She stopped, troubled. She was not a sensitive woman, although she considered herself one. She was sensitive only where she herself was concerned. But she loved her daughter—as she had loved her husband—as much as she was capable of loving. Affections did not go deep with Alva, and were rooted in her ego. She had "adored" Joseph because he had been besotted about her, because he had acceded to her every wish, because until he died he had denied her nothing and had never burdened her with his anxieties. She "adored" Josephine because Josephine was hers, her own, born with pain and resentment, of her rebellious body. She had never wanted children, that had been Joseph's one departure from perfection. He had so greatly wished

114

for a son. And so Alva had come to the realization—like many other women of her type—that if she surrendered to this desire of his and gave him a child he would be more than ever deeply in her debt. Josephine, at first, was a small and rosy club over her father's head . . . for Joseph soon forgot his disappointment and fell completely in love with his daughter. Later Josephine assumed greater importance in Alva's eyes. She was an extension of Alva's ego. And how clever she had been to have her, Alva had often thought, in the last few years, for where would she be without her now?

Someone thumped at the door and Josephine went to admit Bill. He came in accompanied by vitality, noise, laughter, candy for Agnes, flowers for Alva, and a kiss for Josephine, which she managed to elude.

He made and directed the conversation during supper. Most of it centered about the goulash, the remainder around his business activities.

"It's remarkable," he said, "but I've discovered I'm making sales hand over fist."

"Chamber of Commerce?" asked Josephine.

"No, you. I can't stand the office without you. You should see the bucktoothed baby they have in your place. She's a Seymour niece, fresh out of college and business school. Fresh is the word. Wears her hair à la Garbo and her teeth à la elk. She's wonderful."

"Seen Linda Durkin lately?" asked Josephine. "I mean since the Surf Club party."

Bill looked self-conscious. As a matter of fact he

had, he said. He added hastily that it was good business. Durkin had a couple of lots he wanted to unload and if he got his price for them he was thinking of investing in an apartment house.

He added that he was damned relieved that the Rivers sale had gone through.

"That guy Scott," he said, "I thought he'd put the bee on it. Can't understand him myself, he gets a fat job out of it, thanks to Momma."

"Not," said Josephine, "the sort of job he wants. Naturally when Mrs. Rivers plans to build a house she'd want her son to be the architect . . . and his firm would take it for granted. So that ties his hands. But he'd prefer the job if it were for someone else. Any man would."

"Not me," said Bill, cheerfully; "I like a sure thing. Which isn't why I like you, ducky. You're a long shot. What's wrong with you anyway? You look rotten."

"She does look a little pale," said Agnes. "Don't they feed you well at the Rivers's, Jo?"

"Bountifully," Josephine answered. "Hurry up, you two, and get to the early show. Bill and I will wash the dishes."

"Good grief," said Bill with simplicity, "I'd hoped you'd forgotten how."

When Alva and Agnes, losing purses, dropping wraps, and generally creating a minor chaos, had departed, Bill asked, wiping dishes with haphazard fury, "What's up?"

"Nothing. Why?"

"Can't fool me. You're white, you've rings under

your eyes—the wrong place for rings, by the way—
and you didn't hear half what I said at supper . . .
you were miles away."

She said, after a moment, "I'm thinking of quit-
ting."

"Blue Horizons? Are you out of your mind?"

"I thought you'd feel I'd found it again. You and
mother. You were both against it, if you remember."

"My error," said Bill. "You like it there all right,
you're getting good money, and your mother and
Agnes are happy as a couple of clams here, and
besides—"

"Besides what?"

"You can help me," he said calmly.

"You?"

"You did, on the bay-front deal. You walked
around, you said it was perfect. Scott listened to
you. I saw him looking at you . . . as if he respected
your opinion. This is what I wanted to talk to you
about. You come in contact with dozens of people at
Blue Horizons. Some of them are sure to be sold on
the idea of the Beach . . . a place of their own, buy,
build, or rent. Well, that's where you come in."

"I wouldn't dream of it,'" she began indignantly.

"Don't be like that." He dropped a dish towel and
a dish, caught the dish, with a profane remark, let
the towel lie limp on the floor and took her wet
soapy hands out of the water and held them. He
said, "Baby, the sooner I make a lot more dough the
sooner we can be married."

"But I'm not going to marry you, Bill."

"That's what you think. I'll wear down your resistance after a while. I don't mean I want you to give 'em all sales talks. But if you did it wouldn't be out of character. You love the Beach and believe in it. And you know more about it than ninety per cent of the people in this town. No one would think it strange if you gave your home town a boost. Any little boost at the right time means money in my pocket. Of course you'd recommend a sound realtor. Or wouldn't you, stubborn?"

"I don't know." She took her hands away and reattacked the dishes. "I'm pretty mixed up."

"What don't you like about the job?"

"It may not last."

"You knew that when you took it."

"Yes, but—"

"This isn't like you," he said, "chopping and changing. Look here, has someone been making a pass at you? Martin, for instance? I'll knock his block off."

"Of course he hasn't!"

"I don't believe you. So, if it's that . . ."

"Well, it isn't," she said definitely; "skip, it will you?"

"You haven't fallen in love with him?" he asked, appalled at the possibility.

"No, I haven't, and wouldn't if he were the—"

"Don't say the last man on earth," he implored, "because if he were—lucky stiff—you wouldn't have a look in, beautiful, the competition would be too much." He sobered, looking at her shrewdly. "If

118

that's it. . . ."

"It isn't," she said angrily, "I'm not in love, with anyone."

Yet she was. It hadn't helped to admonish herself, to take herself by the scruff of the neck and sit herself in a corner, face to the wall and a dunce's cap on her fair hair. It hadn't helped at all. And she couldn't stay in the house with Jonathan Scott and Elsie Meredith another day.

Yet, she supposed drearily, she must.

"Okay," she said, "you win. You and Mother and Cousin Agnes. I'll stick it out."

He said anxiously, "You sound pretty damned serious. If you'd only tell me what it's all about."

"Nothing, I tell you, except I can't help worrying. It may end in May . . . perhaps sooner. Mrs. Rivers hasn't said any more about keeping me on; either here or in the North after they close Blue Horizons."

"If that's all, don't worry," he said, "there'll be another job. Even out of season. I'll keep my eye open for you. But if you'd marry me—now there's a permanent job," he suggested, "with every modern convenience."

She said, putting the last dish away, "Let's join Mother at the movies, shall we? We won't miss much, there's the short and the newsreel first. And I've got to get back early."

"Heck," said Bill, "I thought . . . an evening alone."

"Think again," said Josephine. She smiled at him.

"And forget it." She thought, I'll go back. What else can I do? Oh, damn families, she thought rebelliously, damn friends, damn everything!

Chapter 11

On the following morning, Josephine leaving Bobbie's room encountered Jonathan in the corridor. He smiled at her. "Busy?" he asked.

"Letters," she explained, waving the sheaf in her hands.

"What about coming to the library when you're free?" he inquired. "I've made some preliminary sketches . . . now that things are under way."

"I'd love it," she answered, before she thought. She shouldn't, at all. She'd hate it, shut in the library, with him. The library was one of the original rooms, that and the long drawing room. Her father had loved it. The Bowens had bought the books when they bought the house.

When she went downstairs, with reluctance, and opened the library door, no one was there. She looked at the big kneehole desk strewn with papers, at the paneled walls and recessed bookshelves. All so much as it had been, even to the flowers and the screened French windows open on the lawn, on trees and bushes, oleander and hibiscus, and a great bignonia vine shedding its golden tears. Birds sang out there and a little fountain splashed musically into a round basin.

Slowly she walked around the remembered room.

Her father had worked at that desk. Her picture had stood there, and her mother's.

She reached the shelves on either side of the fireplace, and on an impulse climbed on the sturdy stool which stood there and investigated a high shelf. She put out her hand and withdrew a volume. What was it doing here, among all the calfbound sets, the classics, the first editions, English and American, which her father had collected?

Jonathan came in, cried, "Hey, what are you up to?" and she jumped hastily off the stool, the book still in her hand.

"What's that?" he asked and came to stand beside her.

Josephine displayed it. A dog-eared blistered copy of *Alice in Wonderland*.

"It's . . . it was mine," she said. "I thought we'd taken all the personal books . . . apparently one got in here. It didn't belong here, it was up in my room," she explained.

"Which was your room?"

"Your aunt's," she said briefly, "that wing . . . the other wing is more recent, you know."

She turned the book over, looking at it with sudden sorrow.

"I treated it badly," she said. "No, it's of no consequence, not a first, not anything. Just a book. Look . . ." She opened it and he saw her name written on the title page in a painstaking childish scrawl. Josephine H. Bruce, Christmas 1929.

"The year of the wailing wall," he said.

121

"It was just another year to me," she told him, "a wonderful one. I had my pony that year and Father bought the cruiser. We had fun."

"Cruiser?"

"We'd fish," she said, "off the Keys . . . I loved it. He hadn't much time but when he had he'd get a crowd of men together . . . and sometimes he'd take me along. My mother never went, she dislikes the water and small boats."

"Do you like to fish?" he inquired, his eyes kindling.

"Terribly . . . it's the best sport."

"We'll go out sometime," he promised. He laughed. "I begin to think there are compensations in this job, after all. I'd forgotten about fishing for the moment."

She was turning the pages of *Alice*, looking at the drawings. She murmured, thinking aloud, "The Mad Hatter's party . . . I think of it often."

"I don't wonder," he said. "This house, that is, what goes on in it."

Josephine flushed a little. "I didn't mean . . ."

"Of course you did and how right you are. Whatever happened to the covers of this book?" he inquired.

"I used to read in the bathtub," she confessed, "and whenever my nurse came in I'd sit on the book."

"For heaven's sake," said Jonathan, "a water vandal. Now, what are you doing?"

"Putting it back."

"Let me, you'll fall. But you shouldn't, it's yours. You'd better take it."

"It isn't mine," she said, "not any more."

"Nonsense . . . my mother would . . . Gosh, I forgot, it isn't hers either!"

"No, it's the Bowens' . . . and honesty is the best policy."

"You're stretching a point," he said. "All right." He took the book from her and their hands touched and such a definite shock of excitement invaded her that she felt faint and sick. It was the briefest possible contact but through it she was aware of him, every nerve and fiber, beating in her blood and racing in her pulses.

"What's the matter?"

"Nothing."

"You're white . . . sure you're all right? What did you have for breakfast?"

She recovered a little and managed to smile.

"Coffee, fruit, toast."

"You girls are all alike," he said, "starving yourselves. You're crazy. As if you needed it."

"I don't starve and I haven't changed in weight since I was sixteen," she said with vigor; "I can eat anything."

"Then why don't you?" he inquired crossly.

"I never have, mornings. What in the world are we arguing about?" she demanded.

"I wouldn't know." He replaced the book and smiled down at her. "Want to look at the sketches?"

They went to the desk and he sorted them, spread them out . . . rough but workmanlike drawings. The façade of a house, a terrace, a loggia.

Rough floor plans.

"They're lovely," she exclaimed, and drew a deep breath. She looked up, her eyes shining. "The sort of house you dream about—"

"Do you?" he asked intently.

"Sometimes."

"Not—like this?" He waved his hand and said quickly before she could speak. "I want to know . . . really. I'm not—I don't mean to hurt you."

"You haven't," she said. She thought, Darling, you don't . . . ever—except all the time. But you don't know it, you never will. She added, "No, not like this. I love Blue Horizons because it's part of my life, the happiest part. I loved it better the way it was, of course. But it was always too big and too formal. This"—she indicated the sketches—"is right."

"I've been talking to Thayer," he said, "he's a very sound man—I'd like to use caystone . . . it's native, very beautiful . . . that brown-flecked cream, the coral rock formation, I like the way it varies and is pitted . . . I thought of doing the terrace in it, and some of the decorative stonework."

"It would be perfect," she told him.

He frowned down at the sketches.

"Mother," he said, "tells me to keep it small. Small, that is, from her point of view. Three master suites, hers, Lanny's, Aunt Susan's."

"Lanny's?" she asked quickly.

"He's never away for long."

"What about you?"

"I am. Two guest suites, and perhaps a room, not

124

en suite, for the droppers-in."

"You?" she asked, smiling.

"Exactly. But I'm not satisfied. I'd like to keep the main house smaller and build a guest cottage. There's plenty of land. Two rooms, two baths, living room, dressing rooms. . . . I haven't sold Mother the idea yet. I've made a sketch." He pulled it out and showed it to her. "Like it?"

"Oh, that." She caught her breath. "But that's it."

"What?"

"My house," she said, "my sort of house."

Simple, classic, but not cold. A livable little house . . . Jonathan had indicated some of the planting. It had its own small terrace, overlooking the bay.

He said, smiling, "If it's to be for you, I'll have to add a kitchen and a dining room, won't I?"

"We'll eat in the corner of the living room," she said.

"We?"

Her color rose. "An impersonal 'we'."

He said musingly, "I suppose almost every girl wants to build a house and most of them know exactly who makes up the component parts of 'we'. That's what I like to do most, you know."

"What?"

"Little houses, for young people. Room for themselves and their friends of an evening; and a nursery. One guest room," he told her firmly, "for who wants more than one guest? One is all you can enjoy and when he or she or they go—providing one's a couple in this case—you're glad. You look at each other and say, 'Isn't it fun, being alone?' "

"I know," she said softly. She was dreaming herself into the sketch. Alice walking through the mirror. A little cream-colored house with soft pastel-colored blinds—pale green, pale yellow? A terrace for two, an emerald lawn sloping to sapphire water. A fireplace and bookshelves. And when he came home from golf or work or fishing—

She said, aloud, "I have a recipe for a planter's punch which is the last word . . . a friend brought it to me from Hawaii."

"What's that?" asked Jonathan, amazed.

She looked at him, startled. She said, "I'm sorry. I was thinking. . . ." She laughed, to hide her confusion. "I was," she admitted, "just dispensing hospitality in your mother's guest cottage."

The door opened and Elsie Meredith came in. "Hello, Miss Bruce," she said pleasantly. She was always pleasant. Just as she was always meticulously groomed, from her coral toenails to her coral finger tips, to the short thick waves of her dark hair and her sleek fine eyebrows. She had cool gray eyes and they rested on Jonathan with resigned amusement.

"Have you forgotten our date?" she asked.

"Date?" He looked bewildered. "Oh, good Lord, golf!"

"Golf. You said you wouldn't have to see Mr. Thayer until after luncheon. I'm ready," she said; "in fact, I have been for some time."

She wore a practical shirtwaist dress in dull pink . . . with matching shorts. Her legs and arms and face were a clear even brown. She strolled over to the table and looked down at the sketches.

"Nice, aren't they?" she commented. "But," she added, "you won't get anywhere with them, Jon."

"Why not?"

"Not unless they're elastic. I was talking to Bobbie this morning and she's decided on four guest rooms."

"Good Lord!" said Jonathan. He dropped a paperweight on the sketches and said briefly, "Okay, let's go."

"Won't you come with us?" Elsie asked Josephine. "We'll round up Lanny and make it a foursome. Unless, of course, you're busy?"

Her tone did not indicate by a shade that she thought Josephine should be busy.

Josephine smiled and shook her head.

"I'm sorry," she said, "I've played very little recently, I'd be pretty rusty. . . . Now and then I get a chance to prove that to myself. Thanks, just the same."

Jonathan said, "I wish you would; we'd have lunch and—"

"Change your mind?" Elsie asked.

"No," said Josephine, "I mustn't. Miss Wilton has asked me to do an errand for her in Miami this afternoon and Mrs. Rivers has people coming for cocktails and there are arrangements—"

"In that case," said Elsie, "we'll let you off. But we'll insist on giving you a rain check."

The door closed behind them. Josephine stood,

looking down at the sketches. She's nice, she thought, she's kind . . . to inferiors. Because she's beautifully brought up. I shouldn't say that. Perhaps she doesn't mean to patronize. I'm sure she doesn't, but—

Jonathan opened the door and thrust his head in. "I forgot," he said breathlessly. "What does the H stand for?"

"H?" she asked, startled.

"Josephine H. Bruce."

Josephine laughed. "I won't tell you. I've promised myself I'd never tell anyone. It's a dark secret and all mine."

She was still laughing when the door closed for the second time. But suddenly she was silent and her eyes slowly, inexorably filled with tears.

Chapter 12

Josephine lay flat on her back on the beach and contemplated the universe. Small woolly white clouds scudded across the sky like sheep before a shepherd's silver crook of wind. Whitecaps, far out, were ponies tossing dazzling manes. Gulls screamed and cried, and the Gulf Stream was dark violet in the distance. She heard the muffled roar of the mosquito fleet racing far out, at practice.

Elsie.

You couldn't dislike her. She did not give you an opportunity. Besides, why should you? She was uniformly kind, amiable, pleasant. All those rather negative words, Josephine thought. Why should I hate her? She's done nothing to, taken nothing from, me. That which she has I have never possessed. If I envy her, if I covet, is that her fault?

Everyone liked Elsie Meredith. Liked. You couldn't go further, you couldn't feel any rousing tingling emotions of excitement . . . hate, anger, fear, love, enthusiasm. The servants liked her, she was generous and gave no trouble. She listened to Bobbie by the hour, discussed house plans, decorative designs, color schemes, mutual friends, and gossip. She held Susan's knitting, accompanied her to the Red Cross rooms, sat with her through various charity relief entertainments. She played golf and tennis with Lanny and with Jon, when he was free, and acted in any of Bobbie's sudden absences as hostess pro tem—without, however, in any way encroaching upon Susan's responsibilities.

She was pretty, efficient, correct. She dressed simply and beautifully, she wore few jewels and those she wore were suitable and lovely. She was a competent pilot, a good all-around athlete without being good enough to antagonize any man with whom she might compete.

Her attitude toward Jonathan was definitely, yet not offensively possessive. It seemed to Josephine the possessiveness of a pampered younger sister, rather than that of a lover. If she called him darling—well, everyone called everyone else darling in this era, and ménage. She called Lanny darling too.

Her diction was the illegitimate, unmistakable offspring of Best Boarding Schools and Britain . . . you

129

hear it all over, at the seasonal resorts, on Park, on Fifth, on Sutton Place. You hear it in hotels and restaurants along the Fifties, on the American stage, in boxes at the opera, and at polo.

Josephine sighed and stirred in the fine warm sand. She must dress and go over the seating arrangements for dinner tonight. Two guests were arriving, Mr. and Mrs. Rollins from Chicago, on the afternoon train. She hoped Bobbie—off to a fashion show at the Roney Plaza—would not forget to be on hand. The South American poet who was visiting friends of Susan's was coming for cocktails, and the war correspondent, now at the Pancoast.

She had not seen Jonathan last night. He had gone off with Elsie somewhere and Josephine had filled in at contract for Bobbie. This was not easy as Bobbie's guests played for stakes, and high ones. Josephine couldn't afford to play for money. "Nonsense," said Bobbie, "the table will carry you."

She had hated that, but the table had carried her despite her protestations. She held good cards and played well. Lanny, who was her partner, was a reckless but intuitive player. They had won.

The spoils were not for her. Lanny could pocket his share, she said firmly, and could figure out the high finances with their opponents.

Someone spoke and she turned her head. Lanny sat down and dangled his legs over the retaining wall. "I was just thinking about you," she said.

"A step in the right direction," he approved. "You're looking very lovely this morning. Relaxed, delectable. A little lonely, but that's soon remedied."

He slid off the wall and came to sit beside her. "Tennis with Elsie," he remarked, "is something to be remembered. I'm practically a wreck. That girl plays with all that's in her. Or almost all. I proxied for Jon, who is off with his friend Thayer, talking to builders, and speaking learnedly of estimates and bids. All quite beyond me and beyond Bobbie, I'm afraid. She's perfectly at home upsetting architectural applecarts, and changing plans but when it comes to mundane things like digging, drainage, plumbing and muntings. . . ."

"Muntings! What are they—or, is it?"

"I wouldn't know," he admitted, "I overheard a snatch of conversation, that's all. Something to do with windows. And for heaven's sake don't ever speak of pillars. It's columns."

He smiled at her, sifted a handful of sand over her shoulder.

"Don't . . . that tickles," she expostulated.

"Been in?"

"Long ago, I'm all dried off, and ready to go back to the house."

"Wait. You've been avoiding me lately, young woman."

"That's silly."

"It is. Of you. My intentions," he assured her, "are far from honorable, I can't afford honor. But they're sincere."

She said, smiling, "I doubt it. The sincerity, I mean."

He said gloomily, "Look at me, wasting my youth. Youth?" his brows drew together. "That's a euphemism. All the draft means to me is a sneeze. I'm getting nowhere, fast . . . and becoming bored. It's probably a symptom of middle age."

She asked casually, "Did it ever occur to you to go to work?"

Lanny raised his eyebrows.

"My dear Jo, how unutterably crude," he said solemnly. "Perish the thought."

Josephine regarded him with indifference. "Well, I don't suppose you'd be much use . . . still, you could dig ditches."

"I'm allergic to 'em." He laughed. "You think rather less of me than usual, now, don't you?" he asked.

She said, "I don't think of you at all."

"Liar. You just said—"

"That was in passing. I was post-morteming the contract game."

He said, "We held all the cards, didn't we? We're excellent partners. Good Lord, Jo, if only you had money. I'd kidnap you—and a preacher."

She was amused, rather than affronted.

"If I had," she said serenely, "I wouldn't shop for a husband."

"I suppose not. Then, let us say, if only I had— Look at Jon. Them as has gits. Despite hell, high water, war and taxes, he'll be a rich man someday and he's not exactly on relief now. And Elsie, moreover, has a mint, in her own right, from her grandmother, whose parents sunk a little dough in Manhattan real estate, whose husband put a little more in Standard Oil and other lucrative commodities. If oil is a commodity—Good God!"

"What's the matter?" said Josephine, startled.

Lanny jumped to his feet. He said, "A familiar voice, crying in the tiled wilderness. I can't believe my ears . . . but I'll have to. Look at that."

Josephine rose and looked where he indicated at the couple crossing the patio, their voices raised.

A short, fat gentleman in the brightest shirt she had ever seen and the most immaculate white flannels was coming toward them accompanied by Wycherly. All very correct except that the newcomer had his arm affectionately around Wycherly's shoulder and was pleading with him in stentorian tones.

"But, my dear good Wycherly," he was saying, "of course I'm not expected. I'm the most unexpected so-and-so this side of the Antipodes. We'll straighten everything out over a tot of brandy. Does Mrs. Rivers still have the Napoleon? Oh, sorry . . . well, anything'll do, provided it's quick. I've been bitten by a snake," he said sadly, "and it's an emergency treatment."

"Who is he?" inquired Josephine. The Rollinses weren't coming until afternoon . . . it couldn't be Mr. Rollins, she thought.

"The progenitor," said Lanny, "the dear old pater. Tight as a tick. Tighter if anything. My old man. The governor. In other words, L. T. Martin, Senior."

He negotiated the wall and advanced toward the

expostulating Wycherly. "Hello, Dad," he said resignedly.

"Lansing, my dear boy!" Mr. Martin released Wycherly and embraced his son. "How splendid to see you. I've been at Palm Beach visiting Julie. Dreadful," he said sadly, "so much splendor, so many malefactors of great wealth . . . even the lake is Worth!"

"You didn't pull it off, then?" inquired his son unfeelingly.

"No. Julie's interested in a gentleman from Chile. Only he isn't. Chilly, I mean. Good neighbor policy and all that, but I must say she carries it too far. In other words, I was thrown out this morning. I had the good fortune to find a car coming this way. . . . And who is the bathing beauty?" he asked, with interest.

His tones carried. Later Josephine was to discover that he was a little deaf and amplified his own voice in protective coloration.

She went on up the lawn and Lanny made the presentations.

"This," he said, "is my prodigal father, Miss Bruce."

Martin's face, lined, round, florid, was wreathed in appreciative smiles. He said, "You know how to pick them, Lansing. Better than I." He sighed. He added plaintively, "I'm thirsty and I'm broke. Wonder if Bobbie would put me up for the night? Of course there's the little matter of train fare—"

"Suppose we talk it over later," said his son, "meantime I'll take you up to my rooms and—"

"Wycherly," said his father, "has disappeared. He's aging, isn't he? In the wood. Do you suppose he understood about the snakebite? Or maybe it was a horse that bit me. In any case, I'm in need of medical treatment. Where's Bobbie?"

"Ask Miss Bruce," said Lanny. "She's Bobbie's secretary. Oh, I remember. At the Roney Plaza."

Martin eyed Josephine in silence. He said, after a moment, "A wonderful improvement over those I have known and suffered during my short tenure as lord of the manor." He slapped Lanny on the back. "However," he said happily, "comfortable as you appear in this outrageously pictorial setting, well fed and well housed, I don't envy you. My way's more fun. Of course, any port, however colossal, in a storm."

"My father," Lanny warned Josephine, "is entirely without inhibitions."

Josephine laughed, excused herself, and went back toward the house. Neither her social nor her business experience had prepared her for this situation. What to do, when your employer's ex-husband arrives.

Lanny could carry on for the time being. She thought, after she had dressed, But I'd better notify someone. She called Susan Wilton at Red Cross headquarters.

"Josephine speaking, Miss Wilton," she said when she heard the brisk voice at the other end of the wire. "I thought I'd better let you know that Mr. Martin has just arrived . . . from Palm Beach."

135

"Martin . . . Lansing Senior? Good Lord," said Susan. "Does my sister—?"

"She's at the fashion show. I didn't want to call her."

"Very well," said Susan, "put him in the room next to Lanny's for the time being. I don't imagine he'll stay long." She chuckled warmly. "He can't stand us for more than a weekend. But that throws out the table for tonight. You'll have to fill in, Josephine . . . do you mind?"

She said uncertainly, "Why, of course not. No, that will be all right, Miss Wilton."

She had a date with Bill. Dinner at Ruby Foo's and a performance of the little theater group afterward. Well, she'd have to break it, that was all.

Chapter 13

In Lanny's room the elder Martin lay sprawled across the bed, a tray, bottle, glass and ice beside him.

"You'll join me?"

Lanny shook his head. He asked, "Look, what are you up to now?"

"My boy," said his father, "you grieve me. Why should you assume—? But you may. Frankly, I'm flatter than usual."

"But last winter—"

"I know, I know . . . but your late lamented aunt's small legacy went with the Wall Street wind. There was enough left to pay Oscar's back wages—good lad, he left me with tears—replenish the wardrobe and avail myself of Julie's invitation. I thought," he said sorrowfully, "that Julie was in the bag. But someone gave her a pair of scissors. Never involve yourself with a romantic widow of your own—I mean—my age. The first pair of large dark eyes, the first dulcet voice speaking with an accent . . . the first gent, in short, heaving over the equator, considerably her junior—nipped my matrimonial plans in the bud." He caressed his chin, tenderly. "Last night," he said, "Don and I had words."

"Don?"

"Not Duck, not Ameche," said his father. "Just Don. I can't remember the rest of it. Words and action."

"And you?"

"Came out a little the worse for wear. Julie sent me packing. Fortunately the Ennises were motoring here or I must have hitchhiked. The necessary tips—pernicious practice—cleaned me out. How much money have you, Lansing?"

"Too little. I'm overdrawn and I can't go to Bobbie."

"Women or horses?"

"Horses," said Lanny, with the ghost of a smile.

His father sighed. "A chip," he murmured, "off the old block. Well, I'll stick it here a day or so until Bobbie finds it in her heart to grubstake the old prospector again. She's a nice woman, you know. We should be damned grateful to her. I sometimes wonder if I'm not a little in love with her still? We had our moments," he said reminiscently. "The day she married Rivers—of whom the less said the better—I got drunk and stayed drunk for a week."

"That's not unusual," said Lanny. "Don't blame it on Bobbie."

" 'You're a hard man, McGee,' " quoted his father, chuckling. "I see by the columnist that old man Rivers is all washed up. I wonder," he added thoughtfully, "if Bobbie would reconsider me?"

Lanny shook his head. "It would be a solution," he remarked, "for us both. But I'm afraid its out of the question."

"Me too," Martin agreed, reaching for the bottle. "I couldn't stick it, not again. I did, as long as I could. It made an alcoholic out of me . . . a three-bottle man out of a four-drink guy. Never," he warned Lanny, "marry out of your income."

Lanny regarded his father with affectionate exasperation.

"The gypsy's warning?" he asked. "Well, just give me a chance. I wouldn't muff it as you have."

"You haven't my temperament," said Martin. "You have your mother's . . . underneath."

"Underneath what?"

"Whatever it is," Martin evaded. "She had brains. I, thank God, have none."

"Good-time Charlie," said his son. "Well, that's that."

"Speaking of girls," Martin said idly, "that's a very tasty little dish you were lolling on the sands with when I turned in."

"Very." Lanny grinned. "I like it," he said, "but

138

I'm on a diet. She, by the way, was asking me why I didn't go to work, just before your untimely arrival."

"Why don't you?" asked his father. "Or have you inherited that from me too?"

Lanny asked, "What in hell could I do? I don't play good enough golf or tennis to turn pro. I don't dance well enough to knock on Mr. Murray's door. I could, I suppose, wait on tables."

"How about your writing?" asked his father. "When I saw you some eight months ago you were agog with the thought that you were a Pulitzer prize winner in embryo."

Lanny said, shrugging, "The typewriter paper's still virgin."

"Your Muse is no lady. But there are jobs," said his father. "Newspaper, publishing houses. And you'd make a good publicity man."

"I tried that once. I got fired."

"Have a drink," said Martin sympathetically, "it's always interesting to me to rediscover that I have fathered, legitimately and in my own image, a completely worthless son. When do we eat, and where?"

They lunched, Lanny, his father, and Josephine, on the terrace under the palms. Martin, appreciative of beauty and of excellent food, excellently served, tinkled the ice in his glass and looked thoughtfully out to sea. He said, "This sort of thing saps my determination, weakens my backbone. Almost it persuadeth me to rebecome a parasite."

Josephine had recovered from an embarrassment engendered by the frankest, and most intimate conversationalist she had ever encountered. She liked Martin Senior. He had definite charm. His short-legged, rotund body was not a thing of beauty, nor his moonlike face, cratered and creased. Yet charm exuded from him and she could understand Bobbie's second marriage—to a Martin thinner, younger, and less alcoholized. She could also understand Lanny better now, the inherited charm, the inherited tendency to drift. But it was a drift in another direction.

"Money," remarked the elder Martin, "is a curse. Unless you can swear right back. I couldn't take it. Believe it or not," he added, fixing his protuberant, bright eyes on Josephine, "I was born lazy and complacent, a minister's son, in a midwestern town. My father scrimped pennies and saved souls to send me through college, where, along with a smattering of classical education, I acquired a terrific thirst, but not for knowledge. I graduated, I went into business. I married the lady who—rather gratuitously, I have thought since—presented me with my son Lansing. We were happy together, and moderately prosperous. And then," he said, "she died."

His face looked older, and defenseless. He set down the glass and smiled at Josephine.

"After which," he went on, "I pulled up stakes and came to New York. Wall Street was a job in those days and you made money at it. I met, eventually, a widow with one son. I had been a bachelor for thirteen years, officially anyway," he interpolated with a slight grin. "I was ready once more for the love that endures, for peace and domesticity. So, I remarried."

"You've had three drinks too many and Josephine isn't at all interested in your saga," said Lanny.

"But she is," his father contradicted. "Josephine. That's a pretty name. It has historical allure. . . . Where was I? Oh, at the altar. Well, I gave up Wall Street and became a competent, respectable gigolo. I spent my wife's money. After a while it palled. To be frank, it palled on her too. But at that," he said mildly, "I think I was an improvement on her last venture."

Josephine rose, and made her escape, as soon as luncheon was over. There was something lost and empty, and pitiable, about Lanny's father. Lanny hadn't inherited that. You'd never be sorry for him, no matter what happened.

Susan came home, Bobbie arrived. Bobbie was delighted on being informed that her ex-husband was now in residence. She cried, "But how like him . . . why didn't he let us know? Of course he can stay. Where is he? I'm dying to hear all the gossip. Where's he been all these months?"

The cocktail party was a success, dinner was pleasant enough. Josephine was put below the salt, with Lanny on one side and his father on the other. Bobbie's guests took the senior Martin's appearance in their social stride. Only Elsie was a little, not too markedly aloof, and Jonathan appeared troubled. But whether by Martin's appearance, or by something that had happened during the day, Josephine could not tell.

141

After dinner someone suggested jai alai and presently they had climbed into various cars and were at the Biscayne Fronton, that huge, boxlike building which houses so much grace, speed, and excitement. Josephine had telephoned for reserved seats and they made their way through the crowd in time to see the last three games.

Music and a rhumba were in progress between the fifth and sixth games as they entered, the betting windows were crowded, the bar was amply patronized. When they reached their seats the players were parading with amusing solemnity, saluting the audience with upraised baskets. The sixth game was a six-point singles and Lanny's father nudged him. "If you've a couple of dollars on you," he remarked, "I think I can pick a quinella on this one."

People applauded, groaned, shouted encouragement or disapproval. Back of the Rivers party a large, slightly soiled blonde kept rising to cheer her Mexican hero, "That's the boy, Izzy," she clamored happily, "give him hell!"

Elsie had never seen jai alai played before and Jonathan, sitting between her and Josephine, explaining the rebote, the carom shot, the fault and pass lines, said, "The basket is called a cesta. . . ." He pointed out the intricate spin, or English, on the ball as it reached the cesta and was difficult for the players to control and return.

Jai alai had been one of Joseph Bruce's enthusiasms. He had seen it played first in Havana and Josephine had been brought up on the game. She

142

followed it, forgetting her companions, watching the incredible speed, the sheer, breathtaking beauty of the plays, and was startled when Jonathan turned and spoke to her.

"You really like this, don't you?"

"I love it," she said sincerely; "there's no more fascinating game to watch."

"Want to place a bet on the seventh?"

She shook her head. "No, thanks," she said, smiling, "this is excitement enough."

Elsie spoke. "I'll bet on the seventh . . . let me see, I pick two players for the quinella?"

"That's right."

"Number two," she decided—"that's the lad in the blue shirt, isn't it?—and number five. And five, on the nose." She gave him a little wad of bills. "I haven't taken the handicapper's selections," she said. "I'm following my hunches."

When after the sixth was over Jonathan had gone down to the betting windows, Elsie moved over in his vacant seat.

"I suppose this is an old story to you," she said to Josephine.

"I used to come a good deal," Josephine said, "but not lately. It's a game I like very much to watch. You know its history, Spanish and Basque. It's pelota, really. . . ."

"So Jonathan told me. Pelota's the ball, isn't it?" Elsie slid one of a very beautiful pair of diamond bracelets up and down her tanned slender arm. She yawned slightly and said apologetically, "I'm so sleepy—too much sun and air, I suppose, and I stayed in the water a long time at the Surf Club."

They left after the last game, stopped in at the Royal Palm Club for a time, and reached Blue Horizons very late.

The Rollinses and Susan drifted upstairs. Josephine, going out on the patio for a last deep breath of the salty warm air, heard Bobbie talking to Lanny's father, by the open French windows.

"Suppose," she was saying, "we talk about it tomorrow. And you've had quite enough to drink for one evening. Lanny, take your father up and see that he gets to bed."

"Can't he go by himself?"

"No," said Bobbie, very firmly for her. "No, he can't. Run along you two. Yes, Susan, I'm coming."

Jonathan asked, "Where's Elsie?"

"She was out on the patio a moment ago," Bobbie told him. "Good night, dear."

But Elsie was not on the patio although Josephine thought that she had seen her, tall and slim in her white frock, a moment ago. The patio was deserted. Josephine crossed it and stood alone under the fronds of two leaning palm trees. Her dress was white too and shimmered faintly in the starlight. She had tied a black chiffon handkerchief over her hair.

She stood looking out to the dark sea, spangled with stars, and wondering why she was there; wondering why she couldn't move, couldn't drag herself upstairs to bed. It was very late. The sky held that special quality of darkness which is apparent before it begins to pale, before the stars are blown out.

Someone came up behind her, caught her in his arms and turned her around. Lanny, she thought before she could speak. But it was not Lanny, it was Jonathan.

It was so dark under the palms. She felt herself held very close, felt it with every nerve in her body. She could speak, she could dispel the enchantment. But she did not. She permitted the hard, searching pressure of Jonathan's mouth on her own. She returned it, she blossomed under it, her arms about his shoulders, drawing the tall head down to hers.

"Darling," said Jonathan, a moment later, "I've been so—uncertain. But now . . . you've never kissed me like this before, Elsie . . ."

Josephine drew away, shaken with an intolerable sorrow. If she had moved, if she had spoken. But she had not wished to move or speak. She had wished to stand there forever, in the magic circle of that mindless moment . . . knowing that the kiss which still vibrated through her, the kiss for which, for many days, she had hopelessly longed, was not for her, and would never be.

She and Elsie were of equal height, they were both in white, and Josephine's yellow head was obscured by the dark veiling of the handkerchief. He had every reason to be mistaken.

"It's not—Elsie," she said.

"Josephine! But you didn't . . . you said nothing, you kissed me . . ." he began incredulous.

Someone laughed near them, moved out from

the other side of the palm trees, where an umbrella, forgotten by the graceless Holmes, cast a
heavy shadow.

"Is this," asked Elsie lightly, "a private game or
may I take a hand?"

Chapter 14

Josephine answered, before Jonathan could speak,
and he stood there, an unwilling audience, much as
man has stood from time immemorial when confronted by a situation in which he feels supremely
ridiculous and which is taken over, under his very
eyes, by two inimical women.

She said lightly: "It isn't my game at all, Miss
Meredith, it's yours. I was merely substituting . . . as
proxy, or understudy—to mix a metaphor . . ."

Elsie said gently: "Now you're angry with me. You
shouldn't be, you know, I should be the one,
shouldn't I?" She moved closer to Jonathan and put
her arm through his. She added, and her voice
smiled in the darkness, "Funny thing, I was looking
for Jon, to tell him I was ready to make our engagement official. It isn't his fault that we haven't before,
poor dear; but now with the draft looming on the
horizon next summer, and his number probably
coming up . . ." Her voice strengthened and she
went on, with animation, "It's amusing, isn't it? Of
course I'm not at all astonished that Jon made a
mistake . . . if it was a mistake."

Josephine said shortly, "It was."

146

"Why don't you speak for yourself, Jon?" inquired Elsie, laughing. She pulled a little on his arm, moved out of the palm shadows with him. She added, "But Miss Bruce was under no misapprehension, I think."

Josephine's control snapped. She made a strangled sound and fled precipitously across the patio, into the house and upstairs.

Lanny, coming out of his father's room, ran into her, literally, in the corridor. "Hey, steady," he warned, caught her arm, halted and swung her around. "What's the matter? You look as if you were being pursued by ghosts."

Her face was flushed, her eyes black and stormy, the handkerchief had slipped from her hair, she was disheveled and utterly lovely. She said imperatively, "Let me go, please."

"No. What's wrong? If I hadn't tucked my incredible parent in the hay I would think that he'd make a pass at you. I wouldn't blame him. Alas, I was in no position. That leaves only Jon," he deduced, "as everyone else has gone to bed. Jon? I can't believe it. But—"

Josephine wrenched her arm away. She said, "Let me go, this instant," and escaping managed to reach her room. He heard the door slam and stood motionless, his hands in his pockets, thinking, his eyebrows drawn together, his mouth shaped to a soundless whistle. After a moment he went on down the corridor and downstairs.

Out on the patio, Elsie confronted Jonathan, smiling. "What an awkward situation. You know,

147

Jon, you should give me a medal or something. I think I behaved beautifully whereas I could have torn her limb from limb." She laughed, still retaining her hold upon his arm. "It was very awkward for you," she added sympathetically, "but I can't believe my eyes—after all, unless she thought you were Lanny. But she didn't, she must have seen Lanny go upstairs. Not a word, not a struggle. I can hardly credit it, she seems such a nice little thing, not at all the sort of a girl who would—"

Jonathan said harshly, "Suppose we stop fencing. I didn't mistake Josephine for you, Elsie."

She was silent, assimilating that. Then she said slowly, "Oh . . . I wondered, I wasn't sure. But I gave you the benefit of the doubt. This puts the matter in an entirely different light."

She was thinking swiftly, coolly, But Josephine doesn't know that. How could she? Neither of them spoke at first and then Jon spoke and called her Elsie and then she spoke.

There was one point on which she must be entirely clear. She said evenly, "Before we discuss it I'll ask you one thing. And I want, I demand, an honest answer. You owe me that much. Was this the first time . . . or has this been going on for some time, since, perhaps, before I came down?"

He said, "It was the first time."

Elsie drew a deep breath. She thought, That's all right then—as long as she doesn't know.

She asked, "Will you tell me *why?*"

"I can't," he said, "I—like Josephine, I admire her.

148

She's a very fine person, as real a human being as I've ever met. And she's lovely. So, when I saw her—"

She asked logically, "Why did you go to all the trouble of making her think it was a mistake? You said—I remember your exact words: 'You've never kissed me like that before . . . Elsie.' "

"Because I heard you move, there by the umbrella. I wasn't sure it was you. But I knew it was someone."

"Saving your face or Josephine's?" she asked lightly.

He did not answer.

Elsie said presently, "I'm tired." She thought, I don't believe you, Jon, it's too lame, it's too absurd. It was a mistake . . . so why do you wish me to believe it was not? Aloud, she said, "I'm going into the house. It's very late. Suppose we talk this over in the morning?"

She reached up, kissed his cheek, said quietly, "I can't believe it was anything but a normal masculine impulse—call it anything you like. I can't believe that it means anything serious, anything that would or could jeopardize our future together. Perhaps tomorrow you'll be able to explain."

She touched his shoulder and was gone, walking across the patio without haste. She thought, If he follows me, if he catches up with me, takes me in his arms, begs my forgiveness . . .

But he did not.

He turned after a moment and walked down to the beach and stood there looking at the dark and shimmering water, hearing the heartbeat of the ocean, feeling the wind cool upon his face.

He would not, he told himself savagely, let Josephine down and humiliate her pride—no matter what the consequences. He would tell her to-morrow, as he had told Elsie, that he had not been mistaken, that he had known all along.

Coming up behind her, seeing the white dress glimmer in the dusk, the bright hair veiled, he had taken her in his arms . . . thinking her Elsie . . . as, many times during the past years, he had embraced the girl who when they were six years younger had promised to marry him, someday. "But don't let's say a word, darling, it's too soon, there's so much to see and do, and we'd be crazy to tie ourselves down now. You've a career to make and I want to have some fun first."

Taken her in his arms, turned her around, and bent his head to hers quite without passion, wholly without desire, until the shock of the responsive lips under his had brought him certain knowledge. He did not need his eyes to tell him that it was not Elsie who stood within the circle of his arms, neither pas-sive, nor casual, nor mildly amused, amiably tol-erant; but another, a wholly different girl, vibrant and warm and generous, giving him kiss for kiss.

Elsie was not easily stirred. She openly disdained demonstration. What little she gave she gave gra-ciously, as a bestowal. You learned to be grateful for that much. She had told him once, "But I can't help the way I'm made, Jon. I do love you, I'm terribly

150

fond of you—but I'm just not matchwood, darling. You have to take me as I am . . . and we'll be very happy. We like the same things, we are the same sort of people."

He had been very unhappy for some time, six years ago. But gradually, as his work absorbed him, as he grew older, he became resigned. It wasn't her fault. She was affectionate, after her fashion, and devoted to him. She would make him a very creditable wife. He had never cared for anyone else. He had been violently in love with her for two years, despairingly, miserably, half starved, hopeful. But that had passed and his love had settled down, to match hers, perhaps, having so little upon which to feed.

In all these years he had not met another woman who had moved him more than briefly, and upon such occasions he knew exactly how much it meant and why . . . and how far it could go. He had been unfortunate in the few episodes, in the type of women who were willing that they remain episodes. He had not felt any especial guilt, or any important infidelity. He had taken nothing from her which was of any value to her.

Tonight, for Josephine's benefit, Elsie had practically announced their engagement. Jon had urged her to for so long, but not lately—latterly it had not seemed to matter much. He simply supposed that someday they would be married. It would please his mother, it would please Elsie's parents, it was taken for granted by their small, mutual world—and there was no one else whom he cared to marry.

He thought, I'll see Josephine tomorrow and I'll tell her—

What would he tell her?

He had not known love, that much was clear to him . . . not until a short time ago when he had experienced it, giving, ardent and without reservation, in his arms. And had recognized it in one miraculous flash of awareness. Josephine, he thought, had been under no delusion. She had known him, she had not suffered his embrace in silence—what would have been the point of that? She had, in silence, returned it, measure for measure. Had she been shocked, reluctant or revolted, she would have spoken at once, drawn herself away, made his mistake instantly known to him.

So he would say to her, "When I took you in my arms I knew it was not Elsie. You will forgive me . . . you are too kind not to forgive me, Josephine."

Yet, curiously, he did not want forgiveness, he wanted nothing tame or negative or gentle. He wanted sparks flying, and anger, a sense of excitement and conflict.

Elsie went into the house, her head high and her heart heavy with misgiving. It isn't pleasant to contemplate failure. She had always been so sure of Jon. When she was through amusing herself, Jon would be there, faithful, dependable, the sort of husband she wanted, the sort of husband necessary to her . . . especially now. Six years ago, even before that, when she was a gangling youngster with dark flyaway hair and more vitality than she needed, she had been told by a practical mother that she could pick and choose. And when Jon began haunting her, a tall, serious ghost of a boy, her mother had said it again, "There's no hurry . . . I married too young, I missed my good times. Jon's a fine boy but don't make up your mind too soon."

The world at her feet. A rotogravure girl whose debut was stupendous, whose chances were unlimited. A girl with looks, intelligence, background, and means.

She still had the looks, the intelligence, and the background but she no longer had the means.

People knew vaguely that the Merediths had lost considerable money in the past few years. But only Mr. Meredith's family and business associates knew how much. They were still considered very upper bracket. If they had closed the Massachusetts place and put it up for sale and rented the Palm Beach house for the season, that was not at all unusual. In these days of mounting taxes and expenses everyone was doing just that, cutting down in staff, paring here, saving there. It was a national pastime. Most of Elsie's acquaintances were of the New Poor. Yachts were vanishing, you no longer saw two men on the front seat of an automobile. Private school enrollments were falling off, more and more girls were refusing debutante parties, and finding some sort of paying work to which they were adapted.

Mrs. Meredith had said, just before Elsie left for Miami Beach, "It would be a good thing to announce your engagement now . . . you can be married this summer, in the country. A simple wedding, out of doors, if the weather is good." She had laughed shortly. "Everyone applauds simplicity these days." She added, "It's extremely fashionable. Anything else seems in bad taste. Which is fortunate for your father."

Elsie remembered thinking, But I don't want to be married—

Married she must be. She had thought, If Jon goes to camp—

She was vague about that procedure. Perhaps he would want her to live near the camp, wherever it was? But it might not be feasible. If that was the case, she would have a year of comparative freedom.

She met Lanny at the bottom of the stairs. He said cheerfully, "You appear a little shaken. I just met Josephine looking as if she were being haunted by the horrors. Very becoming too. But what's the matter with everyone? Where's Jon?"

"Outside," she said, trying to smile. "I just left him."

"Lover's quarrel?" He looked at her, smiling, "That's too bad," he went on with commiseration, "You're not getting any younger, my girl. I was about to look for your boyfriend and invite him to have a drink. It's so nearly morning it seems a waste of time to go to bed."

She said, "I'll have that drink if you don't mind."

"You? Can I believe my ears? You've avoided being alone with me for so long—"

She said, "Let's not talk about that, shall we?

Where do we go for the drink?"

"The pantry." He caught her hand lightly with the air of a conspirator. "Come along then, baby," he told her, "and tell Uncle Lanny what's bothering you. Because something is . . . You are not often released from your marble. Besides, I've been waiting for just this . . . I want you to give me—shall we say?—some advice."

"All right," she said. She knew that this was probably the most idiotic thing she had ever done but it was too late now to change her mind and she followed him with extraordinary docility, into the pantry.

Chapter 15

Wycherly's pantry was a miracle of gleaming porcelain, chromium, and linoleum. His own large icebox yielded soda and ice cubes, his stock on hand of liquor afforded excellent Scotch. "Say when," warned Lanny, pouring with a lavish hand.

They were sitting down, facing each other across the porcelain top of the table, on high stools. It was warm in the pantry and Lanny turned on the electric fan. It was very quiet, beyond them the big, almost aggressively modern kitchen was cloaked in darkness and silence.

He asked, "What's up, Elsie?"

"Nothing . . . nothing at all. What did you want to ask me?"

He said, shrugging, "I've changed my mind, I

think, you wouldn't be interested."

"You haven't changed your mind," she said evenly, "you're just waiting for a good opening."

"One of the many things I dislike about you," he said, "is that you read me like the proverbial book and you don't skip, either. But perhaps you've peeked at the ending?"

"I hate that tone," she said shortly. "What's the matter . . . money?"

"Money," he said agreeably. "As usual. I need some, quite a lot, and now."

"Debts?"

"No."

"Horses?"

"No."

"A woman?" she asked, after a moment, distastefully.

"Wrong again. I haven't had much experience with venal women," he said calmly, "I've managed to avoid them."

"Of course," she agreed, "with your charm—"

"How you hate me," he said evenly, "and how much more you hate remembering having loved me. Because you did love me, and no one else. Not before, not since, not ever. Perhaps you still do. That," he reflected, "would be very amusing."

Her hand shook, raising the glass to her lips. She said, "I thought you promised—"

"Oh, I did, I did! You were the loveliest thing I ever saw, the night you made your debut. Do you remember? A white frock, wasn't it, and white orchids?

156

And good old Jon, so patently devoted, so humbly attentive, so besotted, so infatuated. Do you remember the winter which followed, all the little places we had to meet because you were afraid Jon would find out, or your people? The French restaurant way over on the West Side and the inn on Long Island, with the log fires, the frozen brook, and the car tires skidding over the rutted roads? And Pete's apartment . . . good old Pete, generous with his keys, and hospitality, off somewhere reporting the world's woes, fighting the battle of the press on every beleaguered front, not caring about us, warm and secret and—"

"Will you keep quiet?" she said savagely.

"All right. But, lately, I've been remembering."

"Why do you want the money?" she asked sharply.

"To get away. I can't stick it any longer. I thought I could—all my life, if necessary. But apparently I have a little of my father's restless blood. Bobbie's a darling, I'm very fond of her. But I'm sick of being under this everlasting obligation."

She said, "You could go to work."

"You too? First Josephine, then my old man, who never works if he can avoid it, and now you, sitting there, immaculate and judging. At what, may I inquire?"

"Anything. A clerk in an office, a messenger boy."

"At thirty-six? Don't be comic. And I'd go mad in an office after a week. I tried it once. It was a strait jacket for one, or quit. So I quit."

She asked curiously, "But, if you had the

money—what then?"

"Cut loose, go to New York, have my own place, write. Oh, don't look at me like that, I know I can . . . but not here."

She said, "Why don't you ask Bobbie?"

"She wouldn't give me a cent. She makes me an allowance to keep me around, to amuse her, God knows why. But the last time she cut the apron strings, and let me do as I pleased, I slipped up. She didn't like the company I kept or what I did with her money. So I came back into the fold." He shrugged, setting down his glass. "I've been thinking of London. Newspaperwork. Oh, I know I'm no one, no experience, wouldn't rate a by-line in fifty years but if I could get over . . ."

She said sharply, "That's a supremely silly idea."

"You wouldn't lend me the money?"

Elsie laughed. "I haven't any, beyond enough for tips and travel perhaps. I can't sell the damned plane, so I fly it. That's how things are."

He said slowly, "I had some premonition but I didn't know they were that bad."

She said, "We're ankle-deep in debt. Very few people know it. I don't know why I tell you except that, oddly enough, you can keep your mouth shut where it's not to your advantage to open it. And it wouldn't be, in this case."

He said, "Well, why don't you marry Jon?"

"I intend to," she said serenely, "this summer."

"That should help matters," he agreed. "Jon's income isn't in the proportions that would cause a revolution in his neighborhood but it would support you and your children." He smiled at her, over his glass.

"Don't," she said shortly.

"All right. And when Bobbie dies—"

She said, "I know all that, why go into it?"

He said thoughtfully, "The sooner you marry him, sweetheart, the better for me. Because when you do, then perhaps we can make a financial arrangement."

Elsie's dark eyes were wide and bright. "You expect me to give you money—Jon's money?" she demanded.

"It would be nice of you," he said, laughing.

"Why don't you ask Jon?" she demanded.

He said soberly, "I don't mind trying a touch now and then. But, no, I wouldn't ask him for the golden scissors with which to sever the bonds of my luxurious servitude. Good line, isn't it? Ten, twent', thirt' . . . I knew I had it in me to be a writer of purple patches. But that's beside the point. I like Jon," he added, "too much."

"Of all the crazy reasoning!"

"Isn't it? Too much to ask him to take me on if Bobbie throws me over, yet not enough to refrain from blackmailing his wife."

Her face grew very white. "Blackmail," she repeated quietly. "You mean that?"

"I do," he assured her cheerfully. "If I kept a few souvenirs, who can blame me. I was insane about you, Elsie. I still am, in a wholly illogical way. It's all entangled with resentment and dislike and perfect

159

insight into your alleged character. If you remember, I begged you to marry me—"

She said, "Yes, I remember you wanted to make an honest woman of me."

"No one could do that, not even God," he said.

"I don't deserve that," she said, low.

"I think so. You were eighteen and I was much older. I had no prospects and it was unlikely I ever would have. Yet I was willing to dig ditches if you'd run away with me. I knew that your parents would do anything under their authority to take you from me. I had a chance to go to South Africa. You could have gone with me. But you wouldn't—"

She said, "Even at eighteen I wasn't entirely insane."

"No, you kept your head . . . at least." He laughed shortly. "I was the one who lost mine, who went all chivalrous and gallant and Sir Galahad. You were eighteen, but you knew the answers, and how to get your way. That was all you wanted, wasn't it? Excitement, adventure, romance behind locked doors. Funny," he said, staring at her, "because you were a cold little thing, not just because you were young and unawakened or whatever the pretty phrases are, but because that was *you* and always will be—"

"Not then," she said, almost inaudibly.

"No," he agreed, "perhaps not then. Or was that merely a vicarious sort of emotion, prelude to adventure, something you felt only in your perverse and wicked little mind?"

She cried, "You know that isn't so!"

"And—since?"

160

She shook her head.

"But one hears . . . at least I have . . ."

She said, "Whatever you've heard, it isn't true."

"Don't lie to me. Whatever I've heard has been, in some measure, true. I could name names . . . two of them."

"Has Jon . . . ?"

"Of course not. People are careful what they say to Jon. And would he believe it if he heard? You've kept him dangling for years. He's been in love with you since your pigtail days. I've watched you together. It hasn't been pleasant, but, at least, always amusing. What I know of hearsay and of my own knowledge would be perfectly incredible to Jon. He has quite another picture of you firmly in his mind. What sort of picture? Don't answer," he said, "let me guess."

She said, "You're utterly despicable."

"On that," he said lightly, "we are agreed. If, since my sudden entrance and more sudden exit, you have not been stirred by any other man—then why . . . ?"

She was silent, her bead bent, her dark hair falling over her white face, a heavy, silken screen.

"I think I know," he said. "You like to pull the strings, you live on excitement, on danger. No one would ever dream that, would they? Better marry me, after all, Elsie."

She said, with an effort, "I'll marry Jon." She raised her head and looked at him. "Were you trying to tell me," she asked, "that unless I promise to help you, you'll tell Jon?"

"I'm afraid so," he admitted.

"But," she argued, "if you did that, if you prevented our marriage, what would you gain?"

"It would be a financial loss but a personal satisfaction," he told her. "However, I'm not worried. You'll marry him, and we'll come to terms. But summer's a long way off."

She said, "You *are* in debt."

"A bookie, here and there."

"You said . . ."

"I love to lie."

Elsie slipped one of the pair of bracelets off her hand and put it on the table between them.

He looked from the shining circle to her, picked it up and put it in his pocket. He said, "You can collect the insurance . . . or have you let it drop?"

"It's not insured," she said, "none of it—what's left."

"I see." He said thoughtfully, "Too bad. That's done, you know. You lose a wad at roulette, say, or the races, you don't want to tell your husband so you leave a bauble or two in exchange for your debt and immediately run home to announce that you've left your pearls or your ring or your service stripe in the powder room. All the machinery is set in motion and your husband, poor wretch, collects the insurance and buys you another trinket. He's accessory after the fact and in imminent danger of going to jail, but he doesn't know it and you won't talk. Although now and then a woman does, to her dearest friends, drunk with her own cleverness.

It's just an idea, darling. In case you and Jon don't always see eye to eye on finances."

Elsie slid off the stool and stood there looking at him. She was sick with fatigue. She said, after a moment, "Well, I know where we stand."

"You should," he said amiably. "It cuts both ways. Marry Jon, or else. Marry Jon and buy me a one-way ticket to Hades, or else again. We understand each other perfectly."

He rose, came around the table, took her roughly in his arms and kissed her, not once, but many times, without tenderness. Releasing her abruptly he watched her sway a little on her feet, saw the rare, difficult tears in her eyes.

"That," he said gently, "is for remembrance."

"I've still forgotten," she told him stonily.

"No. You've remembered, these last years . . . you'll go on remembering and you'll remember most of all when you're married to Jon."

He went ahead of her, held open the pantry door. He said, as she passed him: "I've always been a heel, I never pretended to be anything else. Perhaps that's slightly to my credit. Bobbie recognizes it, bless her, and old Jon. Why, they're fond of me, God knows why. I don't. And I'm as fond of them as I can be of anyone but that wouldn't prevent me from stabbing them in the back."

"I don't doubt it," she said.

He walked beside her, through the big rooms to the foot of the stairs. He said, "For your own good—and mine—I'm about to deliver a warning. Work

163

fast, darling. Because you've competition."

She stopped with her hand on the stair rail.

"You mean Josephine Bruce," she said slowly.

"You're very quick on the uptake. Yes, I mean Jo. She's everything you're not. If Jon once realizes that . . ."

She asked sharply, "Why should he?"

"I haven't the least idea. Announce the engagement tomorrow, telephone your doting parents; how relieved they'll be. It's pleasant to contemplate their relief, isn't it? For Josephine isn't like you, my sweet, she isn't like us. She wouldn't disregard a NO TRESSPASSING sign. She's a thoroughly nice girl. I found that out. I wish of course I hadn't."

Elsie's hand tightened on the rail. She asked coolly: "Just what is that supposed to mean?"

He said, "You know. I haven't been in love since I fell in love with a girl in a white dress at a debutante party—a girl who seemed to embody all the lovely gentle things I thought I'd forfeited long ago, a girl who made me feel young, decent, and absurdly honorable again . . . and who disillusioned me completely, yet gave me, at the same time, all the happiness I'll ever know, in Pete Daly's shabby little flat. Still, since then I haven't been averse to the pleasant interludes. Why should I be? Only little Jo doesn't play at interludes."

"I'm not interested in character analysis," she said, "or in your success or failure with women."

He said softly, "I'm not blind. I was once, but not

164

for long. Jo's in love with your suitable young man, my dear. I can recognize the symptoms. She looks at him when she thinks no one else is looking. It's pitiful, it's magnificent . . . heaven help her. I'd help her, I swear it, if it weren't that my financial stake in your marriage is more important to me than the chivalrous impulse."

He watched her high heels hurrying up the stairs, saw her white skirts flutter along the landing, and went back to the pantry to pour himself another drink.

Chapter 16

Josephine sat at the windows in her bedroom, and looked out over the dark, moving waters. She said to herself, not for the first time, I must have been out of my mind. I don't care; I'm glad.

Her white frock was heaped across the bed, the black handkerchief on the floor. Her slippers lay where she had kicked them off, an evening bag spilled compact and lipstick, change and cigarettes on the dressing table. The rest of her clothes, a negligible heap decorated with trailing stockings, were thrown on a chair. Anyone knowing her well would have deduced her confused state of mind from this total departure from her integral neatness.

Thinking of Elsie, she went hot and cold; thinking of Jonathan, not a vestige of the chill remained. But what must he think of *her?*

She told herself, completely without conviction,

I'll resign. I should.

But she had considered resigning before . . . it would have been easier then. Now she regarded the idea as if it was to be a major operation without benefit of anesthetic, and found herself marshaling all the arguments against it, the arguments she had fought not so long ago . . . her mother, Agnes, her own uncertain future. If she had possessed any will power—and surely she had, in the beginning, before she came to Blue Horizons and even after?—it was gone . . . it had been kissed away, under a dark and lovely sky.

The curious and decisive factor in her present psychological state was a complete unawareness that she had betrayed herself, in surrender. As far as her personal memory of that moment in Jonathan's arms was concerned, she was more kissed than kissing. She had retained no mental photograph of her response, none whatever. She remembered nothing except the wild unreasoning happiness, hence was neither abashed nor ashamed, beyond the natural embarrassment of the surface situation.

What did it amount to, anyway? she inquired of herself. Jonathan had come upon her suddenly, in the shadows and darkness, had taken her in his arms and kissed her, believing her to be Elsie Meredith. Elsie had interrupted, had been, Josephine, in honesty, admitted, neither unkind nor dramatic nor hysterical . . . and had simply accepted the obvious explanation and that was all there was to it.

You must admire Elsie. You'd like to wring her

neck, hang her higher than taxes from the nearest palm, send her out to sea, in a storm, in a leaky boat. But you must admire her.

Josephine had, she told herself, no regrets. She had been given something that didn't belong to her, and was therefore no tribute to her charm, her desirability, her appeal. Yet she would treasure it, her life long, for it was very likely all she would ever have. She told herself sturdily, sitting there, in her funny boyish pajamas which made her look about fourteen years old, I'll get over it . . . everyone gets over everything. I'll marry someone, someday. Bill, perhaps. No, she couldn't imagine herself married to Bill. Someone I've never met, then, someone a thousand times more interesting, more exciting, more attractive than Jonathan . . .

How could such a man exist? her heart inquired.

She didn't know, she could not picture it. But it would happen. Not, of course, just anyone. Someone special. And when it happened she would look back on tonight, on the memory of Jonathan, and laugh, and wonder why she had been so torn, so agonized, so stirred.

I thought you said you'd treasure the memory always, her heart reminded her.

Oh, perhaps. First love, romance, all that sort of thing. Laid away in a wooden box in a trunk in the attic, like the other things you collect, squirrel fashion, as you go along, a dance program, a brown, dry gardenia, photographs, the snapshots of your first pony, your closest school friend, your biggest fish . . .

She wouldn't resign; why should she? It was a mistaken . . . the error detectives and heroes made in books . . . mistaken identity. No one's fault, not hers, not Jonathan's. Poor Jonathan, she thought, and smiled a little, how uncomfortable he had been . . . she hadn't been able to see his face, it was a pale blur in the darkness, nor his eyes. But something about the way he stood, moved his hands, his voice when he spoke . . . yet he hadn't looked silly, she told herself fiercely, or awkward or any of those things you'd associate with other men in a like position.

The wind rose, the sky grew a shade lighter, it was very late or very early, whichever way you looked at it. Josephine shivered and rose, turning from the window, crossing, barefoot, on the thick soft rug, to her bed. She lay down, drew a light blanket over her, and turned on her side.

She thought, I'll feel like an idiot, seeing Jonathan tomorrow.

But they were in the same boat.

And seeing Elsie?

That was something else again, she thought, and her mind went relentlessly to the one fact she had been trying to evade, avoid, completely escape since she had reached her room.

The fact that Elsie's engagement to Jonathan would, presently, be announced.

What was so terrible about that? she asked herself; or rather, what made it more dreadful than it had been all along? You knew they were engaged, didn't you? Sending announcements to papers, setting a wedding date, can't make any difference. It's like an undeclared war. You know it's war, undeclared or not. China and Japan. That was war, wasn't it, no matter what they called it? What did they call it . . . an incident? Very well, but people suffered as much, were as homeless, helpless, and afraid, people died, just as terribly.

She saw nothing at all funny in her comparison. Her sense of humor was, for the moment, in abeyance.

She told herself, You've been a crazy, romantic idiot, you should be sixteen instead of twenty-two. Just because it wasn't *official* . . .

There's something so final about a wedding date and pictures in the papers, social dossiers, and Cholly Knickerbocker's final seal of approval.

Don't think about that, Josephine. Tonight has altered nothing; tonight has merely given you something to remember.

Just as she was sure she would never sleep again, she slept, suddenly and soundly as a child, relaxed and innocent, dreaming herself back in Jonathan's arms, smiling in her dream. And once, with the sunshine bright across the foot of her bed, she laughed aloud in her sleep. She was still sleeping when Rhoda brought her tray.

Rhoda was perky. Holmes had retrieved, in a measure, his wretched luck; a dollar here on a slot machine, a couple on the dogs, ten on the last races. Of course, he hadn't made it all back but he would, he told her with the incurable optimism of those who want something for nothing. Last night had been Rhoda's night off; and Holmes's too. They'd worked that rather cleverly. And, as a rule, on the day following Rhoda was cheerful, hopeful of the future. Although, by all the rules, she had every reason to be apprehensive.

She said, "Your tray, Miss Bruce, and there's a note."

The plot thickened. First Mr. Martin, and now Mr. Scott. How does she do it? thought Rhoda; she isn't any prettier than me.

She was, very much prettier. Rhoda's prettiness had been brushed in, with sweeping strokes, and then highly colored. But a different, more meticulous brush had fashioned Josephine, so deftly, and her coloring was pastel and gold, dominated by the dark, astonishing contrast of her eyes. The ancestral artists who had created Rhoda were hearty men and women, who had worked in sunny fields, a world away . . . Rhoda would run to fat someday, she would coarsen, she would sag. Not Josephine; her bones most delicately articulated, her sound, sweet flesh disciplined. When she was eighty she would be lovely, a figurine in ivory and silver. But today, this very morning, Rhoda, conscious of her own lush charms, thought, amazed, What's she got that I haven't?

Mr. Martin, for one, Rhoda decided, and maybe Mr. Scott for another. They wouldn't look at me. Well, not Mr. Scott anyway. And what's he doing looking at her when he's supposed to be in love with Miss Meredith? that pleasant and courteous young woman, a proper house guest, generous with weekly tips and not demanding too much extra service.

"It's a lovely day," said Rhoda, giving up her speculations.

She departed presently with a wicked eye cast on the note. Miss Bruce hadn't opened it. Wouldn't while I'm in the room, Rhoda decided. Stuck up. Thinks she's too good. . . .

An unkind judgment. Untrue. Rhoda knew it. But it still rankled, the fact that Josephine had not become, as it were, the missing link between servants' hall and the boudoir, the liaison officer, the tipper-offer, the purveyor of interesting gossip. Rhoda had once worked in a house in which the mistress's secretary maintained a neat balance between upstairs and below. She'd been ever so useful. Rhoda had repaid her bountifully, by helping her to elope with the oldest son. Not that she'd ever heard from her since. People were that ungrateful. Not that she'd got much either, him being a little vacant in the head. . . .

The door closed behind her.

Josephine permitted her coffee to cool, her grapefruit to stand untouched, the butter on her toast to congeal slightly. She leaned back against the pillows and regarded the square white envelope, the heavy black script, beautifully formed, with the Greek E's. She had seen it before . . . notations on the sketches in the library.

171

She reached out her hand and took it and held it. He had held it, he had touched it. She was afraid to open it, she would never open it, she would keep it sealed, all her life. No, she would burn it before temptation overtook her. Nothing he could write would be all she longed to read. It was beyond the bounds of possibility that she would open that envelope and see . . .

But suppose he said, "Last night changed everything, I love you, I want you—"

She turned it over. She would die if it was to remain unopened another moment. But she could not endure—

She picked up a silver knife and slowly, carefully cut the envelope, at the upper edge. She drew out the single folded sheet, waited a minute. . . .

"I must see you," Jonathan had written, "today, alone. I must talk to you. If I arrange it so that you can go over to the new house with me, will you go?"

Hardly a love letter. Much better to have left it unopened after all. Then she would never have known, she could have gone on dreaming.

Josephine did not appear for her early swim that morning. Lanny waited for her for a time, sitting by the edge of the pool. He couldn't wait forever. He had an errand in Miami . . . where he knew of a pleasant, if Shylockian gentleman who received your offerings, gave you your pound of flesh, no questions asked, in a perfectly legal way . . . bracelet into dollars; dollars for debts. It was a start anyway.

Where was everyone? Elsie wasn't to be seen,

Josephine was passing up her usual swim, the guests slumbered heavily under Blue Horizons' green-tiled roof.

Josephine bathed, dressed, wrote letters at the fragile desk . . . one to her old headmistress at her northern school, one to her best friend, in the Beach, now married and living in Atlanta, one to her closest friend at school with whom she had always kept in touch. She was married too, and living just outside New York. Josephine's fingers rattled determinedly over the keys. She wrote: "And while I like it here very much, it won't last always—Perhaps over the spring, possibly the summer. I don't know. Keep your eyes open, angel, will you and see if there'd be an opening for a good secretary up your way? Of course Mother would have a fit. I could never persuade her to come north. But if Cousin Agnes can stay on with her, she'll be all right. Any kind of work, social or business secretary. I've had experience with both jobs."

A compromise, a sop to her conscience. I'm not resigning but I'm thinking of my future.

She stamped and addressed the envelopes and laid them aside. Someone knocked . . . it was Bobbie's maid who came in and smiled at her. Mrs. Rivers wanted to know, she said, if Miss Bruce was free to come to her now?

She was free. Josephine rose, collected her notebook and sharpened pencils, and went down the corridor. She walked through Bobbie's cluttered office, the equally cluttered but gayer living room, knocked at the bedroom door and was bidden to enter. She did so, on a most extraordinary scene.

Bobbie was at breakfast. Her ex-husband, Mr. Martin, sat negligently on the end of the great swan bed and gnawed thoughtfully on an orange. He wore pajamas and a dressing gown and appeared perfectly at home. Now he laid the flattened orange aside and reached for the coffee pot. Someone had obligingly brought another cup. It all looked to the unenlightened eye as if he belonged in that room, a part of the pretty domestic picture, as if, in fact, he had been there since the night before.

Bobbie said, "Hello, Jo. We'll get started a little earlier this morning, I think. Did you sleep well? You look a little pale." She yawned. "Too many night spots," she said. "Still, what else is there to do?"

"Hi," said Mr. Martin, drinking coffee, "elegant morning."

Josephine agreed.

"Lansing," announced Bobbie, "is leaving today. Will you look up trains and get reservations . . . unless he'd like to fly."

"Not me," said Lansing Senior. "I'm not one of God's chillun."

"Train, then, a compartment," decided Bobbie, "one-way ticket. See what you can do. And make out a check, to cash, five hundred dollars. Get it cashed this morning, as soon as you can. Let the letters go." She yawned again. "There's a wire from Howard Toller. He and Fritzi are coming back. He's putting his boat in commission again, having it sent down from Palm Beach. He wants us all to go on a fishing trip. If you see Susan, will you speak about their rooms?" she asked. "I don't know how many want to go fishing, I'm sure I don't."

The door opened and Jonathan came in.

Chapter 17

Looking at him, seeing him by daylight, was worse than Josephine had expected. Or better. Yet he was just the same, unusually tall, with intensely blue eyes and the right face . . . faces, she told herself wildly, are just a collection of features, eyes, nose, mouth, chin. Why should my heart turn over when I look at this particular collection? Dozens of men look like Jonathan Scott.

Who, for instance?

Well, Gary Cooper, just a little.

He hasn't red hair.

She bent over her notebook and her face was flooded with color. Jonathan hadn't glanced at her except to include her in his general greeting. His brows went up in amusement at the sight of Mr. Martin. And Mr. Martin, looking from him to Josephine, thought, So that's how it is. Well, the poor kid. If I know anything about Elsie she has claws.

Jonathan spoke to Bobbie, cheerfully: "Look here, my child, have you forgotten we were going over to the new house today to talk to the contractors? You haven't been there in a week. We've a nice hole in the ground to show you and some grading. Also I

175

want your final word on the guest rooms. Two, three, or four? You'll have to make up your mind pretty soon."

"Four," she said firmly, "we must keep it small"—she disregarded Mr. Martin's chuckle—"and simple. But, Jon darling, you *didn't* tell me. I've made an engagement to go to Boca Raton this morning for lunch . . . I simply can't break it at the last minute. Everyone's going, Elsie, the Rollinses, Lanny. You begged off, remember?"

"I'd forgotten," he said, "but there are things that won't brook delay—"

She suggested distractedly, "Take Josephine with you. She'll make notes . . . we can talk about it tonight. I'll go over tomorrow. No. I can't. And Fritzi and Howard will be back here next day . . . they want us to go fishing with them. I won't go. I tell you," she said animatedly, "I'll stay home. The Rollinses will have gone then. Lansing's going today. I'll stay here and simply spend my days at the new house. How will that be?"

"I won't answer for it," said Jonathan, "but I'll keep you to that."

"Oh," she said, "but I didn't mean for you to stay. You haven't had a bit of real recreation since you came down. You and Elsie must go, of course, and Lanny . . . Josephine and I will carry on." She smiled at Josephine and added, "Run along, do, dear, and get the check cashed and then you and Jon can go over to the house."

"I'll get your check cashed," said Jonathan, "and

stop back with the money—or don't you need it now?"

"Right away," said Martin. "And also, if you want to get rid of me today, how about those reservations?"

Bobbie said, "Jonathan can stop at the station too." She rang to have her tray removed. "Now tell me your plans," she demanded of her former husband.

Jonathan took Josephine's arm, and led her from the room. He said, "Get your hat, if you wear a hat. I'll go on to the bank . . . I'll be back in no time. What's this about reservations?"

She answered, half dazed because he still held her arm in his firm, warm grip, "Mr. Martin's. A compartment going north, on the first possible train."

"All right, I'll attend to it. Back within an hour, then."

Later she remembered little about that hour. She was waiting, walking around the grounds of Blue Horizons, when he drove up. He ordered cheerfully, "Hop in."

They were driving up Collins. He said, "I left the money and tickets with Wycherly. Bobbie will miss him, you know."

"Wycherly?"

"No, Lansing. That's what I've always called him. Not father, not dad, not uncle. Just Lansing . . . to distinguish him from Lanny." He laughed. "He was awfully good to me when I was a kid, no boy ever had a more sympathetic or amusing step-father. I was very fond of him and shed unmanly

177

tears when he passed out of our lives. That is, I thought he'd passed out. There's something final about Reno to the youthful mind. Maybe it was the mountains, they produce that effect. It's not a true picture, is it? I went along of course, plus a tutor and, oddly enough, plus Lanny, who seemed utterly unconcerned by the oddity of the fact that he was to live in Reno for six weeks while his step-mother divorced his father. He was grown up, of course; and had a whale of a time while we were out there. I admired him enormously, his seat on a horse, his skill at golf, his luck at roulette, and his ease with women."

She said, "But we aren't going toward the bay front."

"No. We're on our way to Golden Beach, for the moment. Just driving along, not too fast. I want to talk to you. You had my note, didn't you?"

"Yes, of course, but—"

He said, "I knew they were all going to Boca. We're just out for a drive. Lunch somewhere. Doesn't matter where, does it? We'll stop at the new house on our return trip, and you can take your notes." He laughed. "This is by way of a snatch," he said calmly. "I knew you'd never talk to me other-wise . . . or let me talk to you."

"Why?" she asked.

He looked at her sidelong. She had bound a bright kerchief over her hair, pale dusty rose to match her linen dress and jacket. Her skin was that pale, unusual gold, rose-flushed, her mouth bright with rosy lipstick. Her eyes were slightly shadowed and she looked very young.

He said, taking a deep breath, "I want you to forgive me."

"Must we talk about it?" she asked faintly.

"I'm afraid so. Let's drive around here, shall we? It's quieter."

She said, "But there's nothing to say. It was all such a silly mistake . . . and I . . ." Well, you have to lie, Josephine, she thought. "I was too taken aback to say a word . . . but I knew instantly that you thought—we were both wearing white," she added.

The bride wore white. The bride was whiter than her frock. The bride wore white. Both brides.

She thought, I must be losing my mind!

Aloud she said, "Miss Meredith behaved—beautifully . . . of course, she understood."

He agreed, smiling a little, "You both understood. But—that leaves me out on a limb, doesn't it?"

"What do you mean?"

He said, "Well, its this way. I—didn't mistake you for Elsie, I didn't think you were anyone but yourself."

She was scarlet, looking at him, her eyes so big and dark that you could drown in them. She said helplessly, "You *knew?*"

That does it, he thought, with great tenderness, that gives her back her—what is it?—not self-respect, not amour-propre, but something akin.

"Yes," he said, "and so, will you forgive me?"

Her heart . . . surely he must hear her heart? She

could hear it. Heavy, pounding strokes. She said unevenly, "But I don't understand."

"You must. I saw you come out, I followed you . . . I was across the patio. You were standing there, alone. You're very lovely, Josephine. And so—"

She said, "I—" and stopped.

"It makes it very different, doesn't it? You thought I had nothing of which to be—oh, not ashamed," he said hastily, "because I'm not that, certainly. You thought, then, that there weren't any grounds for forgiveness. But there are."

"You called me . . . Elsie," she reminded him.

He said quickly, "I heard someone near by . . . I didn't know who it was. Lanny perhaps, his father, possibly Elsie herself."

She said slowly, "It wasn't a bit like you."

She was right. But he said lightly, "How do you know what I'm like? Now you're angry with me."

She was. She was furious. She was crazy with happiness. He hadn't mistaken her, it wasn't Elsie he had kissed but herself, Josephine; he had wanted to kiss her, and he had. But she was angry to the soles of her feet. Thought he could walk up and kiss her, did he, without so much as by your leave? And engaged to another girl all the time!

She said, after a moment: "Yes; you didn't expect I wouldn't be?"

That's the girl, he thought, with delight and that curious pervading sense of protective tenderness, your chin's high and your eyes *are* black. You weren't kissed by mistake, you were kissed on purpose. But it's important that you be angry because that's part of your particular code. You aren't just any girl that any man can catch under the palms on a dark night and kiss and kiss . . .

Suddenly he felt unsure of himself, remembering. What would it be like another time, devoid of the comedy of errors, without deception?

"Please," he said, with real humility, "please forgive me, Jo—I haven't any excuse, except the one you see every day in your mirror."

She asked, "Does Miss Meredith know this?"

"Well, no," he said ruefully, "she doesn't."

"Then it's all right." She drew a deep breath. All right for you, her heart said. But now I'm all mixed up again.

"Forgiven?"

"I suppose so. Now, hadn't we better get on back to the bay?"

"No. We're going driving. You're to show me the sights. We'll stop at that monkey farm or whatever it is. We'll have some lunch. I left word that we wouldn't be in. And on the way back we'll execute Mother's commission."

She said, "But if everyone's gone to Boca, Mr. Martin will be alone, shouldn't someone see him off?"

"His reservations are on the six-o'clock. We'll be back in plenty of time. Stop fussing. You know you've told me very little about yourself."

"But I've told you everything," she said, astonished.

"No. Talk to me about Blue Horizons when you

were a little girl, and about the school in the North and your friends . . . and . . . Bill."

"Bill?"

"You haven't forgotten him, have you? Vital young man in a real estate office."

"We've been friends for years."

"So you won't talk. Never mind. About your father, then, especially about the times you went fishing together. Traffic's heavy here, I have to watch the road."

They lunched at a little out-of-the-way place and came home by a longer route to the bay-front site, swarming with activity. Josephine, standing at a respectable distance from the large maw of the steam shovel, said, "It's always incredible, isn't it, that order can come out of chaos, beauty out of ugliness . . . because all these preliminaries are ugly. The building of a house, any house, never fails to fill me with astonishment. It's magical. A foundation, four walls, and a roof. A new house, big or little, hidden or open. A house which has so much to learn, about people . . . those who will live in it, those who will come and go. Those who will be born, who must die."

"Curious that you feel about things as I do," he said. "You see, I wanted to be an artist. My mother encouraged me. She has never denied me anything, which wasn't wise, of course, though very sweet. But I learned soon enough that, despite a flair for line and color and a real, if small talent for composition, I would never be better than third rate. So all I ever wanted to be as a kid went into architecture. I could use my flair in that." He drew a deep breath. "And I'm completely satisfied."

She thought, There's no one like him, there never has been. She asked, "Isn't that Mr. Thayer coming?"

Thayer and the contractor and someone about plumbing and someone else talking about painting, and something about a strike. Josephine listened, made notes when it seemed indicated, and presently, leaving the men, went off and down to the bay front, where the terrace would be and the loggia. There were palms there and tangled vines on an old fence and overgrown bushes. The water was very blue and no wind rippled across its surface.

She thought, I suppose I'll think this through, sometime. I can't just now.

When they were ready to go she sat beside him in the car looking at the Gregg symbols in her notebook and talking about the house. But he wasn't listening. He was frowning, driving back as swiftly as the afternoon traffic would permit. A plane roared overhead and the sun slipped toward the west.

"Jo . . ."

"Yes?"

"You understand that I'm not sorry about last night."

She said swiftly, "You should be. Have you forgotten Miss Meredith?"

"I did forget her," he admitted. "Will you believe that if things were not as they are . . . ?"

The walls of Blue Horizons were ahead of them,

the open gateway. They turned in, and up the drive, and Jonathan stopped the car and sat there, his hands idle on the wheel. "Elsie," he began, "Elsie and I—"

She begged, "Please don't say anything you'll regret. I do understand. You and she have been engaged for a long time. You belong together. It's—suitable," she said, "it's right."

"Suitable," he repeated. "I wonder. Jo, look at me," he said.

She looked at him, she didn't know how; but she did; and still didn't know—*how*.

"Don't," he said sharply, "not like that. I'm in love with you," he said slowly. "Desperately, terribly. I didn't know it until last night. I didn't believe it then. I do now . . . and you," he said, "you love me, darling."

She did not deny it. She asked, in half a whisper, "What are we going to do?"

"There's only one thing," he began. But the door opened and Wycherly came out and toward them. He said, "It's a long-distance for Mrs. Rivers but they'll speak to Miss Bruce."

Josephine got out of the car and walked, as in a dream, into the cool, flower-scented hall, and through the open door of the little telephone closet. She sat down and spoke. "This," she said, "is Mrs. Rivers's secretary."

After a while she came back into the hall and walked to the stairs. Jonathan followed her. He said: "Jo—"

She paused, her foot on the last step. She said,

"There isn't anything we can do, is there? That was Mrs. Meredith . . . Elsie telephoned her early this morning and she was calling to tell your mother how happy she is about the engagement. She has already sent the announcements to the papers."

Chapter 18

Nothing makes sense; nothing adds up. Life is inconsistent; so are people. Especially you, Josephine, she thought, sitting down at her desk and starting to translate Gregg into Roman script for Bobbie's ultimate benefit. You don't have to do this. You can read it back to her from your notebook. What the contractor said. What Mr. Thayer said. Red-tiled roof or green or one of those newer pastel shades? If you want a swimming pool you'll have to sacrifice some of the planned patio space. Why do you want one? Someone had said, "It isn't necessary, my mother has her club membership."

Who said that, Josephine?

Here it was, the answer, in the oval symbols. "Mr. Scott said . . ."

Look, Jonathan darling, it's an impossible situation. I'll get over it, you'll get over it. We don't mean it . . . not for always. You've given your word. Nothing enduring or substantial, nothing worthwhile was ever founded on a broken pledge and someone else's misery.

What about our misery?

It will pass.

Other people have loved, other people have relinquished their love. Other girls have sat at a desk and translated shorthand, the pages so blurred they could not see them. Other girls have known this battlefield . . . happiness, grief, acceptance, renunciation. It happens all the time. Nothing is new. The basic pattern repeats itself, varying just a little, in all human lives. Why do you feel as if this had never happened to anyone before, not since the world began?

You're nothing very special, neither is he. You're just a pretty girl, normally intelligent, with a normal love of pleasure, good times, gay people. You'd never set the world on fire. You haven't much ambition, you don't want a career . . . you went to work because you had to, it was necessary. You had your mother to consider, and her comfort. You like to dance and laugh, you like flowers and sunsets and stone crabs, you read mystery stories, romances and poetry, you love the movies and you wouldn't miss Fibber and Molly, or Jack Benny or Gracie Allen for anything. You like waltzes and ballad singing and the minor key. You don't care much for hot music . . . or rag cutting. You swim well, play fair tennis, and if you had more practice you might shoot eighteen holes in the low nineties and maybe you could learn to ride again. You like to fish and you're afraid of snakes and spiders and crawly things. You have a flair for dress and if you could indulge in it, it would be fun. You like pearls and sapphires and aquamarines and you'd love a sable coat. That's all there is to you, Josephine . . . a girl like a million other girls, reading the fashion magazines at the hair-dresser's with a sense of complete inadequacy and bewilderment, looking at movie magazines, wondering about the not so private lives of the stars.

Jonathan's not special, either . . . admit that too. He's taller than most men and you think he's better looking. He isn't really. It's just the way you see him. He isn't especially brilliant. He's good in his work, because he loves it. He has a sense of humor, for all he looks so serious. He's kept his head better than many would, growing up in a pretty addlepated household, deprived of the stabilizing companionship of his father, who must have been a fine person, and feeling himself rather handicapped by a lot of money. Admit that he hasn't Lanny's absurd, undeniable charm . . . hasn't even Bill's crazy enthusiasm and vitality. And you haven't known Jonathan long. You don't know what he likes, beyond architecture, fishing, a game of golf now and then, ocean swimming, rare steaks, and deep-dish apple pie. He's average. Like yourself. And he, too, will never set the world on fire.

Stop thinking of yourself as Juliet, of Jonathan as Romeo. Stop thinking of you both as all the star-crossed lovers since time began.

She pushed the notebook aside, and bent her bright head. She asked aloud, "Oh, what's the use?"

There was another side to it, wasn't there? You were entitled to your place in the sun and so was Jonathan. Majority rule. What if Elsie did suffer, not only in her affections but in her pride—wouldn't that be fairer than the suffering of two people, and Elsie's eventually, as far as that went? What sort of a husband does a man make who marries, because of a mistaken loyalty to a childhood understanding, and who loves another woman?

Can't we be modern about this, and civilized?

The door opened, without so much as by your leave and Jonathan was in the room. Josephine got to her feet and steadied herself with a hand flat on the desk. Her knees were water. She looked at him, speechless, white-milk and honey and the only color about her the troubled brown of her eyes, the synthetic rose of her mouth.

He said almost harshly, without preliminary: "I've just had a telephone. My immediate superior has been taken ill. I'm the only one who knows enough about one of his special, very big jobs, to straighten things out until he can take over again . . . at least enough to give directions." He realized that nothing he was saying made much sense, to her; to himself, as far as that was concerned. "Jo . . ."

"Yes . . ."

"I'm flying to New York, Wycherly's packing for me now. If there isn't a plane I'll charter one. I'll be back as soon as it's humanly possible . . . and we'll talk."

She asked, as she had asked herself, "What's the use?"

"Oh, be still!" he cried despairingly. He crossed the room, took her in his arms, kissed her hard and long. "I love you," he said, "I'll love you forever."

Then he was gone and the door swung shut. She

thought she cried, Come back . . . don't leave me, don't go. She hadn't made a sound. After a moment, slowly, carefully, as if she found she had been fashioned from infinitely fragile glass, she sat down again at the desk. She found herself writing over and over in a small careful script, "Notify Mrs. Rivers that Mr. Scott has been called to New York."

After a while the shaking stopped and she could control her hands and her lips. She could even remember Lanny's father, could walk out of the room and down the corridor, and go in search of Wycherly, to make sure that the car had been ordered, and that Mr. Martin's things were packed and ready.

She found Lansing Senior on the patio, with a Scotch beside him and a long cigar in his mouth.

He said cheerfully: "I thought this was a deserted village. To be sure, I heard distant sounds of human activity, phones and bells ringing, footsteps . . . doors slamming. What's wrong with you, Josephine? You look as if you had seen several, not too pleasant apparitions."

She could smile too.

"Nothing," she said. "I—"

"Where have you been?"

"Mr. Scott and I have been over to the new house," she said, astonishing herself, "and he came to tell me just now that he's been called to New York. Someone in his firm is ill. He's flying, but will return as soon as possible."

"Maybe I'll see him there, then," said Martin.

"Nice fellow, Jon. Sound. I recognize these qualities, with detachment, never having possessed them."

She said hurriedly, "You have your reservations?"

"Yes, indeed. Jon entrusted them to the invaluable Wycherly, who gave them to me with the warning that I mustn't lose them. He means, I think, that I was not to sell them and stay on in this *dolce far niente* atmosphere as a superior sort of beachcomber. I have also the proceeds of the check." He patted his breast pocket.

"I suppose you think I'm the father of all heels. I don't mean Lanny. Or do I?" he added thoughtfully.

When you felt as she did, stripped naked, vulnerable and helpless, you spoke the truth . . . almost as if it were someone else speaking.

She said, "No, I don't think that. I like you."

His florid face grew more florid. He said, touched, "I believe you mean it. Yet you don't approve of me, do you?"

"No."

"Why?"

"You take too easily," she answered groping for words, "and you haven't any roots."

"You like roots," he asked, "and believe in them?"

"Of course!"

He shook the ashes of his cigar upon the spotless tiles and took a long drink. He said, after a moment, "Jon's a very lucky man, little Josephine. He likes roots. You've that in common too."

She tried to speak and could not.

He said, smiling, "My hearing's poor but my eyesight's much too good. I even get a good look at myself now and again and wish I hadn't." He lifted his glass and looked into it. "This is one form of rose-colored glasses, you know. When I drink enough I fancy myself a hell of a good guy . . . a fine and upright husband . . . twice . . . a decent, godly father, once—as far as I know. A generous and faithful lover—occasionally. And for the rest a hapless mortal dogged by bad luck who might have been this, who might have had that, who might have done thus and so if it hadn't been for the wrong breaks. Sober, I'm less certain. . . . Well, well," he added and set down the empty glass, "You and old Jon . . . blessings and all that sort of thing."

"Please, Mr. Martin," she said, finding her voice, "it isn't . . . I mean, you mustn't think, you haven't any—"

"Right? Evidence? Okay to the first, but plenty to the second. Lots of evidence. The way you look this minute after being with him all day, after saying goodbye to him for a few days, for a week. An eternity, of course. Do you remember when you were a kid how long it seemed from one Christmas to the next? Years, centuries? As you grew older time began keeping step. When you're my age you'll know that Christmas is always just tomorrow morning but never up to your expectation. Maybe yours will be. I don't know. But this I do know, being in love is, as far as time is concerned, childhood, and ripe old age. Time with the beloved beside you gallops on willful feet . . . but when you're separated, how long, how dragging, how interminable!" He laughed, "Your eyes grow bigger and bigger; it's very becoming. I often talk like this, when in what is known as my cups. I wanted to be a writer once . . . but unfortunately when I'm drunk I can't write and when I'm sober I can't either . . . Lanny inherits," he added, "the flair, or what I fondly believe is a buried talent, and also the incapability. Along with other useless things."

She said, watching the long golden shadows, "It's late. I wonder if you shouldn't be—"

"There's time," he said carelessly. "What you are wondering about is where Elsie comes in. Or goes out."

She was silent, her lips folded like a rose petal, in stubborn hostility against disclosure.

Martin said, "I'm old enough to be your father, worse luck. Curiously enough, you can trust me. I talk too much but not about other people's business—that is, not unless I happen not to like them. It will do you good to tell someone. You're in love with Jonathan and you've just found out that he's in love with you."

"But—"

"You shouldn't leave doors open," he advised gently, "or he shouldn't. I walk like a fat and cautious cat. I passed your door, a while ago. Neither of you saw or heard. Why should you, you were very preoccupied. The heart beats louder than a warning drum or any footsteps and the eyes are closed. I went on down the corridor, came out here and ordered myself a drink. There is something singularly upsetting to a man of my age and habits in the sight of young love. My dear, don't cry," he said, distressed, "don't, I beg of you, I'm a clumsy old—"

She said, "I can't help it. I'm sorry." She groped for a handkerchief and Martin put one into her hand. "It's a little frayed," he said apologetically, "but it's clean. There. I should be shot. Altogether."

She wiped her eyes, blew, definitely, her little nose, and then looked at him. She said, "There's nothing we can do."

"Pish," he said, annoyed, "and even more so, tush. There's a lot you can do. Or rather, Jonathan. He can go to Elsie and say, 'I regret this, but it's off, I'm in love with someone else.'"

"The engagement," said Josephine, "has been announced . . . the announcements have gone to the papers."

"Even the power of the press," said Martin, "can't make an engagement stick."

"She—she loves him," said Josephine, low, "she wouldn't give him up."

"And you will?"

"What else can I do?"

"Hell," said Martin, "is he a man or a mouse? And let's spell it with a capital L. Elsie Meredith loves no one but herself. Her family's in financial difficulties. No one is supposed to know that and I fancy few people do . . . but you'd be surprised how much I know. Sometimes," he explained without shame, "I sell my knowledge to the highest bidder. In this case I happen to know the Meredith brokers. One's a special pal of mine and we got tight together one night. You can imagine the rest. At the moment, it wasn't of much interest to me. If Elsie really loved your Jon," he said, "she might tie him in pink ribbons and hand him over to you because his happiness would mean something to her. But she doesn't love him . . . and she's not giving up a checkbook with a good balance already written in, if she can help it. There's the rub, little Jo. But it's up to Jonathan."

"If I thought that . . ." she said.

"Thought what?"

"That she doesn't love him."

"Take my word for it. Better still," said Martin slowly, "ask Lanny. Oh, not outright, of course, but women have ways haven't they?"

"Lanny?"

Martin sighed.

"I can't even be loyal," he said, "to my own flesh and blood when I see a lovely female in distress. But more than that, I'll not say. There's Wycherly, looking like doom. I must be gone, never again to darken this door—until I am once more without means." He grinned, rose, touched her cheek with his hand. "Best of luck . . . but you didn't tell me what you'd do if you were convinced that Elsie is not emotionally involved with her engagement."

"I'd fight," Josephine said.

"Good girl," Martin approved, "and you have all the proper weapons. Use them, fairly and un-fairly. Hit below the belt if you have to . . . and may the best girl win."

194

Chapter 19

The cars returned from Boca Raton. Bobbie, apprised of her son's departure, was upset. "How too annoying of Jon," she exclaimed. "I don't mean that he could help it. But I was planning a dinner for him and Elsie . . . you know, for the engagement . . . I had such attractive ideas, Josephine . . . I thought we'd work them out, give the party when Fritzi and Howard get here—"

Elsie said, smiling, "It's too bad, of course, but Jon couldn't help it. I imagine he'll phone tonight or tomorrow and tell us how long he must be gone. Don't worry, Bobbie dear."

"I never worry," said Bobbie absently. She looked at Jo, her brows puzzled, "Wasn't someone leaving? Oh, Lansing, of course. Did he?"

"On time," Josephine answered; "Just a few minutes before you returned."

"That's good. But I'll miss him." She said fretfully," He amuses me more than anyone ever—of course, you couldn't stay married to a man who just amused you. I mean, in large doses it palled. Monotonous. Like drinking champagne every day for breakfast. But if that impossible Bertie had been half as entertaining as Lansing I wouldn't be here now. At least not under compulsion . . . not that I don't like being here."

Josephine was having difficulty. She asked, "Bertie?" inquiringly.

"Bertie Rivers. He drank too," said Bobbie, lying

on the chaise longue in her bedroom, her perky flower hat perched on a lamp and the print-lined coat of her dress slithering to the floor from the bed. "But he was so morose when he drank. And women too, of course. You couldn't say that about Lansing. Women, I mean. Or morose."

"Bobbie, for heaven's sake!" began Elsie, lightly but with a warning undercurrent.

"What? You never liked Bertie," said Bobbie, "you know you didn't. He was crazy about you, though. Remember the time we were all at Placid for skiing and he kept following you around and trying to kiss you behind snowbanks? So impractical I always thought."

"Bobbie!"

Elsie was jarred out of her usual control. She was even slightly flushed. Bert Rivers, dark, good for nothing, much Bobbie's junior, was not a man she cared to recall. One of her less attractive episodes. Not that it had gone very far. Yet it might have, only Bobbie, moved by her usual undirected restlessness, had taken Bertie off to Bermuda, or was it Puerto Rico? And by that time Carl had come along.

Elsie thought, suddenly cold with terror, Lanny couldn't have meant Bertie when he said he had heard . . .

"I'm tired," Bobbie complained, "people tire me, motoring, contract . . . and I ate too much. Speaking of Bertie, Mr.—what's his name, Josephine, you know, the lawyer, such a nice man? Well, I was telling him just a fraction of all I'd gone through

196

with Bertie and he said, 'I can't understand, Mrs. Rivers, why you didn't divorce him long ago.' "

"Bobbie," asked Elsie desperately, "is this really—?"

"Oh," said Bobbie, suddenly comprehending, "you mean because of Josephine. Don't be silly, my dear. She's just like one of the family." She beamed fondly at Josephine, "And besides, she knows better than to listen to anything I say, that is, when I'm just talking too much—to be talking, you know."

Josephine rose. She asked, "Is there anything more I can do . . . before I go?"

"Go?"

"You said you wouldn't need me this evening."

"That's right. Run along . . . get one of the men to drive you—have a good time," she said vaguely, "and I'll see you in the morning."

As she left the room Josephine heard Bobbie's light voice running on: "I must dress for dinner. Maybe I won't go down to dinner. I'm dead. Elsie, do me a good turn, take the Rollinses out afterward. Dog races. Or don't they have them at night? I've forgotten. Wycherly will know. Or Josephine. I forgot, she's gone. No, maybe they'd rather play bridge. Don't bother to pick up that coat. I don't like it anyway. Did you ever see anything like the beach hat Patsy Dover wore today? She looked like a hazel nut peering out from under a palm leaf. What an awful woman. I'm sure I don't know why I like her."

Josephine returned to her rooms to change her frock. She went out presently, refusing Wycherly's offer of calling the garage. She'd rather walk, she said, it was a beautiful evening.

When she reached the apartment and rang the bell there was no answer. She fished for her latchkey, opened the door and went in. The place was spotless as it always was; Agnes was a wonderful housekeeper. But it was also empty. She called down to the superintendent on the house phone and he reported promptly that he thought Mrs. Bruce and her cousin had gone out to dinner somewhere. They'd said they wouldn't be back until quite late.

Josephine cast her hat and handbag from her. The apartment was cool, the blinds drawn. She went back to the telephone and called Bill at the office but he had left. She called his house and he answered.

"Night off," she said, with what gaiety she could muster. "I came home but my parent has departed, with Agnes. Giddy gals. Could we have dinner or something?"

Bill cleared his throat. He said, "Gee, I'm sorry, beautiful. I didn't know you'd be free and I made another date. . . . I can't break it. . . . I'm due at the Royal Palm in an hour."

She said, "Ten cents says it's the Durkin child."

He said uneasily, "Well, it didn't seem politic to refuse. Besides, I want to talk business with the old man. He's more amenable after the first six drinks."

Josephine said severely, "You wouldn't be falling for his only child, would you, Bill?"

"Don't be a dope," he said crossly, "she's young enough to be—"

"Come, come, she's at least nineteen."

"And popular," he said gloomily; "you can't get a date with her unless you send six wires and a basket of lilies four weeks in advance—" He stopped, appalled.

Josephine giggled. "I thought so."

"I didn't mean," he shouted, "that is . . . oh, hell, Jo, I'm all mixed up."

Me too, she thought. Aloud she said mildly, "Why should I be annoyed with you, Bill? You don't have to make any pretenses with me."

He was sputtering when she hung up.

So that's that. Bill, good-bye. Not that I ever wanted him but . . . it's funny to lose him, makes me feel a little odd, uncertain and sort of lost. You could always depend on him, always fall back . . . But what real man wants to stand there like a hitching post and wait for you to fall back? He deserves better. I'm not hurt, except, perhaps, in my vanity. It was only last week, wasn't it, that he asked me to marry him? For about the hundredth time. Maybe not last week, but that's near enough. It was habit. He'd been in love with me once, thought he still was, as no one else had come along, until this Durkin business. He deserves the best, not second best. Besides, she told herself, I never said I'd marry him, I never even contemplated it.

All right, Bill, good-bye. . . . I'll make it easy for you.

Perhaps, she thought, men are more single-track and less adaptable than women. Some types of men, that is. Not Lanny, not his father. Men like Bill; like

199

Jon too, although they're so different. Perhaps it frightens and embarrasses them to realize that what they thought was love forever wasn't at all.

She sat on the big couch in the darkness. After a while she rose, turned on a lamp, and wrote a note to her mother. She thought, I can't sit here all evening thinking.

If Martin was right, if Elsie didn't care about Jonathan, if it was only the money . . .

Only the money? But perhaps Elsie wouldn't feel that way. *Only.*

Josephine picked up the telephone again and called a girl whom she had known most of her life and of whom she was very fond. She had seen little of her lately, for Nora was running a dress shop, successfully, and was often out of town on buying trips.

"Nora? It's Jo . . . are you free tonight, could we have dinner together?"

Nora was bright, gay, and a little disillusioned. You'd never tell her anything that mattered. She'd talk about her customers, her buying trips, her profits and losses. She was very amusing. If you were with her you wouldn't think.

Nora, who lived in a small hotel on Indian Creek, would be delighted. "Come here and have dinner," she suggested, "I'll have to throw you out early, I've some people coming."

That meant a man, who hadn't been able to make dinner. Probably he was married; possibly he was from out of town. Nora handled her life with discretion but within its limits she permitted herself

200

enormous latitude. Josephine respected her reticences. It was the best way to go on being friends, possibly the only way. And Nora had no people now, no one to whom she need account.

They had dinner together, under the stars on the patio of the pleasant little hotel. And shortly after nine Josephine's taxi turned into the gates of Blue Horizons.

Someone called her as she walked into the hall. It was Lanny beckoning from the doorway of the card room. He, the Rollinses and Elsie were playing contract.

Bobbie hadn't appeared all evening he said. "Gone to bed, tired or something. Susan, too. What have you been doing?"

She told him, smiling, trying to make her escape. Yet she didn't wish to escape. She was afraid of being alone, of her thoughts. Almost as afraid of seeing Elsie. But there she was, her black hair shining, her linen dinner dress as severely cut as a golf frock, her bracelet on her arm.

That's funny, thought Josephine idly, she always wears the pair.

"I'm dummy. Come talk to me. Did Pop get off all right? He left me the damnedest note."

"Yes," said Josephine, "I saw him for a little while just before he went. I wonder if there is anything I could do for Mrs. Rivers?"

The hand ended. Elsie rose and came toward them. She said, "Have a nice day? Isn't it too absurd about Jon?"

201

The telephone rang and Wycherly came to report that Mr. Scott was on the wire.

Elsie said, "Take my hand, Josephine, there's a dear," and went to the hall telephone leaving the door open. "But, Jon darling," they heard her say, dismayed, "not for a week!"

Josephine closed her ears and went on arranging her cards, concentrating on the hand and the play. When Elsie returned she finished out the hand.

"Good work, partner," said Lanny. He looked at Elsie. "We're still in the hole," he said, "thanks to my cards."

Josephine rose. Elsie said, "Thanks," carelessly and slid the bracelet up and down her arm. And Josephine spoke idly.

"Your bracelet?" she said. "You haven't lost the matching—"

Elsie spoke quickly. "No . . . but the clasp was weak. . . . I won't wear it until it's repaired."

"I'll take it for you if you like," Josephine told her, "I have some errands to do on Lincoln Road tomorrow."

"Oh, it can wait," Elsie said.

Lanny spoke. "Did you forget you gave it to me for safekeeping, Elsie? I don't think there's anything wrong with the clasp. Perhaps you didn't fasten the guard," he said.

Under the incurious eyes of the negative Rollins couple he took the bracelet from his breast pocket, folded the handkerchief which had contained it and slid it across the table. Josephine thought, There's something queer about this . . . something very strange about the color rising to Elsie's high cheekbones, something off in her voice. She said, "Why, thank you, Lanny, I had forgotten."

He said gallantly, "Let me," rose, came toward her and fastened the bracelet about her slender wrist. "There, you see," he said, "as good as new."

She said slowly, "I remember. You were going to have it fixed."

"I changed my mind," he said; "it didn't need fixing."

Mr. Collins rattled the cards impatiently, shuffling them expertly.

Josephine went upstairs. She thought, What was wrong about that? What was so—so queer?

How could you forget you'd given a bracelet worth, at a venture, three thousand dollars, to someone to have fixed for you?

Two days later Fritzi and Howard Toller arrived brown from the Nassau sun and full of gossip. Josephine was astonished to find how glad she was to see them, how much she liked the fat, genial, sometimes impertinent Mr. Toller and the wholly incalculable countess. The boat would be along presently, Toller reported; it had been delayed because of some engine trouble. They'd all go to lunch at the Quarter Deck Club, first chance they got. "You too, Josephine," he said sternly; "won't have you begging off." And then they'd plan the fishing trip. Couldn't undertake that until Jon came back.

Fritzi was in high spirits. No one in Nassau knew

how to play poker, she said.

Except herself.

On the next day the Rollins couple arrived. "Just one big happy family," said Fritzi, strolling on the patio with Josephine. She wore a broomstick skirt in a thousand different colors, very short, very fetching. She wore a sheer white blouse with puffed soft sleeves and her narrow waist was bound with a broad girdle. "Why are you looking at me like that, my child?" she inquired.

Josephine said puzzled, "You look—different."

Fritzi's green eyes were bright with laughter, and she smote herself lightly upon the chest. She said, "Hays office . . . Lana Turner . . . is that what you mean? When I was a girl, a thousand and one years ago, I used to use tissue paper. I rattled when I breathed. It distressed my poor mother, it startled St. Louis. But the pancake-chested female was not then in vogue. When she was, boy, was I a knockout! Latterly I have again become conscious of my deficiencies. This time it isn't tissue paper," she explained, admiring her new curves.

She looked at Josephine and added, "You'll never have to worry," and laughed, delighted. "It's nice to see a genuine blush now and then. The only way I can manage one is to stand on my head in a corner—so I don't, because I don't want people to think I'm a little pixillated. Matter of fact I remember the first and only time I ever blushed. I was going to school, and the minister's son was walking beside me carrying my books. I was eight years old and on a busy corner,"

Fritzi remembered happily, "I lost my pants!"

She added thoughtfully, "It gets to be a habit. And I don't mean *blushing!*"

The boat arrived, a sleek and shining fifty-six-foot cruiser, the *Alice T.* . . . with two tall outriggers, fishing chairs, and complicated gear, and a radio telephone; with a couple of men in crew, plenty of cabin space, and sleeping quarters. They sailed on it, the day following its arrival, down to the Quarter Deck Club, that enchanting structure which is its own complete island, rising out of the water, astonishing and unique. They spent the better part of the day there, having cocktails and a leisurely lunch, fishing afterward, and came back over the sunset-still water, under a fantastically colored sky.

The day's mail lay on the hall table. And Elsie, reaching it first turned it over, selected hers, put her hand on an envelope with clear black writing and little Greek E's—"from Jon," she said. "I—"

She stopped and her face changed. "I'm sorry," she said, and gave the envelope to Josephine, "It's for you."

She said it very clearly. Lanny looked from her to Josephine. Fritzi grinned and said lightly, "If there's anything for me, it's bills, I don't know anyone who can write," and Bobbie asked, "For you, Josephine? That's *very* strange."

Josephine said, after a moment, "It may be something about the house."

Lame, lamer than lame. No one believed her. It was a long way to her room. She mustn't hurry. She mustn't seem in haste.

A little later in the library, Elsie drew Lanny aside. She said, "That's very odd."

"What?"

"Jon—and—"

"I warned you."

"I didn't believe it. I won't now. Not that it could make any difference, as he's mine," Elsie said.

"Oh, sure," said Lanny.

She looked around her, walked swiftly to the door and closed it.

"Why did you return my bracelet?"

"I've told you. I changed my mind."

Walking up to the shop where the gentlemen waited who would give him a fair price; walking in, dropping it on the counter, making the bargain, and then picking up the damned thing, unable to go through with it . . . what a fool he had been.

"Why?"

"Don't offer it to me again."

"I didn't in the first place."

"You might now."

"Why did you change your mind, Lanny?"

He said gently, "You wouldn't understand, Elsie. I don't myself."

Chapter 20

Josephine sat on the edge of her bed and read Jonathan's letter. It was not very long; but it was definite.

"My darling," he wrote, "I have written you every day, and many times, since I left you, yet sent none of my letters, they have been so inadequate. Anything I can put down on paper is inadequate. I cannot even say how much I love you. I need all our lives together to say it, and to prove it. And I miss you. Here under gray skies and whirling snow, with a bitter wind blowing, I think of you and the blue sky and the bluer sea and I'm happier than I've ever been and miserable because we are not together.

"Things are going well enough, Mr. Forest has been operated on, is doing well, and I have been able to talk with him for a short period. I will be back very soon, to you and Blue Horizons. And when I return I will tell Elsie. It is the only thing to do.

"I am living here in this hotel for the few days I must be here. Mother's apartment is closed, as is the little place I maintain as my own. Will you not write me here, air mail, special delivery? Please don't say any of the things you feel you must say . . . the sober, pedestrian, utterly absurd things. Say only that you love me and that one day we will be always together. . . .

"It does not seem at all strange that I have known you so short a while and yet have already loved you a lifetime.

"Jon."

Josephine locked the letter in the small drawer of the desk and put the key in her handbag. She thought, I can't answer it.

She tried. She was not very articulate on paper.

She wrote slowly in her round, pretty script:

"Elsie saw your handwriting, she thought you had written to her. She was—annoyed, although she tried not to show it, and of course, curious. Your mother, too. Have you thought about your mother at all, Jon? She'll be dreadfully upset. She's so fond of Elsie and she takes your marriage for granted. She is planning an engagement dinner when you get back.

"I don't know what to say. We have no right to each other. How could you be happy with me, with everyone you know hostile to me? . . . It's strange, people never seem very upset when a girl breaks her engagement but when a man does . . . that's different somehow."

She stopped and looked at the sheet of paper. She folded it so that it blotted and made queer, fantastic pictures in ink. She tore it into tiny pieces and dropped it in the wastebasket and took a fresh sheet.

"I do love you, Jon," she wrote, "I can't help or deny it, but loving each other doesn't solve our problem. Don't write me again, it's better not."

She sealed and stamped the letter and just before dinner was announced, slipped from the house to mail it at the nearest box.

The night was unusually warm and they dined on the patio by starlight and the more practical illumination of tall hurricane candles in their etched-glass shades. Howard dominated the conversation, planning the fishing trip. As soon as Jon came back, he said, and the weather was favorable they'd start out, go down and fish off the Keys. What about a run to Bimini later? And there'd be plenty of room on the boat . . . two cabins each with four bunks, exclusive of crew quarters. Everyone could go. Bobbie, he remarked, was just being stubborn.

Bobbie shook her head. She hated boats, she said, any boat under thirty thousand tons. She didn't like fishing, or fish smells or blood or getting wet and being uncomfortable. Deep-sea fishing was not her idea of sport and as for climbing into a skiff and rowing in and out of deserted keys! The way Howard described it gave her the horrors, she said definitely. Anyone who wished could go but she wouldn't and that was that.

Fritzi said promptly that she agreed with Bobbie. Howard looked at her reproachfully.

"But I thought . . ." he began.

"I doubt it," said Fritzi. "I've just kept quiet, that's all. I think it's a ridiculous idea. Ruinous to the hair, the skin, and the manicure. Also I'm too old. There are a few things," she added, with her emerald twinkle, "for which I am too ancient. Fishing is one of them. Tennis another, golf a third. Age has its compensations. Thanks, no. I'll stay here with Bobbie if you don't mind and even if you do. We'll scare up some form of entertainment. There are always the races."

"Well, that's fine," said Howard, gloomily; "plan a

good party and everyone backs out. What about you, Elsie? Good. Lanny?"

Lanny said sadly that he supposed he'd have to go—

"Josephine?"

Josephine looked up, startled. She had been sitting quite still taking no part in the discussion, thinking her own faraway thoughts, immersed in her own problems. She said, "Thanks, Mr. Toller, but I couldn't, I'm afraid."

"Why not?" asked Susan Wilton suddenly. "It will do you good." She looked at her sister. "Don't you think so, Roberta?" she inquired. "You can spare Josephine for a few days, and you won't be alone, as Fritzi is staying home."

"Of course," agreed Bobbie, "I thought that was understood." She had completely forgotten her project to remain home with Josephine, practically hanging over the excavations at the bay-front site.

"Fine," said Howard heartily. "You, Susan?"

"I'm going, of course," said Susan cheerfully, "even if I'm seasick."

Josephine spoke to Susan after dinner. She said, troubled, "It's awfully kind of you, Miss Wilton, but I don't feel that I should go on this trip." She hesitated and then added stoutly. "That's not what Mrs. Rivers pays me for, is it?"

Susan patted her shoulder. "You need some fun."

"It's all been fun," Josephine said. "I feel dreadfully guilty—"

"Guilty?"

"I do so little."

"Nonsense, you do a great deal. You've been oil on the troubled social waters, you've taken over all the niggling little arrangements which consume so much time, you've been unfailingly amiable, cheerful, and also too self-effacing. You deserve a little jaunt. I wouldn't suggest it if my sister was to be alone. But she won't be."

"I'd love it," Josephine admitted, "if you're quite sure that it's truly all right."

"Quite, And stop arguing. Anyone playing contract?" asked Susan. "I feel lucky."

It had been late when they finished dinner, too late for Josephine to slip away and go home. Moreover, Bobbie had remembered the report Josephine had made on the progress of the new house. She'd been too busy, too sleepy, too anything to bother with it until tonight. Tonight she sat at Jonathan's desk in the library, looked at the latest plans, glanced over the notes, until she was tired and decided to take a hand at contract. Josephine was not needed and she slipped upstairs to her room presently, with a new mystery novel in her hand. Susan doted on them, and lent them generously. A Lincoln Road bookshop kept her supplied with the latest fashions in annihilation. "Vicarious revenge," she explained; "every time I dislike anybody to the point of frenzy I read the newest, most blood-curdling thriller I can find. It relaxes the tension."

Josephine went to bed, turned on the reading light, and opened the book. On the very first page

Squire Harkens was found done to death, by a blunt instrument, and in his locked and shuttered library. The butler who had been with him for forty years was all of a dither. His handsome but graceless nephew who stood to inherit was darkly suspect. A pretty girl turned up, a dumb policeman, and an erudite secretary. But during the third chapter the nephew also departed this involved life. . . .

It was a good yarn, hard boiled and fast moving, but Josephine's mind was not on it. She put it down on the bed table, and closed her eyes. There was only one thing to do. She would tell Jonathan that she could not marry him.

A mid-Victorian heroine, she told herself scornfully. Not a modern heroine at all. Honor had an alien sound nowadays. People did not much consider honor . . . people, politicians, diplomats, entire countries. Under dictatorships and expediency, the word no longer existed.

Joseph Bruce had killed himself because he had felt dishonest, if not dishonorable; because in his own enthusiasm be had overreached himself and, in his fall, had taken with him many of his friends. He had been unable to face that outcome, unable to excuse himself, although he had meant no harm.

She told herself, Jon's given his word.

Yet she had told Lansing Martin that she would fight.

Only if she was sure that Elsie—

She wasn't sure. How could she be sure of anything?

She turned off the lights and lay there listening to the murmur of the sea, her eyes wide and aching, fixed on the darkness beyond the windows. The curtains stirred, the wind rose. . . . She thought, sensing its direction, sensing the pull of the tides, tomorrow will be cloudy, tomorrow it will rain.

She must have slept eventually, but woke startled, her heart pounding, conscious that someone was in the room. She smelt cigarette smoke, and saw, when her eyes were open and focused, the little spark of light. She sat up and asked, "Who is it?" more frightened than she had ever been. But burglars didn't walk into your room smoking cigarettes. She thought, I forgot to lock the door.

"It's I," said Elsie, "don't be frightened. The game's over, we had something to eat. I thought, possibly, you'd be awake. I want to talk to you. No, don't turn on the light. I'll sit here, by the window."

She was a shadow among shadows. The cigarette glowed and Josephine heard the tinkle of glass. Elsie had moved an ash tray on the small table near the window.

"You don't seem astonished," said Elsie after a moment.

"No."

She wasn't. It was like a dream, the quiet voice in the darkness, the odor of tobacco, the shadow stirring by the open windows.

Elsie said: "It's time we talked, I think. You had a letter from Jon today. Your explanation convinced no one. Bobbie's forgotten, I dare say. She has a

213

mind like a sieve. Of course should I decide to re-mind her, with footnotes, you'd be out of a job. But that isn't my way, exactly. Tonight I saw you running down the drive with a letter in your hand. It didn't take a Peter Whimsey to know you'd answered Jon's letter and weren't trusting it to anyone else to mail. I'm not going to ask you what he wrote or what you replied. I don't much care."

Josephine spoke. She asked, "Do you love him?"

"That's an odd question," said Elsie. "Naturally, I love him. I have for years."

"Would you," asked Josephine, "if he weren't Roberta Rivers's son?"

"If he hadn't money, you mean? How delicately you put it. And what an absurd question. Would you?"

"Yes," Josephine answered, making the ultimate admission.

"That's what you think," said Elsie, and ground her cigarette in the ash tray. "How can you separate him from his background? If he weren't Bobbie's son he wouldn't be Jon. He'd be someone else. Simple—isn't it?—and logical."

"Neither," Josephine denied.

Elsie laughed, without malice. "Look . . . Jon and I have been more or less engaged for years. He's never looked at anyone else—as far as I knew. It's been understood between us that as soon as I made up my mind we'd be married. I was quite frankly having too good a time to surrender to a cottage for two and a white picket fence or its equivalent. Par-ties and visits and trips and people," she said

214

vaguely, "and even a fling at the stage, one year—only summer stock of course and I wasn't very good, but it amused me. Then latterly I've discovered that I'm competent, an organizer. That's been amusing too. Yet when I came down here I was quite ready for the—picket fence. I'd had what used to be called my fling and it looked as if Jon would be on his way before long, off to training camp. I realized, too, that if we were in the war before that time came that he'd volunteer and naturally we'd marry first."

She waited, but Josephine said nothing. And presently Elsie went on: "When I came here, I found you. You're very pretty," she said carelessly, "very appealing. I don't blame Jonathan for his—shall we say temporary?—aberration, and I don't blame you. You haven't had many opportunities, have you? I didn't, however, take you seriously, not even after that romantic interlude on the patio—you must admit, my dear, that you took advantage of a ridiculous mistake."

"It wasn't a mistake."

"Even that," said Elsie calmly, "is hardly world-shaking. I expect Jon has kissed a lot of girls—and not by mistake. We neither of us took any monastic vows—I was, however, warned about you. When and by whom doesn't matter but that didn't bother me either. You see, I know Jon . . . his loyalty, his basic fidelity. You don't know him; how can you, in so short a time? He's not—what's the old-fashioned word?—a philanderer. And he loves me. I'm telling you this so that you'll understand. I won't give him up," she said definitely, and rose, "no matter what happens. And what is more, as soon as he returns here we will make arrangements to be married as soon as possible. From this house, if it can be arranged."

She walked to the door and put her hand on the knob. She said with silky quiet: "Even if you have any valid reason for feeling that Jon should terminate his engagement to me and marry you . . . I wouldn't know, of course, and I'm not asking—it would make no difference."

The door closed behind her and Josephine sat upright in the darkness with her hands clenched, consumed with anger and a clear sense of outrage. She thought, But she gave herself away, she doesn't love him, no woman who loved him could speak like that; that isn't love, that's hate.

"You shan't have him," she said aloud, "you shan't!"

Chapter 21

Elsie walked quietly along the corridor and as she passed Lanny's door it opened and Lanny stood there. He asked, smiling, "Been calling?"

"Calling?"

"Don't stall. I came along a moment ago and heard voices, or rather yours. Putting Jo through the jumps, weren't you?"

"What business is it of yours?" she inquired.

"I can make it my business," he said, and caught her hand. "Come in here . . . or do I have to drag you in? Pretty picture that'll make. And be quiet. Susan's next door."

His hand was relentless on her wrist and she yielded and went into the room. Lanny locked the door and put the key in his pocket. He grinned at her, without merriment.

"Ha, me proud beauty," he said.

"Lanny, you're absurd. Let me out of here."

"Nope. Cigarette?" She took one and he lighted it for her. "Sit down," he said; "we're going to have a fireside chat. Drink?"

"No, thanks."

He said rapidly, standing in front of her: "This highly complicated situation is getting more so every minute. But it's very simple really. You've finally come to the conclusion that Jon and Josephine Bruce are in love. So you've told Jo to lay off and you're hell-bent on marrying Jon the first minute you get your hands on him."

"What of it," she demanded negligently, "since you're so clever? He'll get over her!"

"Perhaps. You'll hold him to his word?"

"Naturally."

"You'll have a wonderful life," he prophesied. "Jon's such a sap he might permit himself to be held. But I don't know. What will you do if he tells you to go jump in the lake? Any lake?"

She said evenly, "I will sue him for breach of promise."

Lanny's jaw dropped. "My dear girl, if you do that your shoestring existence will be exposed for the world to see."

"If I don't do it," she retorted, "and Jon doesn't marry me, it will be anyway. What have I to lose?"

He said thoughtfully: "Bobbie's odd. She's whizzed through widowhood, one divorce, and another impending without the slightest breath of scandal. She always married her man, she always had public opinion on her side. My father drank and caused her considerable confusion. Bert Rivers is no good, he drank too much and kept, practically, an entire floor show. Bobbie doesn't like scandal. She'd especially dislike this sort. She dotes on Jon but, good Lord, your mother's the closest thing to an intimate Bobbie has and—"

"Exactly," said Elsie.

"What would you get out of it? I doubt if Bobbie would put up a cent . . . millions for defense, but not a penny for tribute. Do I quote correctly? Blackmail, then."

She said carelessly, "You're talking about blackmail. And, by the way, what happens to you if I don't marry Jon?"

"I've changed my mind about that."

"Like the bracelet?"

"Exactly."

"Why, or aren't you telling?"

"I'm telling," Lanny informed her. His jaw set, he looked lined, and much older. "You won't believe this. It started with Jo, really. Watching her, watching Jon . . . both of them troubled, and not knowing what it was all about. . . . I felt like a grandfather. I

218

felt like hell. Just seeing them together, not knowing anyone was spying on them. They're young and decent and deserve a break. Jon doesn't deserve you, my sweet. As much as I can care for anyone these days I care for him. . . . I have ever since he was a kid and I was a big, swaggering, sophisticated brat who'd come home half plastered from some place I'd no business to be, with the smell of stale smoke and stale liquor and stale women on me, sit on the edge of his bed and make up a yarn to tell him . . . because it was fun to see his eyes and hear him laugh—because I knew he admired me, thought me all his storybook heroes rolled into one."

"Very touching," said Elsie, and smiled slightly. "Don't tell me you're going into a psychological confession."

"Shut up," he said; "what a filthy mind you have."

She said, "We always got along so well, you and I."

Lanny tossed his cigarette into an ash tray. He said, still standing over her, looking down: "I thought it would be easy to sell your damned bracelet, and to make things so uncertain and unpleasant for you that after you and Jon were married I'd be able to cut the apron strings and go my own way. Well, it wasn't. I can't do it. I don't want Jon's money . . . and I'm getting out. I've been cultivating certain acquaintances lately . . . there are a lot of South Americans here this season and I've been offered a job. It wouldn't interest you. There isn't much money in it. There's a lot of hard work and I won't like that, and it will be as far from civilization as I've ever been. But I'm going to take it."

"I don't believe it," she said flatly, and was white, suddenly to the lips.

"Whistle for me," he said, "in a few weeks. I won't be here. I'm afraid I can't be at your wedding, darling," he added.

Elsie rallied, leaning back against the deep upholstery of the chair.

"Bluff," she said scornfully. "You and work . . . you and reform. It's out of all reason."

He said, "I like to believe that if you had really loved Jon and he loved you I would not stand in your way."

"You can't," she said, "now or at any time."

"I can. If you'd cared about him, Elsie, I wouldn't have asked you to drink with me in Wycherly's pantry."

"What do you propose to do?" she asked. "Tell Jon about us?"

"Amazing," he murmured. "Jackpot."

Elsie laughed. "You wouldn't. I realized the other night after I left you that you wouldn't. You wouldn't want him to think that of you . . . and besides," she added, "what about *my* side of it? Ignorant, romantic, eighteen years old—you were much older, my dear, and very experienced."

"A good act," he agreed, "but he wouldn't believe it. Oddly enough, he'll believe me. I don't lie to Jon about important things and I don't intend to begin now. "

She said, "You'll see. He'll think it more than ever

220

his duty to marry me."

"He's not that much of a sap," Lanny said, "and I can name names. One of my choicest exhibits is a letter Bertie Rivers wrote me at the time Bobbie first decided to give him the matrimonial brush-off. I was away at the time, looking in Chicago gutters for my incalculable father. Bertie—never a great mind—was panicky. He was in Puerto Rico with Bobbie and they'd had their first rousing quarrel. He wrote to ask me to exercise my influence over her. He admitted this, that, and the other thing, blonde, redheaded, or what have you. But, he added, as far as you were concerned there wasn't anything in it, matters hadn't progressed that far— no matter what Bobbie thought. It appeared that she twitted him with some episode in Placid and he jumped to the conclusion that she thought it impor- tant—which she didn't. Because it would never occur to Bobbie, not in her most confused mo- ments, that you and Bertie—"

She said, "Jon will listen to me. He'll understand it's malice on your part and jealousy."

"I have Bertie's letter," he said, "and several of yours. The best. I didn't keep them for this purpose, or for any purpose except that I was a fool and wanted something of you. I have the cigarette case, too, Elsie."

"You told me you'd lost it!"

"I hadn't," he said.

She asked, after a minute, "What do you want me to do?"

"When Jon comes," he said, "you can tell him you've changed your mind."

"And if I don't?"

"Think it over," he advised her. He walked over to the door and unlocked it. He said, "When I told you I was going to South America you turned very white. Why? What difference does it make to you where I go? You despise me, you're afraid of me, you could murder me—you would, too, if you had the guts and could be sure of escaping the consequences. But you don't want me to go away. You want me around. You want me to be best man at your wedding, you want me to sit at your table, drink your cocktails, deal your cards, occupy your guest room. It would amuse you, very much. You want to think, as you have thought all these years, All I have to do is beckon and everything goes overboard. You wouldn't beckon. But you'd like to think that you might. Wait a minute, don't go yet." He held her pinned against the door, and bent to kiss her. "One more thing. If you'd be interested in seeing South America. . . ."

"Let me go!"

"Certainly. You should," he said easily, "marry me, you know. Because I'm about the only man on the face of the earth who deserves to have you. It would be very suitable. We'd probably be poor, we'd never be honest, we'd quarrel incessantly. We'd dislike each other, as we do now. But we couldn't break away, never completely away, because we are the same kind of people and we belong. And what's between us is authentic. It's not the sort of thing you talk about over a tea table, and it hasn't anything of youth in it, or of hope or joy. It's dark and rather dreadful and unescapable. But it's *real*. It's all the reality we will ever know, either of us."

He opened the door and Elsie went out without a word and walked, quietly and carefully, to the turn of the corridor.

Lanny went into his dressing room. His heart shook, he felt physically ill. The sweat stood out on his high forehead, his scalp and hair were wet with it. He went into the bathroom and undressed. Standing under the shower he surveyed himself without illusion. His muscles weren't as good as they had been. He was flabby. He was beginning to acquire a small but definite paunch. His wind wasn't anything to brag about. South America and the oil-fields. Keeping books in some God-forsaken jungle. Danger, monotony, and disease. It wasn't a pretty picture.

He turned off the shower, rubbed himself down with a sheet-size towel, and went to bed. He thought, I've a hell of a headache. He thought, I can't face Jon, I couldn't, and tell him. She knows that. She thinks I haven't what it takes to go to South America. Maybe she's right. No, she isn't. I'll go, I'll wash my hands of this whole business.

Bluff.

If Elsie knew it was bluff, was convinced of it?

He thought, I can't give Jon this way out. It's a dirty way. It's a door opening on unspeakable things. It's not a way he'd take. She's right. He's just that much of a damned chivalrous fool.

He got up and turned on a light. He opened a bureau drawer. Piles of custom-made shirts . . . Bobbie had them made for him. She was always good to him, generous, too generous. Under a pile, the chamois case and in the case the gold cigarette case with his initials in enamel, severely plain, and inside the case the inscription in Elsie's handwriting, with a date and an utterly damning quotation.

He weighed it in his hand, satin sleek, cool, heavy. He remembered the day she had given it to him and why. He thought, She's utterly beneath contempt, she isn't human, she's out of another world. She's strong where I'm weak. The wrong kind of strength but strength just the same. She hasn't a vulnerable fiber. Once perhaps, long ago. But not now.

Funny, wasn't it, this persistent ache, this denied longing, this enduring desire . . . a love that wasn't blind at all, a love with far too excellent sight—thirty-thirty, didn't they call it? Something like that. A love that saw, understood, despised yet went on living somehow, hating its own existence.

He thought, She may guess that I can't do this to Jon, but she'll never guess that I couldn't to her.

He went back to the bureau and took from the bottom drawer, from under the soft cashmere sweaters, a small battered box. The key was on his watch chain. He opened it and took out the letters, Bertie's, Elsie's.

After a while he went to the desk and sat down.

He took a sheet of paper and wrote:

"You were right. I can't. You're the only human being I've ever loved. What other affection I know is for Jon—because he once looked up to me—even then I knew how crazy that was, and for my father, because he's such an amiable crackpot. But what I feel for them wouldn't stand up under fire.

"The letters will burn, the cigarette case will melt down.

"You're going to do something so wholly, bitterly wrong, Elsie, that I wish I might warn you you will regret it all your life. But I doubt if it's in you to regret anything. So I'm going away. I'll leave word for Bobbie, but she won't be surprised, she'll guess I'm off on a bender. I do it now and then when things get too thick and as long as I don't do it in her presence she accepts it. When I come back you'll be on your fishing trip. I'll tell Bobbie about South America and when you return, I'll be on my way there if I can manage it.

"If I loved you a little less I'd go through with my melodramatic gesture. If I loved you a little more I'd probably kill myself—and you too. That would be an interesting and complete solution.

"Funny thing, I've always known you intended to marry Jon yet I never believed it would happen; not even when I urged it upon you in a sort of dim-witted belief that it would solve my future financial problems and set me free in more ways than one. That was before I was sure about Jon and Josephine.

225

Once I *was* sure . . . bighearted Lanny . . . I wanted to show you the error of your ways and give them both handfuls of happiness in one easy lesson. Well, it wasn't that simple. I wish I was as uncomplex as you, Elsie. But I'm not, so when I discover a spark of decency it always starts a forest fire . . . and destroys things . . . so it isn't much good, is it?

"I wish you all the happiness in the world. I'd prefer that Jon didn't have to share it. But I can't have everything."

He folded the letter, sealed it, and went searching in the tidy closet for paper and string. He found them, folded, on a high shelf. There was sealing wax on the desk. Susan was such a good housekeeper, he thought. He'd miss her, and Bobbie. Bobbie exasperated him but he'd miss her. He'd miss a lot . . . the ease, the luxury, and the good times; not that they were very good, but they got you through another day.

He took off his pajamas, dressed, dragged a small suitcase down from the closet shelf and packed it. He opened his wallet and shrugged. Lucky at cards.

Before he left he sat down and wrote briefly to Bobbie.

"Angel," he said, in his careless scrawl, "the wilderness calls. In, other words, I'm off on one of my little excursions. Don't worry, I won't land in jail this time. Make any explanation you like to the rest—I'll be back sometime soon, probably when the crowd's

226

off to the Keys, and you're alone. I want to have a talk with you anyway. And don't fret about me."

He wrapped the cigarette case and the letters in the brown paper and sealed them with the red wax. Then he left the room quietly and made his way toward the back stairs and up to the servants' quarters. Old Wycherly slept lightly, and woke instantly as Lanny turned on the light.

"It's me," said Lanny unnecessarily; "I'm pulling out."

Wycherly nodded. In the last ten years this had happened several times.

"Be careful, Mr. Lanny," was all he said.

"Okay." Lanny whacked him on the shoulder. "Have this note go up on Mrs. Rivers's breakfast tray," he said, "and this brown paper package is for Miss Meredith. Send it up to her in the morning."

He smiled and departed and Wycherly shook his head dolefully. The state he'd be in when he returned! He must remember to replenish the medicine closet, he thought sleepily.

Lanny stopped in his room, picked up his suitcase, went downstairs and let himself out. He walked briskly down the driveway along Collins until he found a cruising cab. He named a small, obscure hotel across the causeway and relaxed, closing his eyes.

You can't escape forever but for the moment, he thought, there are ways and means.

Chapter 22

Wycherly overslept and woke with a headache. His blood pressure was high and the doctor had warned him he must slow up, "take things a little easier." Once he had expected that when this time came it would be simple enough, as his wages had always been excellent, his personal wants few and his sense of thrift acute. Tips averaged well over bad times and good, and there were certain commissions which he considered legitimate. He drank little, his modest gambling was his only extravagance, and he had cared little for women for the last ten years. But little by little his savings had been sent overseas and now, having reached the age at which he had expected to retire, return home and purchase a small, conveniently located pub, he knew that he must go on working.

The last mail had brought word from his sister's married daughter and his brother's widow. Distressing word. Wycherly had had his headache ever since.

He rose and took his shower, moving creakily as was his habit in the mornings. He had completely forgotten Lanny's visit to his quarters until he saw the letter addressed to Mrs. Rivers and the brown-paper parcel. He took them downstairs and into the pantry where he would superintend the trays. Poor Mr. Lanny. Not that Wycherly had any use for him. He merely liked him, despite his shortcomings.

He spoke to Bobbie's maid and she took the

note, laid it on the tray, and went on arranging a gardenia in a bud vase. Rhoda was in charge of the trays for the other women. Holmes would take up Howard Toller's.

Wycherly weighed the brown-paper package in his hand. Mr. Lanny had said, send it up on Miss Meredith's tray. No, he had said, send it up on Miss Bruce's.

Wycherly's head ached furiously, he felt old, tired, and confused. He had not gone back to sleep for sometime after Lanny had left and then had fallen into heavy, anxious dreams.

What had Mr. Lanny said?

He sat down on a high stool with the package in his hand and tried to reason it out. If Lanny Martin was to leave some sort of farewell gift for someone, for whom would it be? Nonsense, thought Wycherly, not Miss Meredith. . . . I must have been mistaken. Yet it seem to me that he said . . .

Holmes spoke. He said, "Mr. Martin hasn't rung."

"He won't," said Wycherly; "he left last night, late."

"Where'd he go?" asked Rhoda, sparkling with life.

"He did not inform me," said Wycherly with dignity, "he merely said he was going away for a time. He left a note for Madame and this package for—"

Rhoda squealed. "Give it here, I'll take it up to her," she said.

"Her?" asked Wycherly heavily.

"Miss Bruce. He's always sending up notes and flowers," reported Rhoda, exaggerating happily, "but he's getting nowhere fast, with her. I have eyes."

Wycherly was above gossip, per se. Now and then he inclined a godlike ear but made no comment. However, this was evidence. Miss Bruce, of course. He gave the little package to Rhoda and turned to his immediate duties.

Josephine rang for breakfast, and spent the time elapsing before Rhoda's arrival under a shower. She thought, As soon as Jon comes back I'll tell him I've changed my mind. We'll go to Elsie together and ask for his release from the engagement. I'm not afraid. I'm not afraid of anything or anyone. Not even of Jon's mother. If she loves him—and she does, I know it—she can't want him to be unhappy . . . she must see his viewpoint, and mine.

Jon, I'll make you the very best wife in all the world.

Rhoda came in and Josephine smiled at her. Rhoda, setting down the tray, announced with the speculative gleam with which Josephine had grown familiar: "Mr. Martin went away last night, Miss Bruce. He left this package with Wycherly for you."

She lingered as usual, fussing over the tray, picking up slippers, retrieving a silk robe from the floor. But the package remained unopened.

Rhoda departed in an aura of wounded disappointment.

Josephine opened the package, and stared, astonished, at its contents—letters . . . addressed to Lanny, one single letter, and then several, secured together with an elastic band. A cigarette case.

And still another letter, thick, unaddressed, in a white envelope.

She shook her head, and opened the cigarette case, which bore Lanny's initials, and stared, incredulous, at the inscription within, engraved in facsimile in the handwriting which was on the envelopes under the rubber band.

"Lanny from Elsie." A quotation . . . and a date.

Josephine closed the cigarette case. She felt ill and dizzy with shock, and utterly incredulous. She thought, Lanny sent these to me . . . so that I'd show them to Jon.

Perhaps the letter would explain. But no explanation was possible, she thought, cold and hot by turns.

She drew the sheets of paper from the unmarked white envelope and read the first line. . . . "You are going to do something so utterly and bitterly wrong, Elsie. . . ."

Josephine thrust the paper back in the envelope, her hands shaking. The letter was for Elsie, the cigarette case, the other letters. Not for her . . . Wycherly, Rhoda, someone, had made a mistake.

She set the tray aside and got out of bed. She put her feet into slippers, belted the silk robe about her. She thought, I mustn't read it, I can't.

She had never known a stronger, more urgent temptation.

She took the letters and the cigarette case, left the room, and went down the corridor to Elsie's room. Knocking, she felt her knees shake and her heart tremble.

"Come in," said Elsie.

Josephine went in and closed the door. Elsie, pushing her hair back from her forehead, sat up in bed and stared at her. She said blankly, "I thought you were Rhoda."

Josephine went over to the bed and looked down. She dropped the case and letters on the blanket cover. She said rapidly: "Lanny went away during the night. He left a package with Wycherly, which was sent up on my breakfast tray."

Elsie put out her hand and touched the cigarette case. She saw Bertie's letter lying there, addressed to Lanny . . . she remembered his hurried, angular writing, the unfinished careless look. She saw the other letters, hers.

Her face was colorless and perfectly still.

She said, "Lanny sent these to you. He hadn't the nerve to take them to Jon himself. So he gave them to you to take. Well, what are you going to do about it? Or am I to have an opportunity to withdraw gracefully? I don't suppose so. I don't much blame you. It's exciting to hold all the cards, I suppose. I assume you've read these?"

Josephine's eyes were very dark. She said evenly, "No. I opened the cigarette case."

Elsie took it in her hands and opened it. She said, "I haven't seen this for a long time. What a fool I was. . . . names, dates . . . and the quotation." She laughed. "The quotation tears it. I was romantic in those days, I read the anonymous poets—I suppose the *Oxford Book of English Verse* was included in your

232

schoolroom culture too?"

Josephine said, "Enough. I recognized this."

"Okay," said Elsie, "I never thought he would." She looked at Josephine with venomous hostility. "Simple and guileless maiden," she said, "confronted by female menace, guilty as hell. I never dreamed Lanny went in for chivalry. I hope he'll never come back I hope he rots in—"

Josephine said: "Lanny didn't send this package to me. He sent it to you. There was no name on the brown-paper cover. Wycherly, or Rhoda, made a mistake."

The color came back to Elsie's face and lips. She asked, "How do you know?"

"There's a letter," said Josephine, "for you . . . in the white envelope."

Elsie put out her hand; drew it back. She said negligently, "You read it, of course."

"I read the first line. Your name occurs there. I didn't read further."

Elsie said, "Curiously enough, I believe you. Don't," she added hastily, "think for a moment that I respect you for it. You're as much of a fool as I was—if in a different way. And it doesn't matter whether you read it or not. You've plenty to go on. The cigarette case in itself is enough. Lanny told me he'd lost it. Dropped it overboard, he said, one night on a cruise. I didn't believe him but—" She shrugged. "Well, there it is, and so what are you going to do about it? You were out of your mind to return these. I'll deny everything, of course, that you

233

tell Jon."

Josephine said, "You're—I haven't words to tell you what I think of you. I'm not going to Jon with this . . . I'm not telling him anything."

Elsie's eyes widened. "You can't mean that?"

"I don't fight that way," said Josephine, "believe it or not. I'm going to tell Jon that I'll marry him whenever he wants me to. . . . I'm going to agree with him that it's only fair for him to ask you to release him from your engagement. He wants to, and I've been opposing him. I had an idea—which must seem childish to you—that promises aren't lightly broken. I thought you loved him. . . . I was willing to sacrifice myself and him too. No, not willing. Yet I didn't see any other way out. Until last night. After you left my room I decided that I'd been very stupid and unnecessarily noble. I knew then that you didn't love him, you couldn't. So I made up my mind . . . before the package came into my possession. It hasn't changed anything," she said.

"You don't expect me to love you for this," said Elsie, in a light, hard tone. "If anything, I dislike you more than I did. Which is saying a lot."

"That," Josephine told her, "is a matter of indifference to me."

She had reached the door when Elsie called her. Her voice had altered, it was strained and harsh.

"Where's Lanny?" she asked.

"I don't know," said Josephine.

She closed the door, as Elsie took the letter from the white envelope.

234

Back in her room, drinking the lukewarm coffee, crumbling the toast, she was giddy with happiness. Jon was free. There wasn't a weapon at her command that she wouldn't use. Except that which Lanny had placed, unwittingly, in her hands.

The least small shadow darkened her bright skies, grew larger. Jon would never feel quite free, perhaps. And she could not untangle that one hard knot of distaste—or conscience, even. But it could not be helped.

Come soon, she thought, tomorrow, today.

Lanny and Elsie. Long ago. It was incredible, it didn't bear thinking about . . . she wouldn't think of it. She couldn't help it. It explained, she thought, so much about Lanny. If he still loved Elsie Meredith—and he must still love her—if he had loved her all this time, stood by, watched her promise herself to his step-brother . . . it must have been like a knife turning in him, the remembrance of love, the knowledge. A knife which had cut both ways, to set Jon free.

While she was dressing, Bobbie's maid knocked to ask if she could come, at once, to Mrs. Rivers.

Josephine said, "I'll be right there," and went as soon as she was ready to Bobbie's room, to find that lady in a state of distraction. Susan was marching around the room with her early morning cigarette, putting in a word now and then, to which Bobbie paid no attention whatever.

She cried, as Josephine entered, "Lanny's gone!"

"Yes," said Josephine, "so Rhoda told me."

"He hasn't done this for months," wailed Bobbie, "it means he'll turn up in a few days or a week or more, in a *state*."

"It means," said Susan at the window, "that he'll drink himself blind and grope his way home again. Sorry to drag you into this, Josephine," she added, "but Bobbie doesn't mind your knowing."

"*Everybody* knows," said Bobbie vaguely. "Josephine, couldn't you go out and find him for me?"

"I?" asked Josephine, startled.

"Don't be silly," said Susan tartly. "That's a fine mission on which to send a young girl. Besides, what makes you think he's still around the Beach or Miami? There are trains, planes, boats. He may be anywhere. Cuba for choice, or en route to New York or off to Nassau."

Bobbie said firmly, "No, he never goes far. Just to some awful little hotel until his money gives out."

"It's your fault," said her sister. "Lanny's weak and you encourage him. If you kicked him out to-morrow, he'd survive . . . and be better for it."

"But I'm fond of him!" wailed Bobbie.

"You've ruined him," said Susan; "not that it was difficult. Because you are fond of him, because you want someone to fetch and carry for you, make you laugh, and flatter you. Jon wouldn't. Jon is very like his father, you know."

Josephine murmured, "If you no longer need me . . ."

Wycherly knocked and came to stand in the doorway, his head still pounding, but his dignity unimpaired. A telephone from New York he said, from Mr. Scott's office. Mr. Scott had taken the morning plane, and would be home today.

"In the nick of time," murmured Susan, "whatever that is."

Wycherly having departed, Bobbie lay back among her pillows. She said happily, "Everything will be all right. Jon can find Lanny. Men know about these things."

Elsie looked in at the doorway, smiling. She asked, "May I come in or are the morning audiences over?"

Chapter 23

Josephine attempted to pass her but Elsie held her back with a hand on her arm. She said pleasantly, "Don't go, Josephine. I happened to overhear a little. Why bother Jon with Lanny's gypsy blood? I fancy the fishing trip will be on for tomorrow. Howard's champing at the bit. . . . I've decided not to go." She smiled at Bobbie. "I'm subject to seasickness and allergic to fish. . . . I'll stay here with you and Fritzi, Bobbie, and when Lanny turns up we'll all kill the fatted calf."

"Not go on the fishing trip!" asked Bobbie incredulously. "But Jon will be furious with you . . . he'll want to go. And if you don't, he won't."

"I don't think so. You see," said Elsie carelessly, "I'm breaking our engagement. I've just sent Holmes out with some wires—too intimate over the telephone, don't you think?—and in that case it might be awkward for Jon in the close confines of a cruiser. . . . I'll be gone when he gets back."

Susan swallowed an exclamation. Susan was feeling very happy. She had never liked Elsie Meredith, she never would. She thought, But what's happened, whom has she met, it couldn't be Howard, could it? No, that's out of the question.

"Josephine," began Elsie and then said, "Oh, she's gone. . . . I tried to stop her but—"

"What's she got to do with it?" Bobbie demanded. "I'll never forgive you as long as I live. What *will* your mother say?"

"I dread to think."

"And your father! Elsie, you're out of your mind. Have you quarreled with Jon? Surely a little quarrel isn't important," Bobbie said, and began to weep in a soft, becoming fashion. "I think we're all crazy this morning, I've never heard of anything so absurd. Why, you've been going to marry him for years!"

Elsie sat down on the edge of the bed and patted the quivering shoulder. She said, "I know, dear. But I don't love him, and he doesn't love me. It was just one of those things, we drifted into it when we were too young to know our own minds really and ever since he's been away I've been thinking how best to drift out. Don't cry. He'll be relieved, no matter how politely protesting, and as for me . . ." She drew a deep breath and flung out her arms. "I am too, oddly enough," she murmured, and Susan, turning, gave her a sharp, astonished glance.

"The papers," began Bobbie feebly.

"Pooh," said Elsie lightly, "when did the papers ever worry you?" She bent and touched her lips to Bobbie's forehead lightly. "Try to forgive me," she said; "you can, you know. I'm not hurting your ewe lamb . . . not nearly so much as I would if I married him."

"You don't love him," Bobbie mourned, unbelieving.

"Not a bit," admitted Elsie cheerfully. "My heart beats no faster when he comes into a room, I don't turn giddy, I haven't softening of the brain. I'm fond of Jon, but that's not enough, is it? I mean, not at my age. If I were thirty years older . . . But I'm not. You'll hate me," she said mildly, "for a while, and I don't blame you. But when you realize what I've done for Jon, you won't, you'll even like me again."

She rose, smiled at Bobbie and departed.

"Aromatics," said Bobbie feebly.

Susan fetched bottle and glass from the bathroom, and administered a dose.

"You don't need this any more than I do," she said, "and I don't need it at all."

"I do too," said Bobbie stoutly; "the shock, the disappointment. Of all the ungrateful . . . after the way I've treated her, as if she were my own daughter. After the way Jon . . . I'll never forgive her."

"Oh, do," said Susan negligently. "If you hadn't been so blind, Roberta, you would have realized that Jonathan hasn't been in love with her for years. Oh, at first, of course. But things grow a bit stale, waiting. She was always putting him off. Most men tire. Jon's not that rare creature, the singlehearted lover who goes on sighing for eighty years—for the same girl. He's a man like other men. He couldn't survive on the little she gave him. It's the best thing that ever happened to him."

Bobbie cried, "There's another man, I'm sure of it. She's a—a—"

"Relax," advised Susan, "let Jon handle this. It's his affair, you know, and not yours."

"All my plans," said Bobbie plaintively.

"Mice and men," remarked Susan inevitably. "And now, for heaven's sake, let me send down for some fresh coffee and do stop sniffling. Do you want Josephine to come back?"

"No. I don't feel well," said Bobbie. "Send for the coffee and then I think I'll have a massage and stay in bed the rest of the day. I'm having such palpitations. I shouldn't be upset like this, you know I shouldn't, it's bad for me."

Josephine was out on the patio when Elsie came out of the house and walked over to her. She said agreeably, "So Jon's coming back today."

Josephine said, "Yes," and waited.

Elsie said, "Howard's gone off to see his captain and arrange the trip. You and Howard, Jon and Susan." She smiled slightly. "Want me to wish you luck?"

"No," Josephine said calmly.

Elsie said musingly, "You think I'm afraid because of your hold over me?"

"I hold nothing over you," said Josephine shortly.

240

"I'm not a blackmailer."

"You'd be surprised how many of us are," said Elsie. "Well, you won't believe this, but that's not the reason I'm breaking my engagement. I could put up a fight, couldn't I? I know you don't think so but that doesn't matter. If you knew the real reason—"

"I don't want to know it," Josephine said.

"Nice, you're so interested. It's Lanny," Elsie said. " 'His honor rooted in dishonor stood.' Is that how it goes? The letters have been burned. I'll return the case to him . . . for a wedding present."

Josephine tried to speak and found she could not.

"Don't you understand?" Elsie said impatiently. "He sent the letters and the case to *me*. Not to you. He couldn't go through with it, so I *can*. I mean, I can take it; Lanny or what's left of him, the horrible life we'll lead, and even South America."

"South America?" Josephine repeated faintly.

"That's where we're going," Elsie informed her. "My father will have a stroke, and as for my mother—They're broke, you see, that's why it was pretty important for me to marry Jon. You asked me if I'd love him without Bobbie's money. . . . I said you couldn't separate him from his background. Well, his background was the only valid reason for marrying him. I'd be off the Meredith hands at least. It doesn't matter now. They'll have to join the New Poor and so will I. Would it be difficult for you to absent yourself this evening?"

"Why?" asked Josephine doubtfully.

"Ask for the afternoon and evening off," said

Elsie. "I want to talk to Jon without complications. Or don't you trust me?"

"Why should I?" inquired Josephine reasonably.

"You shouldn't," Elsie said pleasantly, "only, as it happens, you can. I burned my bridges—as well as the letters. You heard me tell Bobbie that my engagement was to be broken, didn't you?"

"No," Josephine said, "I made my escape. Did you?"

"Take my word for it. She's probably up in a darkened room now weeping over the way her pet plan has gone glimmering. She won't take very kindly to a substitute plan, but that's your battle and not mine. I think she'll come around eventually. Susan's never liked me although she's done nothing about it. She's a noninterventionist by nature.

"Here comes Fritzi," she added warningly, "looking like the Witch of Endor after a visit to Antoine, Elizabeth Arden, and a gland specialist. Have you noticed her new figure? Very fetching. But fetching what, I wonder? Surely not poor old Howard, or has she come to the end of her emerald rope? Before she gets here, will you clear out . . . tonight?"

"All right," Josephine said, "if you will tell me why."

"It's just that I'd like to save my face. Not that it's much of a face. It would be harder with you around."

Presently Josephine went back to the house, found Susan, asked her if it would be possible to have the af-

242

ternoon and evening free. She said, truthfully enough, that if she was going on the fishing trip there were some things she wanted to get at home and, besides, she had not seen her mother for some time.

Susan said, "It will be all right. My sister won't need you, I'm sure, today." She smiled, adding, "I'm looking forward to the trip, you know. Poor Howard is distracted, his guests have fallen off in large numbers, but I imagine we'll have a very good time."

Josephine lunched alone; Elsie was not in, nor Susan. Howard Toller was conferring with his captain and Fritzi had gone to the races. Afterward, she left Blue Horizons, walked in on her astonished relatives, and telephoned Bill from the apartment.

"The forgotten woman," she announced gaily. "No, don't stammer and make excuses, I want to ask you a favor. Will you be out showing the wonders of the beach to a client this afternoon? No? Then may I borrow your car for a little while? I want to take Mother and Cousin Agnes gadding."

He said, obviously relieved, that she could have his car, she could have anything of his she wanted. He was sorry, he added, that he couldn't go along.

"We don't want you," Josephine said sweetly; "just girls together."

Bill delivered the car in due time. Standing on the sidewalk he said, "Look here, Jo, I—"

She patted his hand soothingly. "Bill, don't say another word. Would it interest you to know that I'm in love?"

His jaw dropped. He said, "But I—but that's—"

"That makes two of us," she deduced, smiling, "but not with each other. Wish me as much luck as I wish you . . . and some day I hope you'll let me tell the future Mrs. Gamble what a fortunate young woman—"

"Jo, who is he?"

"I'm not at liberty to tell," she said, making a face of extreme demureness. "Here come Mother and Agnes. Please close your mouth. You look half-witted. And don't say a *word*."

They drove out through Golden Beach and back again. They paid three calls, they had tea. They drove along Indian Creek Drive, by the blue waters smiling in the sun, at the edge of the green lawns, and the boats at anchor, and when they reached home again it was dusk.

I wonder what time the plane . . . Is he home, has he spoken to her? When will I see him? . . .

"You're very quiet," said her mother, anxiously. "Has anything happened, dear?"

"No. I'm still brooding," Josephine said, "over our narrow shave. I would have loathed returning Bill's car minus a fender."

"You aren't eating," said Agnes reprovingly.

"I'm not hungry, I had too much tea."

"One cup, no sandwiches, no cakes. Jo, dear, aren't you well?"

"Never better." She rose from the table, flew at them, hugged them both. "Let's leave the dishes and go to an early movie," she suggested.

She went into the bedroom to pack her oldest

slacks, her stoutest shoes, her ancient fishing gloves, anklet socks, warm underwear—you never knew how cold it might be—a sweater, a disreputable leather jacket. She came out again, radiant, lugging the suitcase. "I'll stop by for it," she said, and dashed back for something she'd forgotten.

"Oh, of course," said her mother understandingly, "she was always like this when she went off on a fishing trip with Joseph."

Agnes shook her head. She said, "There's something more to it than that. I never saw her like that before. She said she was starved and then she didn't eat. She's always been such a careful driver, Alva, but I declare my hair stood on end half a dozen times. And at supper she was so quiet and then she talked so much and so fast. If I'm any judge, there's only one explanation—the girl's in love."

"Why, Agnes," said Alva, "how would you know? And with whom?"

Agnes, crushed, subsided.

They went to the movies and it was Clark Gable but when they came out Josephine said dreamily, "Gary Cooper's wonderful, isn't he?" and Alva opened her mouth in astonishment to reply but Agnes clutched her arm. "See," she whispered, "that's what I mean. She simply isn't *here*, that's all."

Josephine and the suitcase went back to Blue Horizons in a taxi. She thought, approaching the house, feeling her hands grow cold and her heart start to pound, suppose he hasn't told her—suppose she—

Wycherly opened the door and took the suitcase

from her. He said, smiling, "Good evening, Miss Bruce."

"Good evening, Wycherly." Josephine hesitated. She asked finally, "Did Mr. Scott return?"

"Oh, yes, miss," said Wycherly, "and they all went out for dinner—to the Surf Club, I believe, and they were going on somewhere afterward."

"Oh," said Josephine blankly, "I see. I thought Mrs. Rivers—"

"Madam didn't come downstairs until time to leave," said Wycherly. "Miss Bruce, there's a little matter—" Holmes appeared and Wycherly waved him upward with the suitcase and went on anxiously: "Just a moment, Miss Bruce, if you would be so good. The package Mr. Lanny gave me. . . . He came to my quarters late, while I was asleep. I woke but was, I suppose, a little confused. I thought he said I was to give you the package, but all day it has been with me that he said Miss Meredith."

Josephine said, "It was just a mistake, Wycherly. Yes, it was for Miss Meredith. When I opened it, I found her name inside, so I took it to her at once."

Wycherly drew a deep breath. He said apologetically, "I have had a bad headache all day, and I wondered . . ."

"It was perfectly all right; no one was in the least upset about it," said Josephine, "so you mustn't be."

She went on up to her room. She thought, I can't sleep. He'll come in sometime, late perhaps, near morning. He'll be under this roof again—

The flowers were on her dressing table and the

note. What if Rhoda had read it? . . . it looked very much as if the envelope had been unsealed and hastily sealed again.

"Darling," he had written, "why aren't you here? It isn't like coming home . . . I knew you'd gone the moment I set foot in the house and it frightened me. I have to go out, Mother insists, but I'll talk to Elsie tonight . . . and in the morning I'll see you . . . it is years since we were last together. I hear we're going fishing tomorrow. I shouldn't. I should be over bossing the job, but I'll go over early and talk to the men, as we aren't starting until noon. Goodnight, and I love you."

She went to sleep with the note under her pillow and did not hear them come in, from the Brook Club.

Elsie said, yawning, "I was too abstemious at the Brook. Maybe that's why I lost Jon. Let's have a drink, shall we?"

Bobbie expostulated.

"It's late." Her small face was haggard under the pink hair. "Elsie, perhaps tomorrow—"

"I won't change my mind," said Elsie, "but it was smart of you not to give us a moment alone, as it's not the sort of thing you announce from a dance floor or in the middle of Hildegarde's song."

"What's all this?" asked Jon lazily, his thoughts elsewhere.

"Nothing," said his mother resignedly and Susan

took her firmly by the arm.

"You come to bed," she said; "you're just in the way here."

"Pantry?" asked Jon. "As if we were housekeeping?" He stopped. Why in Hades had he said that? he thought. He had been very much perturbed when, reaching Blue Horizons, he found Josephine had gone. Had she run away? But Susan had reassured him quickly—almost as if she knew he needed reassurance. "Josephine," she said carelessly, "has gone home for the evening to get the things she'd need on the fishing trip. . . . Everyone's dropped out," she added, "except Josephine and Howard, you and I."

He could hardly tell Elsie at dinner or on a dance floor or at a table or over roulette. He couldn't ask her, "Elsie, will you release me from our engagement?"

He could now.

"No," she was saying, "not the pantry . . . get the makings and let's go in the library."

She was there waiting for him, fingering the books along the shelves, when he came in. She said, turning, "Pour me a short one, will you?"

Presently she strolled back to the table where he had set the little tray. She was wearing a crepe frock, cool mint green, her lips were newly reddened, her dark hair brushed off her face. She picked up her glass.

"You look very fit, or have I said that before?" she said. "I forgot to ask you how the work went."

"Everything's all right. Office in a sort of turmoil, a matter of government contracts," he said, "consulting architects, all that sort of thing. For the new camps, you know. Party politics . . . I—"

She interrupted, smiling, "Here's to our engagement," she said, and raised the glass. "I mean to its dissolution."

He said blankly, "Dissolution?"

"I'm breaking it," she told him. "It was a stupid mistake, the sort you make when you're very young. I can't go through with it, Jon, I thought I could, but I can't. I came down here determined to set the date and keep my promise, but now, my dear, you'll have to let me off."

He said, "Elsie, I—"

Don't say it, she thought, don't be honest with me; this is the better way.

She said, smiling, "Don't tell me you're sorry, Jon, you're not. Perhaps your pride will be a little hurt, I wouldn't know. But it was your mistake too. Habit . . . and feeling that it was expected of us . . . I told Bobbie this morning. She was upset, of course, but she'll get over it. And I'm not worried about you. You haven't loved me for a long time and I don't in the least blame you. For I never loved you, not even at first."

She set down her glass, moved swiftly, reached up to kiss him lightly on the cheek. She said, "Sorry I couldn't. It would have been a nice solution, all told. But you deserve a lot more than I have to give."

He said gravely, "Wait, Elsie, I came back from

249

New York to tell you that I had reached the same conclusion and to ask you—"

She asked, "Must you always be honest? It would have been so much gayer if you had pretended a little." She held out her hand and he took it in his own. She said, smiling, "Well, no hard feelings . . . ever."

"None," he agreed, "and, if there is someone else, I hope you'll be very happy."

"Am I to return the compliment?" She looked at him with her narrow dark regard. "There is someone else," she said, "there always has been—I wish there weren't. I've tried not to believe it and we won't be happy but that's the way it is. Good night, Jon, and, I think good-bye."

The door closed after her and he stood staring at it, trying to realize that he was now as free as any man can be who is bound by every nerve and fiber in him to another woman . . . free to go to her and tell her so, tomorrow.

Chapter 24

Josephine woke with the morning, and assured herself that she had not slept at all, but had lain awake all the dark night through and had just this moment drowsed off.

The day was so new that it shone with a unique luster, the memory of dawn, a patina of thin and delicate gold. The sea was as calm as wise old age, as guileless as a baby. It stretched like a lake on a windless day, pure, and flawlessly blue, to the deeper blue of the Gulf Stream. Looking from her windows Josephine saw a small fishing boat stealing out, an early water bird. Even the gulls were quiet, triangular white shapes against the sky or mincing along the beach.

A small, modest breeze ruffled the palm trees and a bird sang for the sake of singing, the true artist, indifferent to lack of audience and applause.

It was a warm day and tender, a day for beginning again.

Josephine looked with distaste at the bed, at the four walls of her room. This small space could not, today, contain her, nor all the space of Blue Horizons. She wanted to stretch her arms and push away the boundaries, she wanted to sing and dance, to laugh and to weep. Because she would see Jonathan this morning. Not someday, not tomorrow, but today.

Suddenly she could not quite remember what he looked like. Tall, yes, and with intensely blue eyes and a straightforward, direct smile. He would not be still and pose for the camera of her memory. Instead she saw him in a series of shifting pictures on a screen: Jonathan laughing, Jonathan frowning over a blueprint, Jonathan standing in a group of workmen talking, his hat pushed back on his head and his hands in his pockets, Jonathan crossing the polished surface of a dance floor.

She could not think, this morning, she could only feel.

I'm not afraid, she told herself, whatever's happened, I'm not afraid.

Elsie could not, nothing could, harm her. Whatever Elsie had said or left unsaid last night, this was today.

Dressing, some lines from the beautiful little prayer attributed to Mary Stuart came into her mind and she found herself repeating them mutely.

"May we never be hasty in judgment and always generous," Mary Stuart hid prayed, and at the end, "Let us not forget to be kind."

Josephine brushed her thick honey-gold hair, and it curled back around her face. Powder, lipstick, a brown linen dress, strapped shoes. She went softly from the room and downstairs and Holmes, dusting the hall, looked at her with amazement. She smiled at him and went out on the patio and down to the beach and stood there, her hands clasped behind her back, looking out to sea. The air was as fresh and sweet as a flower.

Jonathan spoke, from the sea wall. He said, "I knew you'd be here."

She turned, spoke his name, and found herself stammering.

He jumped down and stood beside her, taking her in his arms, turning her face to his. He kissed her, and there was no time, no world, no sorrow, only now, the immediate, treasurable moment.

She warned, "Someone will see us from the house."

"Who cares? Must you be so practical?" he

laughed down at her, and she fell silent, memorizing his face and altering expression, as if this was the first time she had seen it or the last time she would look and look—

"Your eyes are as big as brown, velvet dollars. When are you going to marry me, Jo?" he asked.

"Elsie?" she asked, "You haven't told me—"

"Elsie broke our engagement last night," he told her. "She informed me that it had been a mistake. I managed to remark that I had come to the same conclusion but it must have sounded like self-defense." He grinned, his arm around Josephine's shoulders. "Let's walk down the beach," he suggested. "If I don't translate my present state into active exercise, I'm likely to go berserk, shout, stand on my head, do nip-ups."

"Can you?" she inquired doubtfully.

"Shout?"

"No," she said hastily; "nip-ups."

"Naturally, my good woman. Want to see? A cartwheel, for instance . . ."

He executed one neatly and stood upright again, disheveled, sandy, laughing.

"Jon, you're absurd."

"I know . . . and you're very beautiful. You haven't answered my question."

"What was it?" she demanded, knowing but wanting to hear it again.

"When are we to be married?" He took her arm, held it close to his side, accommodated his long stride to her shorter steps. "Soon? As soon as possible? I had a long talk with my boss while I was in New York. I won't wait for the draft . . . there's no reason. I would have enlisted long ago but there were jobs which the firm felt were especially mine, and then Mother was so very much against it and—"

"Elsie?" she asked with a twinkle.

"I don't think she cared," he said soberly. "We never discussed it, very much."

"Army?"

"Navy . . . for the duration of the emergency. Do you mind?"

"I mind dreadfully."

"Every nice girl loves a sailor," he reminded her.

"Darling, of course. It's just that I couldn't be with you," she said.

"Women aren't allowed on battleships," he told her; "such a curious naval regulation. Fantastic, isn't it? But there are ports, and sailors have wives in every—"

"Bigamist."

He said contentedly, "It's all right then. Of course, you'll have to help me win Mother over."

She said, her heart tightening, "She'll never forgive us."

"I mean, about my enlisting. As for us, she'll forgive us all right, she'll be delighted."

"Possibly, but I doubt it."

"We'll tell her today."

"No . . . please, Jon."

"But—"

She said definitely, "Can't we just have today for

our own . . . or until after the fishing trip, Jon? I know you must tell her very soon. But let's have these few days—it will be best for her too, to adjust herself . . . to—"

"Non-Elsie?" he suggested.

"Don't laugh. She did have her heart set on it. And you know how she feels about—about secretaries."

"Evelyn," he deduced.

"Yes. I have been warned," said Josephine. "I was warned almost immediately. Hands off sons and heirs." She chuckled, remembering, but added thoughtfully, "Still, I needed no danger sign as I didn't like you at all . . . at first."

"And I thought you were a little—"

"Don't say it," she said hastily.

"I could have murdered Lanny . . ." he began.

He stopped and looked at her, laughing. "I must have fallen in love with you then and there," he said, "or else why should I have been so righteously annoyed? Quite out of all proportion; I'd seen Lanny in action before."

"And how I resented your superior attitude. Perhaps I too—"

"Love," he said happily, "is all the sweeter for a touch of antagonism."

"Where'd you hear that?"

"Read it somewhere. What's the matter?"

"Lanny," she said, "I just remembered. You knew he'd—gone away?"

"Yes. Don't worry. Mother's upset, of course. But

255

he always comes back."

"She thought perhaps you'd find him."

"Better not. Better leave him alone. He's an odd creature. He wouldn't like being found. By the way, I saw my stepfather in town. He called me up and we had dinner together. Mostly, we talked about you. He thinks you're quite a girl."

"I like him," she said, "I'm sorry for him. Jon, you should try to do something for Lanny."

"What, for instance?"

"I don't know. If he'd get a job, if you'd encourage him to break away . . ."

She halted. She couldn't say more without betraying Elsie. What had Elsie said about South America? What had she meant?

But Elsie and Lanny seemed to count for so little. How selfish I am, she thought.

"I'm hungry," Jonathan announced. "Romantic thought, isn't it? Let's get back to the house and have breakfast. I've got to get over to the bay front. Here, wait a minute—"

He caught her to him, kissed her long and deeply. When he released her, he said, "I'm going to see Mother."

"You promised."

"No."

"Then, please . . . Not because it's a reasonable request—although it is, actually—but just because I ask it."

"All right, but I don't like it. When we return from the fishing trip then. And you'll take me to see your

256

mother. Suppose she doesn't like me?"

"She will," said Josephine. "She'll cry a little and say she's losing her little girl. But she won't mean it. She'll be enchanted."

He said, "After we're married and settled somewhere she'll come live with us, Jo."

Josephine shook her head.

"Her life's here," she told him, "and all her friends . . . I couldn't take her away." She looked at him, troubled. "It's dreadful, I hadn't thought of her, or of the problem she'd constitute."

"What problem?"

Josephine was very pink. She said, "Let's talk about that later, shall we?"

"My delicate-minded nitwit," he said gently, "it's money, isn't it? And you don't like the intrusion of financial considerations."

Josephine nodded.

"We'll take care of your mother," he promised.

"I know," she told him, "it's just that I—" She looked at him appealingly, "It seems so—so unfair, to bring you nothing but more responsibility."

"I like responsibility, I haven't had enough. I wouldn't have had any if Mother had had her way. That's partly what's wrong with Lanny . . . no responsibility of any kind. Long ago I suggested that Mother throw him out, well, not literally, but it would amount to that. The idea upset her. She accused me of being jealous. After that, my hands were tied."

They walked back to the house and Elsie saw them approaching. She watched them from her windows, unsmilingly, she shrugged her shoulders and went swiftly from her room, downstairs, and out the open front door. She walked briskly to the gates and along Collins Avenue until she found a taxi. She stood there, conscious that she was a little lightheaded from lack of sleep and no breakfast, and talked for some time to the driver. The driver said, doubtfully: I wouldn't know, miss. It probably wasn't a regular . . . there's no cab stand near here. The police might help you . . . they can round up the cab drivers."

Elsie hesitated a moment and then got into the cab and it shot away, down Collins.

Josephine and Jonathan breakfasted alone in the great dining room. She said, as Wycherly, apparently unastonished, served them, "Father always wanted to have a breakfast room . . . Mother didn't. She said, why, when practically no one ever comes down to breakfast! I wish he'd known you, Jon—and you, him. You would have liked each other."

He said, "I deplore trays. Never use 'em. Crumbs, and I always spill the coffee. This is the right way. Always. I'll scowl at you over the newspaper and complain bitterly about the eggs."

Josephine looked down at her plate. Wycherly was moving about pontifically. He must have heard. It didn't matter, but her eyes were wet because this was today and Jonathan was himself—and hers.

Chapter 25

That evening, at sunset, the *Alice T.* lay anchored off one of the Keys . . . a small key dense with growth, the mangroves like a green ruffle along the water's edge, their pale, moving roots responding to the stirring of the water until the entire shore line seemed to sway. Standing on deck, Josephine pointed to the dark, crouched shape of an eagle high on a dead tree, his shoulders humped, his bald head thrust forward, like an old man sleeping.

Their trip had been uneventful save for the awareness of beauty. A calm sea and green keys, the passing boats, the hot sun, tempered by a little breeze . . .

"Someday," said Jonathan, "we'll have a boat and come down here and do this . . . a lot. You'd like that, wouldn't you?" He smiled at her. "You'll be homesick, away from here," he said anxiously.

"Not with you."

But she was Florida born, she had sand in her shoes, the sea in her heart, the wind along her veins.

"You'll have your little house," he told her, "after I'm out of the navy. The house you've dreamed of, remember? I have the sketches to show you . . . and we'll come down, vacations. Your mother and—who is it?—Cousin Agnes can keep it open and ready for us, until we come. You can run down and visit them . . . but not for long," he said jealously, "not for long unless I'm with you."

There were good smells from the galley and they

heard Howard Toller prowling around happily, talking to his captain.

"I must help Miss Wilton," Josephine said reluctantly.

"Aunt Susan to you, and not yet." He put his hand in the pocket of his jacket. "I brought you something . . . besides the sketches."

She opened the small leather box and gasped.

"It's—beautiful! Jon, you shouldn't . . ."

A ruby, like the heart of sunset, with the evening star rising.

He said, "Once when we were dancing—at the Surf Club that night, I think you said you didn't like diamonds. So I thought—"

"I love it," she said. "Will you keep it for me?"

"Put it on."

"Not now, afterward. When you've told your mother. Besides," she added, "I can't go fishing in rubies, can I?"

"That's what you think. Have you ever been to Cat Cay? Rubies, raw silk slacks, and bandannas." He laughed. "You're not giving me the brush-off?" he inquired as she held the box toward him.

"Not for the next eighty years," she assured him. "Be careful of it. Maybe," she added, "you'd let me just look at it when no one's around, a little later."

"I never," he told her, "bought an engagement ring before, so I don't know the regulations. Am *I* supposed to wear it?"

"What about Elsie?"

He said, "No ring until the announcement. The

announcement, if you recall, took me rather by surprise. And, by then, it was too late."

"Silly of me," she said, "but I'm glad."

Howard came out from the cabin. He asked, "How about a drink you two?"

After supper, when Susan and Josephine had washed up, they sat around the table in the cabin and played contract. Jonathan admitted, at the end of the second rubber, "Sorry, can't keep my eyes open much longer. How about the rest of you?"

Susan nodded. "Well, if we're to get an early start—"

Josephine shared a cabin with Susan. It was completely shipshape, and comfortable, with built-in lockers and drawers, reading lights, bunks.

"You look about twelve," commented Susan, watching Josephine emerge from the shower, her hair shining, her face scrubbed clean, her childish pajamas.

They heard the men talking on deck, they heard them come into the adjoining cabin, heard water running in the shower room. And Susan said sleepily: "I should do this more often. No household. No servants. It's marvelous. No orders. No menus. Come and get it and take what's there. Sun and wind and sea. I—"

She thought enviously, The child's asleep. She thought, with tenderness, I've never seen anyone so happy. If Roberta makes a scene . . . for the first time in our life together I will slap her down, I will shake some sense into her. I should have done it when we were children. That's the right girl for Jon, the one he needs, the one who needs him. I knew it the minute I laid eyes on her. She thought, Where in the world did I put the sleeping tablets? But she was too comfortable to get up and find them and she told herself resignedly, Well, even if I don't sleep, I can at least relax.

She slept, and almost instantly it was morning and the smell of coffee and of bacon frying was creeping through the cabin and Howard Toller was shouting, "What's the matter with you women . . . are you going to sleep all day?"

They had breakfast, weighed anchor and were off, sailing through the gold and pearl morning, anchoring again for an early lunch off one of the small, lost keys.

"Hurry," said Howard, "we're supposed to be fishing, not cruising."

But Susan wasn't going fishing. She had brought three detective novels and her knitting. She was going to have a completely restful afternoon she said, for once. Let Jo go with the men.

The captain and mate stayed aboard, Howard and Jonathan and Josephine rowed off in the skiff, and finally poling over the shallows, literally wrenching the boat over the heavy white sand, through about three inches of clear water, watching the crabs scuttle through the waving undergrowth, until they reached deeper water and the little winding creek where they were to fish.

Snappers drowsed under the mangrove roots, and

baby barracuda slid by, long, gray and vicious, even in miniature. Jonathan rowed slowly, quietly, and Howard and Josephine cast deftly under the writhing roots into deep still pools. A snapper rose to the bait and Josephine braced herself. "Good girl," said Howard, as she reeled in and Jonathan seized the net.

A red-winged blackbird protested sharply and flew out from the tangled trees. The creek widened and opened on a stretch of sunny shallow water. Herons waded there, great white herons which are almost extinct, smaller more delicate herons, white and blue, and out beyond them hundreds of pelicans were gathered together, as in conference.

So still the water, so motionless the herons that each had a twin reflection in the water. White bird looking down at white bird, and where one began and the other ended, you could not tell, nor which was living and which but the image.

Across the flats they could see the cruiser racking in a little swell, they could see Susan lying on deck, reading, and hear the voices of the two men.

Red fish went by, in a school, and Howard rose to cast. He missed and swore, heartily.

The herons waded and fished and stood still, the substance and the reflection, dazzling white, against the blue of the water, under the blue of the sky, like a dream.

There was no wind. And Howard said in disgust, "The damned fish see us coming."

They rowed back and down the creek again, stop-

263

ping to fish in a place Jonathan had marked mentally, tying the skiff to a bending branch and standing up to cast in the narrow space. "What a girl!" said Howard with admiration, watching Josephine, her wrists sure and supple, her eyes and aim exact. He caught his own hook in a mangrove root and swore. "If I weren't so busy I'd put my hands over my ears," commented Josephine.

Jonathan was neglecting his fishing. He sat down and watched Josephine, faded blue slacks, anklet socks, and stout weatherbeaten shoes, a blue shirt open at the throat, a sweater tied around her slim waist. He could not see her eyes behind the disguising dark glasses, but he could watch her smile and frown a little, intent on her lure.

When plentifully supplied with fish, they came back to the boat by the route they had taken, only now the water was a little deeper over the shallows. "Thank God," said Howard piously, "I'm getting too old for that type of exercise. You can supply all the muscular strain this time, Jon, old man."

Supper, and the dishes to wash and wipe. And then they sat out on deck, replete and lazy. Howard was a shade darker, Josephine's even gold tint deeper, but Jon was delicately shrimp-colored. He lay flat on his back on a long, leather-covered seat and bedaubed himself liberally with tannic acid.

"We must go to Bimini," said Howard, "next time. It isn't much of a sail and even if it's rough, the *Alice T.* can take it. There's sport for you."

"Never been," said Jonathan, so contented that he

was economical of words.

"I visited there once," said Susan, "a thousand years ago . . . people I knew had a fishing camp."

"My father and I used to go," said Josephine. "It's a wonderful place, I doubt if it's changed, the rickety dock, the steps leading up to the government offices and the natives lounging on the wharf and a lot of fishing boats at anchor. People fly there now, they didn't then. You went on your boat and lived on it. Trees and sand and the bay on one side where the bonefish twinkle along the surface, almost; and the ocean on the other . . . sand and coves and rocks, sharks and devilfish. I caught a blue marlin once. I was sitting watching the outriggers when it exploded on the surface."

"Not for me," said Susan definitely, "I went big game fishing once off Catalina. I've never had a baby," she added superfluously, "but I think landing a fish of that size must be something like it. You hurt all over, you can't stand it another minute, the sweat drips off you and there are a dozen people all yelling advice. And suddenly you make up your mind . . . no matter what happens or how much you suffer, you've got to go through with it. I did," she said, "and once was enough."

"The water down there," Josephine said dreamily, sitting cross-legged on the stern seat, "is like liquid jewels, aquamarine, sapphire, amethyst, emerald, all mixed up . . . and as clear as air. You look down twenty feet . . . and it feels soft as silk on your skin, and volatile as quicksilver."

265

"Nice place for a honeymoon," said Jonathan, "fly over, have a boat meet you there . . ."

Howard swallowed the question, "Thinking of getting married?" But Jon couldn't be. Howard, as well as Fritzi, had been informed of the broken engagement. For a man whose heart might be supposed to be broken, Jon was taking it very lightly, he thought.

He said, instead, "Good idea. How about marrying me, Susan, and going to Bimini?"

She said serenely, "Why don't you ask Fritzi?"

"She doesn't like fishing."

"Neither do I."

"But you can cook!" said Howard.

It was growing dark, the last traces of the afterglow had faded and the water was still and dusky and stars shone. A little while ago, while they had been at supper, the sunset had poured out on the water like brilliant oil, rose and green, gold and sulphur, and the sky had been a blaze of color, the little white clouds turning pink, like the wings of flamingos.

It was so still they could hear the stir of strong wings in the mangroves to their left . . . another eagle possibly, the one they had seen coming back to the cruiser, sitting like yesterday's with hunched shoulders, the look of an old campaigner, the waiting look of the patient and powerful killer.

Near by something, a fish probably, troubled the still water with a sudden small sound.

The captain appeared on deck and spoke to

Howard. He said, "I was fooling with the radio, sir, there's a call coming through."

Howard yawned, rose and went below. He said, as he disappeared through the door, "Dunno why I have the blasted thing. But—"

Every hour or so one of the men listened in to see if any calls were coming through or to talk to another boat. It amused the captain, an amateur wireless fan.

Howard shouted, "Miami Beach calling you, Jon . . . I think it's Bobbie. Hey, marine operator? Wait a minute!"

"Bobbie?" said Susan apprehensively, and rose to go into the cabin and Josephine, anxious and startled, followed.

Jonathan sat down and spoke. He asked, "Is that you, mother? Yes. Wait a minute. Talk a little more slowly. What's that? Lanny? Tell me again . . ."

Bobbie spoke wildly into his ear.

"Can't you understand me, Jon? Elsie went out yesterday morning without a word to any of us and has been gone ever since. She came back half an hour ago. Yes, with Lanny. She found him in some dreadful place. No, she didn't say. Something about tracing the cab driver who had taken him there, through the police. No . . . Anyway they came back together. They've just gone. I can't believe it."

"Believe what?" inquired Jonathan patiently, listening to her light voice hollow and flattened by its progress through space.

"They're going to be married," said Bobbie. "Isn't

267

that dreadful? I thought I'd better tell you. He has a job or something silly in South America and they're going there as soon as the details can be arranged—passports and vaccinations and things like that, I suppose. Elsie's sold her plane to a commercial firm here. They'll go by clipper—"

"Good!" said Jonathan heartily. "Wait a minute." He was still a little dizzy from the shock. He swung around and reported briefly and Susan exclaimed, watching Josephine's transfigured face.

Jonathan returned to the radio telephone.

"Don't cry. It isn't dreadful, it's fine. No, why should I care? I'm going to be married myself," he said.

"Hell's bells!" said Howard Toller, startled.

"Jon!" cried Josephine.

"Yes. To Josephine . . . who else? Of course you're not going to faint. Think it over. You're going to like the idea very much, once you're used . . . Yes, we'll come back. Tomorrow."

"That tears it," said Howard gloomily; "no fishing."

"Here," said Jonathan, "talk to Bobbie, will you?"

Susan moved forward to take his place and Jonathan walked over to Josephine.

She said, "So she found him?"

"I believe you knew," he accused her. He thought, That was it then, Lanny all along, why didn't I guess?

He fished in his pocket and produced the jeweler's box.

268

"Jon, you didn't take it out fishing!"

"No." He put his arm around her and took her out on deck. "You stay where you are," he told the gaping Howard.

Susan was still talking practically and soothingly to the completely undone Bobbie. She was saying, "I know it's too much to have happen in one day. But it has happened, and—Oh, relax, Roberta. Of course. But we can't discuss that now. Yes, tomorrow. Let me speak to Fritzi."

She said, a moment later, "Fritzi? Give her a bromide or something, will you, and hold the fort till we get back? Yes, of course you're delighted, we all are, even Roberta. No, I haven't any designs on Howard, and if you have you should be here. . . . What do I think of Lanny and Elsie? Let that wait till tomorrow too." She laughed. "All right, good-bye," she said, "till tomorrow . . . oh, toward night, I suppose, I wouldn't know."

She turned to Howard, who was the only other person left in the cabin. The captain and mate had vanished, Jonathan and Josephine were not within sight.

She said, "Fritzi is enchanted at the idea of Lanny going to work and taking Elsie with him. She says that when she sees the dugouts on the beaches she is reminded of covered wagons. From covered wagons to dugouts . . . and now, back again, as far as Lanny is concerned. You really should marry her, Howard, she's most amusing."

"She's somewhat my senior," he said with dignity,

"and besides . . ."

"She doesn't look it," said Susan, entertained, "and haven't you compromised her enough?"

"Compromised Fritzi? Good God!" He jerked a thumb over his shoulder. "What about those two out there?"

She said, "Let's play Russian bank, shall we? And do keep your eyes away from that door. Let them have their moment in peace."

Josephine stood on the deck, at the stern, and looked down into the dark water, shining with stars. The star ruby was on her finger and her hand was in Jon's.

She said, "Your poor mother—"

Jonathan laughed.

"You mustn't worry," he told her. "She's liking it, really . . . thanks to Elsie. Mother could never hold up her head if she believed the world thought her son had been jilted for another man. But if *he* had done the jilting . . ."

"You didn't."

"I meant to!"

"But—"

"Mother told me," he said, smiling, "that she understood . . . She's a little mixed up about it, thinks I'm chivalry itself permitting Elsie to speak the final word, and she's determined that Elsie made off with Lanny out of pique. She's going to be grateful to you, really."

"How about you?" asked Josephine.

He took her in his arms.

"Please," she whispered, "some one will come!"

"Nonsense. Aunt Susan's discretion itself . . . she'll keep Howard in line. Besides, it's official now."

He kissed her. "I'm grateful too," he said, "and I'll be grateful all my life. I love you, Jo—Wait!"

"What?" she asked, startled.

"The mystery in your life. You'll be filling out a marriage license pretty soon. Josephine H. Bruce. What does the H. stand for, Jo?"

"I can't bear to tell you. No one knows," she said firmly, "except Mother and me."

"Come clean, woman, no secrets, ever!" He shook her.

"Jon, stop! It's—well," she said desperately, "I've told you about Father, how he adored the Beach, how he fell in love with it, with all of Florida . . . and so, when he named me—No, I can't!"

"It will be on the records. Your mother will tell me. I'll wheedle it out of her, I'll threaten her, I'll—"

"*Hibiscus*," said Josephine faintly.

Susan smiled at Howard, listening to the laughter from the deck, the helpless, contagious laughter. And then it stopped, and there was silence.

She laid down a card and said, "They're young, in love, and happy . . . and life is all before them. They're telling each other that now."

Howard strained his ears.

"I don't hear a thing," he said testily.

"They don't use words," said Susan.

The water spoke softly against the cruiser's sturdy sides, the wind rose a little, the stars shone down.

"Will you be afraid?" asked Jonathan.

"Of what?"

"Of anything, Jo—what's to come, in this crazy, bewildered world, what's to be, for us, for our children."

"Anxious perhaps," she said, "and wondering, but never afraid, not really, as long as we are together."

Center Point Publishing
Brooks Road ● PO Box 1
Thorndike ME 04986-0001 USA

(207) 568-3717

US & Canada:
1 800 929-9108